AFTER THE WAR

A Coming Home Novel

JESSICA SCOTT

Thirty One Fox Books

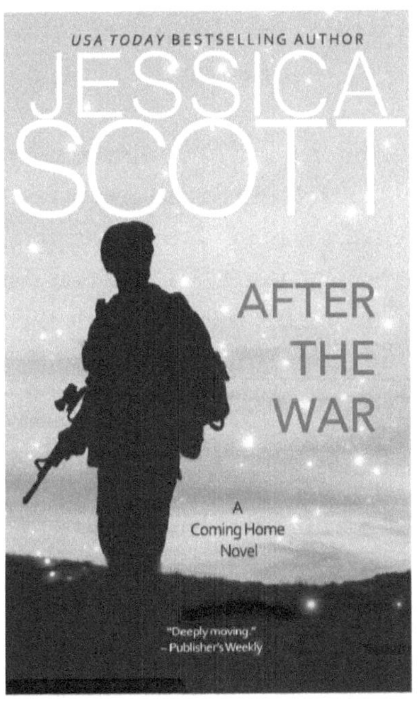

"After The War is Jessica Scott's best book to date. It was a powerful and emotional book" - Smut Book Junkies

From USA Today bestselling author Jessica Scott, a compelling story of daring to love again. New York Times bestselling author JoAnn Ross calls it "beautifully written."

A touching story about finding forgiveness and love filled with emotional second chances

Sarah Anders has been running from the worst day of her life ever since the day the chaplain knocked on her door. Throwing herself into her Army career after the loss of her husband, she's been trying to be a mother to her young daughter and a good soldier. But a freak accident has nearly derailed her career and losing the Army means

losing the one thing that keeps her connected to her husband.

Sean has never been good at commitment but he never forgave himself for letting Sarah slip away all those years ago. But wars have a way of distracting you away from the loneliness of an empty home. For the last decade, he's been focused on preparing his men for their next deployment and ignoring the quiet longing for something more. The one thing he is not prepared for is a little girl, who wriggles her way into his heart, despite her mother's resistance

When Sean and Sarah are thrown into a new assignment, they come face to face with the past they shared and the man who stands between them, even in death.

AFTER THE WAR was originally published as part of the Homefront series. It has been republished as part of the Coming Home series as it was originally intended.

Note – these books are fiction. Any resemblance to real people or events is purely coincidence

Author's Note

The Coming Home series and Homefront series were originally published as separate series. I have rebranded them to get things organized as they were originally intended.

Come Home to Me: A Coming Home Novella* was originally published as part of the Homefront series

Carry Me Home* was originally published as Until There Was You as part of the Coming Home series

A Place Called Home* was originally published as All for You as part of the Coming Home series

Take Me Home* was originally published as It's Always Been You as part of the Coming Home series

Last One Home* was originally published as Find My Way Home as part of the Homefront series

To my husband
The love of my life
I am so grateful every day that you made it home

PROLOGUE

Al Fallujah
Late 2003

"L T, stop!"

Lieutenant Sean Nichols looked away from the fire and at the soldier holding him back. "Let me go." A direct order, laced with violence.

Specialist Kearney shook his head. "Getting yourself killed isn't going to do anyone any good, sir."

Sweat ran from beneath Sean's helmet and into his eyes, fogging the lenses of his eye pro. He dragged his gloved hand beneath his glasses and took in the chaos around him. Thunder from the fifty cal vibrated through his chest. The heat burned through his flesh to the bone. At the end of the street, one of the aircraft overhead let go with the main gun and pushed the approaching militia back.

The entire fucking city was burning. Smoke from the fire seared his nostrils and tore at his lungs.

Greeted as liberators, my ass.

Chatter and intermittent screams flooded the airwaves over the radios as everyone tried to get medical and fire support.

But the truck in front of them was all he could see. He started toward the truck again.

"Stop, goddamn it!" Kearney smashed his palms into Sean's chest, knocking him back a step. "They're already gone."

The front end of the truck was melting into the asphalt.

The war surrounded them. Hot. Violent. A brilliant flash blinded him, followed by a wave of heat and sound that drove his skin into his bones.

He hit the deck, Kearney slamming into the pavement next to him.

Ammo started cooking off from inside the burning truck, tearing through the thin-skinned Humvee and slamming into the concrete around them.

Gravel bit into the skin of his cheek as a round ricocheted off the concrete. Sean closed his eyes but all he could see was the fire. He hoped Kearney was right. He hoped Jack and his boys had died in the initial blast. There was silence as he pushed to his knees. Or at least the appearance of silence. It wrapped around him and made the battle seem far away.

He looked up, his brain slowly registering the beat-up white sedan weaving through the wreckage and burning trash toward them. He punched Kearney in the shoulder and pointed. Kearney nodded once, his lips moving. Sean felt the vibration from the M249 on his vehicle where his gunner had opened fire. The sedan rolled to a stop near the burning Humvee.

He reached for the hand mike on the seat of his truck as all the sound came rushing back.

"Punisher Main, this is Warlord Blue. MEDEVAC follows." Sean read off the lines required to get the MEDEVAC bird in the air. The number of wounded. Their location. The information rolled off his tongue line by line, ingrained with practice. His voice locked in his throat and he forced the words through the blockade.

When he was done, he doubled over, throwing up the little

liquid and food he had in his stomach, heaving his guts out on the streets of Iraq. Heaved until his ribs ached and his throat burned from the bile or the smoke, he didn't know which.

When he was empty and hollowed out, he felt it again, slamming into him. The cold violence in the pit of his stomach. The rage churning in the empty space his soul had just abandoned.

His hand tightened around the butt of his weapon and all he wanted to do was kill.

ON ANOTHER BASE IN THE CENTER OF BAGHDAD, LIEUTENANT Sarah Anders answered a knock on the door of her CHU.

Her company commander stood on the top of the rough wooden step. The chaplain stood behind her.

Sarah's heart caught in her throat. She took a single step backward, shaking her head slowly, denying the hard, ugly truth of what those two visitors meant.

"No." The word tore from her throat.

She fell to her knees.

Far away, she heard someone screaming.

It was a long time before she realized it was her.

$$ \text{❧} \quad \text{I} \quad \text{❧} $$

Fort Hood, Texas

"You are officially the worst friend on the planet."

Captain Sarah Anders smiled at the sound of a familiar voice. Captain Claire Montoya stood behind her trying to look offended and failing miserably. Sarah squealed as she hugged her friend close.

"You are the only thing good about being at Fort Hood," Sarah said, holding on a little too tight. "God but I missed you."

"Funny way of showing it, you ass," Claire said with a grin. "How long have you been here?"

"Long enough to get settled. I was going to call," Sarah said, knowing Claire wasn't actually offended. She was that kind of friend. The one you didn't talk to for ten months because of a deployment and when you finally did, you picked up right where you left off.

Claire waved aside Sarah's half-baked apology. "How's the munchkin?"

"She turned five while I was gone."

"Wow, that goes by fast. Wasn't she just in diapers a second ago?"

"Feels like it. Now, though, sometimes I feel like she's going on fifteen. She can be so dramatic." Sarah pulled Claire into her tiny nook that passed for an office. She was new here, which meant she had a shitty desk in a shitty space, but she wasn't going to complain.

"Bet you can't wait for puberty, huh?"

"I'm sending her to boarding school and volunteering for another deployment," Sarah said. "Man, I missed you. How have you been since the epic disaster also known as Colorado?"

Claire pulled up a chair. "Oh, fine. Got thrown out of this brigade and sent over to the Cav Regiment. Ai-ee-ya, and all that," she said, pointing to the patch on her left shoulder.

"You sound like you're enjoying it."

"Of course I'm enjoying it," Claire said with an evil grin. Claire was a warrior, through and through. There was nothing she enjoyed more than leading soldiers in combat. And she was damn good at it, too.

"And how's Evan?"

A warm flush crept over Claire's face, matched by the smile that transformed her. "He's good." She held out her hand, revealing a square-cut diamond ring.

Sarah bit back an excited sound. "Now who's the shitty friend? You didn't tell me you were engaged!"

Claire flushed but the smile never left her lips. "Well, he pretty much had to hold me down to get me to agree." She shrugged. "He's...a good man."

"I'm happy for you," Sarah said.

Claire tucked her thumbs into her belt loops. "Okay, so spill. What the hell happened? You were leaving for Iraq the last time I saw you, and now you're here. Which means mostly not good things as far as I can guess."

Sarah looked down at her desk, the shame of failure a hot flush on her skin. "I got fired." She looked up at her friend. "Training accident in Arifjan. I never even got to take my team into country."

"Shit." Claire sank back into her chair. "Is that why you're limping?"

Sarah nodded. "Yep. Fuel exploded. Boss didn't want to hear that it wasn't my fault even though I was literally topping vehicles off. Contractors deliberately failed to properly ground the fuel stop."

"So what you're saying is you're lucky to be alive, and instead you're bitching about being fired?" Claire said dryly.

"Well, when you put it that way," Sarah said. She grinned and shook her head. "The boss was looking for a reason to fire me and he found it."

"Well, I'm not going to complain if that means you're here. I have a shortage of female friends who can put up with me."

"Ha! That's just because you're terrifying." Sarah let the conversation drift away from her failure as a commander. She couldn't face the memories, not today. Not when she needed to get her head in the game and focus on her new job here at Fort Hood. If she was planning on staying in the Army, she needed to get used to riding a desk on the staff.

One of the lieutenants in the ops stuck her head in Sarah's cubicle. "Excuse me, ma'am?"

She glanced over Claire's shoulder at LT Picket and felt positively ancient. The Army was a young soldier's game, and at thirty, Sarah hadn't been a young soldier in half a lifetime or more.

"What's up, LT?"

"Ma'am, Major Wilson directed me to hand this to you." The lieutenant looked like she expected Sarah to rip her throat out.

Sarah hadn't had a run-in with Major Wilson yet, but that didn't mean the battalion executive officer's reputation didn't precede her. She was not a warm and fuzzy kind of leader, apparently. She ruled by fear and intimidation. Always a fun mix with a superior officer.

"Thanks. What is it?"

Picket placed her hands at the small of her back at the position of parade rest. "You've been appointed as the investigating officer for an incident that happened this past weekend. A fight between a lieutenant and a sergeant in Chaos Company over in Death Dealer battalion. Drunk and disorderly with assault. Some sergeant got drunk and was involved in a fight with his company XO. Now the brigade commander wants answers."

"So much for getting integrated with the battalion's logistics mission," Sarah said. Being an investigating officer took time, time she could be using to establish herself as a valuable asset to the logistics planning team. Now she was going to be out chasing sworn statements and picking through lies, instead of doing her job, which was working logistics for the upcoming deployment to Iraq. Fights weren't usually serious incidents, contrary to what most folks outside the Army thought. Why was this one being investigated?

Sarah frowned. "What kind of unit has officers and enlisted men fighting on the weekends?"

Claire smiled. "Oh, trust me, Death Dealer battalion is special."

"And you know this, how?"

Claire leaned back in her chair. "Evan is the ops officer there. Trust me; when I say 'special', I mean 'entire chain of command was relieved a few months ago' kind of special."

"Oh wow. That's really serious."

"You have no idea. New command teams are on board, but they're busy trying to clean house and get the unit prepared for the next deployment coming up in" —she glanced at her watch— "seven months. I haven't met any of the new commanders beyond Bandit Company but Sarn't Ike says they are an interesting mix of characters."

"Well, that ought to be interesting then." Sarah flipped open the folder to look at the memorandum appointing her as the investigating officer.

Cold prickled over her skin. Her stomach twisted into knots

violently as she read the name of the company commander again and again. It had to be a mistake.

Had to be.

"Dude, what's wrong?" Claire's voice came from very far away.

She said nothing, handing Claire the paperwork, her heart caught in her throat.

"Oh shit." Claire's expression hardened as her eyes scanned the paperwork. She looked up at Sarah. "Sarah—"

Sarah covered her mouth with her hand, a thousand memories storming forward all at once, flashing back to a terrible time years ago. Before she'd met Jack. Before she'd lost the man who'd filled the dead space inside her with love and laughter and understanding. Things she'd thought she'd lost forever when Sean Nichols had walked out on her.

The man she'd been engaged to marry. The man who'd left her when she refused to give up her career to be his wife.

❦

"Goddamn it, Sean, I thought you were getting your men under control." Lieutenant Colonel Gilliad jammed a finger in Sean's chest and Sean deliberately kept his expression blank.

Captain Sean Nichols stood in his battalion commander's office, hands at the small of his back in a parade rest stance. It was the preferred position for getting a wire brush run over his fourth point of contact. While the visual might have been funny any other time, right then, Sean wasn't in the mood for a joke.

"Sir, I'm working on it. There's a lot to unfuck in this unit, sir."

"How exactly are you working on it? The lawyer tells me your company is the farthest behind on legal packets."

"Sir, we're processing the medical and mental health before we start the legal proceedings."

The muscle in Gilliad's throat pulsed visibly as he stood, leaning over the desk. "And now you've got sergeants picking fights with the officers?"

Sean ground his teeth. He was going to whip Kearney's ass six ways from Sunday when he got a hold of him. And Sean's executive officer? Oh, LT Smith was going to be lucky to still have a job if Sean had any say so. But like everything, firing any lieutenant, let alone that particular lieutenant, was complicated. "Sir, I'm still trying to get the answers as to what's going on there."

"Yeah, well, you're out of options on that one. I've asked the brigade commander to direct an investigation on this clusterfuck since you can't control your formation."

Gilliad slapped a folder against Sean's chest. Sean kept it from falling and dropped it by his side, feeling like now might not be the best time to read it and take notes. Not with flames shooting out of Gilliad's ears, anyway.

"Roger that, sir."

Gilliad sank down into his chair with a heavy sigh. He looked up at Sean quietly for a moment. "I hired you because you came highly recommended. I'm not sure what the problem is with this particular sergeant, but you need to get him under control or you need to throw his ass out of the Army."

Sean ground his teeth. He really was going to kill Kearney. "Sir, he's working through some difficult family issues."

"Noted. Don't care. He gets arrested one more time, and I'm coming for you. You want to put your ass on the line for this guy, you'll deal with the consequences when he fucks up."

"Roger that, sir."

"Get the hell out of my office."

Sean saluted sharply and left the office quickly, before his mouth decided that discretion was not the better part of valor.

"That was fun." First Sergeant Morgan fell into step with Sean outside the colonel's office.

They stepped outside of the headquarters, and Morgan paused to pluck a fresh cigar out of the breast pocket of his uniform.

"A blast. We should do it again tomorrow." Sean pushed his sunglasses on to shield his eyes from the brilliant Texas sunlight.

The trees overhanging the battalion headquarters offered shade, but the heat was oppressive, and it wasn't even summer yet.

"Heard from the XO yet?" Morgan asked.

"Nope. Where the hell did we get these lieutenants? Clown college?" Sean shook his head. "Fucking Tweedle Dum and his merry band of miscreants."

"I love that you call your XO Tweedle Dum, sir," Morgan said dryly. "It warms the cockles of my twisted little heart."

Sean grunted. He'd nicknamed LT Smith Tweedle Dum out of sheer frustration. He and his buddies were all part of the same class at West Point. All but one had a mother or a father currently on active duty but somehow, they were the least competent officers Sean had ever seen. He'd never encountered more unprofessional behavior in his entire career.

God save him from lieutenants who thought they knew everything because they were related to someone who did.

"Probably time to strategically apply some pressure to their fourth points of contact. You've given them the benefit of the doubt and, well, they're not really rising to the occasion, are they?"

Sean shot his first sergeant a sidelong look that said *no shit*. "Does Kearney have a good story for this one?" Sean wished he hadn't quit smoking. It might have been six years ago but, right now, he'd give anything to relieve the tension winding around his chest, and a cigarette seemed just the thing. Something. Anything to take the edge off.

"Nope."

Sean sighed heavily. "He still at the company?"

"Yep. Bleeding on the conference room table."

"Well, it ought to give the medics something to do," Sean said dryly. "Have them stick him with an IV and patch him up."

"Want me to draw up the counseling packet? He needs a boot in his ass." Morgan clipped the end off his cigar and flicked it into the bush. "Maybe taking some time and money will smarten him up."

"I doubt it," Sean said. "And no, we can't do a damn thing right now. The boss appointed an investigation."

"What'd he go and do that for?" Morgan held the lighter to the tip of his cigar. "Kearney's problems are pretty simple."

"Guess he doesn't believe me when I tell him that Kearney and his wife just enjoy making each other miserable." Sean scrubbed his hand over his mouth. "How do we fix this, Top? This is five weeks running we've had boys arrested."

Morgan blew out a smoke ring. He did his best thinking when he was smoking. "First, we need to figure out what the hell happened last night. Kearney getting into a fight with the XO is bad juju, but the more I think about it, the more I'm with the boss. We need someone else to take a look at this because clearly there's some bullshit going on that we're not seeing."

"I love how you read my mind." Sean grinned. "Want to snuggle?"

"Just because I read your mind doesn't mean we're going to be taking long showers together," Morgan growled.

Sean laughed at the long running joke between them and some of the tension that had been squeezing his chest eased back. He released a deep breath.

They walked in silence to their company headquarters, a small, one-story brick building, with bushes cut in the guitar pick shape of the First Cavalry Division patch. All of the company ops were lined up in the same building.

There was a lone female standing on the front steps. Her hair was tied back in a severe bun, her eyes masked by dark Wiley-X sunglasses.

"Lost?" he said.

She didn't turn right away. There was something familiar about the curve of her neck, the line of her jaw. It nagged at him, just out of reach.

She turned, her face shadowed by the sun. "I'm looking for Captain Nichols."

He stopped, his heart pounding hard in his ears. He stood for a moment, convinced that lack of sleep had him hallucinating. That he was hearing and seeing things he'd long ago tried to forget. He knew that voice. Hadn't heard it in half a lifetime at least, but it blasted him with a sense of *knowing*.

She shifted then, turning until the sun no longer cast a shadow over her features and reality slammed into him. A thousand brilliant points of pain exploded somewhere in the vicinity of his chest. The sounds from the world fell away, leaving him in a vacuum filled with memories and the silent regret of long ago mistakes.

"Yeah, Sean. It's me."

❦   2   ❦

It had been nine years since she'd seen him. Nine years since his words had sliced into her skin with bitter anger and hurt and loss. Nine years since their lives had fallen apart, and she'd relegated Sean Nichols to a memory she tried to forget.

But in one moment, the intervening decade fell away and she was suddenly that twenty-year-old sergeant again, her heart bleeding in her hands as she tried to put her life back together.

She swallowed the dryness in her throat, determined to keep things professional, then get the hell out of Dodge as fast as she could. This was not allowed to get messy. She'd done messy with him once before, and she'd be damned if she was going to repeat that mistake.

She couldn't see his eyes behind the sunglasses, but for the briefest instance, his lips parted. A hint of emotion, then it was gone, his mouth pressed into a hard, flat line. His hands clenched into fists before they disappeared into his pockets.

He jerked his chin toward her nametape. "Anders?"

She nodded briefly. "I was married."

"Apparently." It was amazing how much bitterness could be packed into a single word.

"Well, now that the interpersonal hostilities are over, I'm the investigating officer for the incident in your company last night."

"I figured that one out just now, thanks."

She took a deep breath. So much for keeping things professional. She wasn't going to get drawn into an argument with him. But the standoff continued. Neither of them moved and a thousand memories swirled between them, snapping like live things.

He'd changed. A lot. His shoulders filled out the gray ACU uniform much better than when he'd been a younger man. His jaw was stronger. His tanned skin was creased from the bright sun of Fort Hood and Iraq, if his combat patch was any indication. His dark brown hair was longer than she remembered him wearing it when they'd been young sergeants together all those years ago.

So much for hoping he'd gotten a paunch and gone bald. Guess voodoo dolls didn't work after all.

The first sergeant standing next to Sean cleared his throat. "Anyone going to bother with introductions? Or am I supposed to guess what this awkward interpersonal hostility is all about?"

Sean sighed heavily. "Top, meet my ex, Sarah Delany."

Sarah stuck her hand out, annoyed that he'd deliberately misstated her name. She'd been Delany once upon a time but hadn't been in a long time. "Captain Anders. Nice to meet you, Firs' Sarn't."

Morgan's hand was strong and solid and felt like eighty-five grit sandpaper.

"Ma'am." Morgan stepped around Sarah and unlocked the door to the orderly room, his cigar still smoking. "Well, you two kids play nice."

She had the distinct feeling he was laughing at them, but she said nothing instead as the silence closed around them.

"Married?" he asked, his eyes going to where her left hand was wrapped around the strap of her bag. There was no ring on her left finger. Her hand felt more naked than it had in years.

"Seven years ago."

"Kind of fast, wasn't it?"

She felt the old anger surfacing between them, crawling over her shoulder to whisper terrible things in her ear. "You have no right to question what I did with my life after you left me."

His smile was cold and hard. "So that's how you remember it? I left you?"

She stepped away, out of his space, and sucked in deep breaths. His words hurt. They were supposed to. "Not much to misconstrue, honestly."

His smile could have cracked glass. "Pretty selective memory you've got going there, Sarah. Let's not forget who said no."

"You know what?" She held up one hand. "I'll get the MP and civilian police reports from your first sergeant. It'll be better if we interact as little as possible, since things obviously haven't changed that much."

She walked away before the situation devolved more than it already had. She stalked past the battalion headquarters and went straight for her car, surprised by the force of the anger threatening to choke her.

She'd taken a long time to get over him. Longer to get past the anger and the hurt.

She needed a few minutes, just a few, to put everything back in the box where it belonged. Chained and bound at the bottom of the void where she could pretend the life before she'd met her husband didn't exist.

Because Sean Nichols was nothing more than a bad memory. One she was determined to leave exactly where he belonged.

In the past.

Sean let her go.

Again.

It was a long time before he unrooted himself from the spot and walked into his company ops.

He'd handled that about as poorly as he'd always handled everything with Sarah. He never had a chance to ask her how she'd been. The change of name had rocked him off his axis—and it was a name he knew all too well.

That name carried far too many memories, far too much guilt and sadness.

It couldn't be.

It just couldn't be.

Kearney sat at the conference room table. He avoided Sean's eyes, deliberately playing with his cell phone. Sean stopped at the edge of the counter.

"Did you ever meet Jack Anders's wife?"

Kearney looked up sharply. "Talk about your random question, sir."

Sean didn't respond to the sarcasm from his sergeant. With a sigh, Kearney set his phone down. "Yeah, I met her once when we'd convoyed down to Baghdad with Anders's platoon."

"She was a soldier?"

"Yeah, another lieutenant."

Sean felt the blood leaving his head. He needed to sit down.

"What made you bring that up?"

"Nothing." He walked into his office and shut the door, needing a few minutes to pull his emotions back from the edge of the abyss.

He'd spent more than a few hours over the years wondering where Sarah had gone and how she was. The whole time, apparently, she'd moved on with her life. In the first years after she'd left, he'd often thought of what he'd say if he ever saw her again. Some days, the stupid part of his heart that never got over her would ask her how she'd been. She'd smile the way she used to, and they'd finally talk about how things all went to shit when she'd turned down his marriage proposal.

Other days...other days were darker. Other days, he imagined railing at her. Demanding to know why she'd said no when they'd been so damn good together.

But he'd never imagined this. Never imagined that she'd moved on with her life. That she'd married. Never in his wildest dreams would he have thought that she'd been married to Jack. Holy fuck.

He sat at his desk, turning that revelation over and over in his mind. He scrubbed his hand over his mouth as old memories mixed with new.

Morgan rapped on the edge of the doorframe. "Medics are getting an IV bag from the medical company. How long do you want to leave Kearney out here?"

Sean folded his arms over his chest and sighed. "Restrict him to the barracks, and let him sleep the rest of it off."

Morgan nodded then stepped farther into the office. "Looks like you had a lot of catching up to do with that other captain."

"Don't suppose I can ask you not to pick that scab right now?" Sean leaned back in his chair.

Morgan said nothing for a long moment. "Kind of curious about what has you this fired up, honestly."

Sean breathed deeply through his nose and deliberately changed the subject. "So have we gotten ahold of the XO yet?"

Morgan lifted one brow. "Apparently he's on his way."

"Any reason why it's taken him so long?"

"Apparently, he was still drunk when he woke up. He claims he didn't want to get a DUI."

Sean leaned back in his chair. "Let me know when he gets here," he said simply. Then, "Did you get the paperwork done up on Kearney?" He needed to keep his mind focused on work.

It would be far too easy to disappear on a long winding trip down memory lane.

"Yep, already done." Morgan sighed. "Look, whatever is going on between you and that captain, you need to put it away. We don't have time for you to be pining away like a lovesick puppy. We have privates —" He glanced over his shoulder where Kearney sat at the conference table. "And sergeants for that shit."

Sean looked up at the big first sergeant, grinding his teeth to keep his better judgment from escaping. Morgan meant well and he wouldn't be saying anything if he didn't see the train wreck that

Sarah had turned him into. The unit couldn't handle any more command or leadership disasters. They'd had more than enough already.

"I'm working on it, Top," was all he said after a moment.

Morgan studied him quietly then left him alone. Alone with the silent recrimination in his thoughts and the swirling memories that took him back to another life. To a life before the war, when he'd still believed his own bullshit that he'd be man enough to bring everyone home. That he'd be able to go to war and come home with his honor intact. That Sarah loved him enough to leave the Army behind.

Funny how a decade at war changed everything.

3

Sarah walked into her office an hour later, infinitely more calm. She'd gotten a copy of the police report of the fight from the military police liaison and had sat in her car, flipping through the information. There really didn't seem to be much to it. Basically, Kearney and Smith got into a fight about Kearney's wife.

She honestly could not figure out why she was investigating this fiasco. But, there were times in every officer's life that one simply shut up and colored, and that's exactly what she was going to do. She set the file on her desk and started to log in to her computer.

LT Picket stuck her head into her office.

"Ma'am? There was a call for you while you were out. Your daycare?"

"Thanks," Sarah said as she pulled out her cell phone. No missed calls. Great, Fort Hood was a cell phone dead zone. That was always helpful. *Please don't let Anna be sick. Not today.*

"Oh, and Major Wilson was looking for you." Sarah looked up at the LT. "She said something about the command and staff?"

Sarah looked at the battalion calendar on her desk that she'd printed out the night prior. "There was command and staff today?"

"It was moved because of the meeting for the ball next weekend."

A sense of dread curled around Sarah's heart. "And I was expected to be there?"

Picket nodded. "Yes, ma'am. Major Wilson was, ah, not happy that you weren't there."

Sarah blew out a hard breath. Great. First week in the unit and she'd already missed an important meeting. Command and staff. The weekly meeting between—who else? —commanders and the battalion staff officers.

The daycare had called thirty minutes ago. She looked between the note and her phone and hated herself that she even had to think about which one needed to be dealt with first. Never in her life had she imagined that being a parent and a soldier would tug her in completely opposite directions. She closed the door, dialing the daycare from her office phone.

"Hi, Ms. Silver, this is Sarah Anders, Anna's mom. I had a message you called me?"

"Yes, Ms. Anders. It looks like Anna is running a fever. She's going to have to be out for at least twenty-four hours before she can come back. Will you be coming to get her or will her father?" The daycare manager, Ms. Silver, had the kind of voice that got on Sarah's last nerve every time she heard it.

Sarah closed her eyes and opted not to clarify that she was Anna's only parent. Again. "I'll be there as soon as I can." There was a single rap on her office doorway and she held up one finger over her shoulder.

She turned and realized who she'd quite literally given the finger to.

"Put the phone down, Captain." Major Wilson stood in Sarah's doorway.

She'd never met Major Wilson before, but she didn't need to know much about her to know she was going to be highly unpleasant to work for. Her gray blond hair was cut short around her face. She wore neither makeup nor a smile, and her eyes were cold and merciless.

Sarah was fucked. She knew women like this. Women who made it their life's work to push other women out of the Army because they weren't the right type for the job.

Sarah clicked her phone off and stood immediately. Her half-formed apology was barely a sound in the base of her throat before Major Wilson cut her off.

"Captain Anders, I don't know what kind of standards they had in your last unit, but here, my staff officers are on time and present for my meetings." Major Wilson's voice was gravelly and filled with napalm.

"Roger, ma'am." She thought about mentioning that she had no idea the meeting had been changed then decided against it. Major Wilson didn't look like she handled excuses too well. Sarah had a sudden vision of *Mortal Kombat*, with a player getting her spine ripped out.

Not exactly comforting imagery at the moment.

Major Wilson didn't raise her voice, but still managed to make Sarah feel like she was two inches tall. "I'll see you at 1800 tonight for your initial counseling."

Sarah opened her mouth and Wilson's ice blue eyes narrowed quickly. "Is that going to be a problem?"

Sarah snapped her mouth closed and shook her head. "No, ma'am." She bit the inside of her lip while she waited for Wilson's response.

Her gaze flicked to Sarah's phone. "You have childcare issues." It was not a question.

"Ma'am, my daughter is running a fever. I have to keep her out of daycare tomorrow. My family care plan is current, pending my local childcare provider getting the last form notarized." Sarah would forever be grateful to the fates that had sent Mel and Jamie Sorren her way. Mel had volunteered to take care of Anna whenever she needed it. It was just that Mel was a little preoccupied with her ex, who'd gone and had a heart attack a couple of weeks ago. Sarah just couldn't bring herself to ask Mel for help right then.

Wilson blinked rapidly, her jaw flexing. "Where's your husband?"

Sarah breathed in through her nose and out through her mouth. She wondered if she would ever get used to the callousness of that question from her leaders. Even if Jack hadn't died in the war, maybe she'd left an abusive relationship. Maybe she'd decided to have a child on her own. But no, the default for officers was white, heterosexual couple with a stay-at-home Army wife and a husband who sold his soul to make the next pay grade and wow did she sound bitter.

"My husband died in Iraq, ma'am." The hurt no longer blocked her throat like it once had, no longer crushed her lungs and kept her from speaking, but the lump was still there. Still made her clear her throat so she could breathe again.

She was still off kilter from the altercation with Sean. That was all.

"I'm sorry for your loss." A bland platitude. It wasn't always. Most people meant it when they said they were sorry.

But Wilson didn't. She was the kind of officer who punished other women who dared do the Army differently than she did— single, childless, and as manly as the men.

Sarah had forgotten that there were officers out there like Wilson. She'd been so fortunate to work with other women who lifted each other up rather than tore each other down. Women like Claire, who pushed her to do better instead of tripping her up. Guess her luck had finally run out.

Sarah remained silent, figuring there was nothing she could do or say at this point to dig her ass out of the hole she'd gotten herself into by missing a meeting she hadn't known about. Awesome first impression with the battalion XO. Fantastic start in the new unit.

Everything that was important to her slipped a little further out of reach as she stood beneath the unflinching scrutiny of

Major Wilson. Her hard work to stay in the Army even after Jack died. Her need to stay in the fight, to be a soldier. To make a difference. All of those reasons that mattered so much to her slipped a little further away.

"Submit a leave form for tomorrow and any future days you need to take off work to care for your family." Wilson paused, her expression cold. "I hope you don't have a sickly child."

"No, ma'am."

"Good. I can't afford to have staff officers missing work. We've got too much to do with the current deployment cycle."

Sarah waited until she was alone before sinking into her chair and cupping her face in her hands.

Had she kicked puppies in a previous life? Drowned kittens or something?

"Major Wilson can be really tough, but she's not that bad once you get to know her," LT Picket said from the doorway.

"I'm sure she's normally charming," Sarah said dryly. She looked over to find Picket still in the doorway. "Can I help you with something, LT?"

Picket chewed on her lip, and Sarah couldn't decide if the gesture annoyed her or not. "Is it true? You're really a single mom because your husband died in Iraq?"

The lieutenant's earnestness was such a stark contrast to the banal chill in Major Wilson's eyes. God, had she ever been that young and naïve? And holy hell, when did all these personal questions become normal for people to ask?

"Yes." Wow, she did not want to have this conversation tonight. Or ever, for that matter.

Picket's expression was instantly sad, the way only a young soldier who had not yet gone to war could be. It was honest and real and it reached in and squeezed Sarah's heart. "I'm so sorry."

There was nothing Sarah could say to that.

Sarah finished her leave form. "Can you drop this off at the company for me?"

"Sure, ma'am."

"Thank you. I'll be back in a little bit. Have to get my daughter, before my late night meeting with the boss."

❧

"THIRTEEN HOURS AFTER I CALL YOU, LIEUTENANT, YOU DECIDE to show up?"

Wilford Paul Smith, III stood at the position of attention in front of Sean's desk. His white button-up shirt was stained with blood and his khaki pants were ripped at one knee. He reeked like a Porta-Potty in Iraq in August even from six feet away. "I came as soon as I got your message, sir."

"Clearly, we need to come to a common understanding of what ASAP actually means." Sean rocked back in his chair and folded his arms over his chest. He remained silent for a long moment. Long enough to make Smith squirm.

The little fucker was lying to him. Sean had already gotten the report from one of his platoon leaders. Smith hadn't come as soon as he'd gotten the call. He'd stayed out partying until he passed out in LT Biggs's back seat. The only reason he still looked like shit was because Biggs had left him in the car when Biggs had reported to PT formation that morning. "So make it a good one," Sean finally said.

"Sir?" Smith broke his hundred-yard stare from some point over Sean's head to meet his gaze briefly.

There was something smarmy about his stance, something Sean couldn't put his finger on.

"The story. Why you're getting into fights with one of my NCOs? Make it a good one."

Smith's nostrils flared. "Are you going to read me my rights first, sir?"

Heat crawled up Sean's neck. He ground his teeth and yanked his temper back viciously. It was forever before he leaned forward. By some act of God, he did not raise his voice. He kept his voice perfectly calm and flat. "You can invoke your rights, LT. That's perfectly fine. There's a 15-6 investigation ongoing as of right now." Smith's expression flickered, then shuttered closed once more, revealing nothing more than a hard night of drinking. "I encourage you to think long and hard about the content of your statement."

Smith's red-rimmed eyes narrowed and landed quickly on Sean's face before finding a spot over Sean's shoulder. He cleared his throat. "I already gave my statement to the Harker Heights PD, sir."

Sean let him squirm just a little inside of his hundred-dollar khakis.

"Stand fast in the ops," Sean said.

Smith left the office less sharply than he'd entered it. There was uncertainty in his movement now. Good. Sean wanted him to squirm.

Sean stepped out of his office. Morgan sat at the conference room table, the *Army Times* spread out before him like he was reading the Sunday paper. "What's your plan, sir?"

"I'm going to find the investigating officer," Sean said. "See if she'll interview him tonight instead of waiting."

Morgan glanced up, then back at his paper. "I take it I'll be keeping him and Sergeant Dances-With-Fists separated?"

Sean shook his head and fought a grin. "Roger that. I want this over with sooner rather than later."

"And you think she's going to come skipping down here because you ask her to?" Morgan asked.

Sean stopped at the front door of his ops. "I'm a commander. Staff officers work for commanders."

Morgan looked up at him. "Clearly you haven't been paying attention in command and staff."

Sean pinched the bridge of his nose. "I need this wrapped up. We don't have time for outside officers to be getting into our affairs."

"We don't have time for lieutenants and sergeants to be coming to blows at bars downtown, either."

"What's your point, Top?"

"My point is that if you'd dealt with Kearney the first time I recommended you throw the damn book at him, we wouldn't be dealing with his bullshit now."

Sean swallowed hard. "So this is your way of saying I told you so?"

Morgan stood and gripped Sean's shoulder. "I get it, sir," he said quietly. "I understand why you're reluctant to take action against a man you bled with in combat. But he's detracting from the mission in a big way." Morgan released his shoulder. "I'll support whatever you want to do, sir, but I strongly recommend dealing with Kearney and his shit." Morgan paused before folding up his paper. "He needs to soldier, or he needs to go home, sir."

Sean stood there for a moment, letting his first sergeant's advice sink in. Morgan was sharp, one of the strongest first sergeants Sean had ever served with.

But he was wrong about Kearney.

Sean headed to the support battalion headquarters, hoping to find out what unit Sarah was in so he could get a hold of her.

He hated going into the support battalion headquarters. Their battalion executive officer was known to make grown men cry. She'd gotten a hold of Sean's fellow commander Captain Bello a few weeks back and had damn near ripped his soul out through his nostrils for allowing trucks to be driven without proper equipment in them.

Wilson couldn't be all bad if she was ripping into Bello. It was a perverse sort of pleasure that Sean took from seeing that fucking guy get his ass handed to him.

He rounded the corner leading from the parking lot toward her battalion headquarters and stopped, his heart frozen in his chest.

Sarah was walking toward the headquarters, holding the hand of a small, dark-haired little girl. Her entire body was relaxed as she tipped her head toward the small child and listened intently to whatever the child was saying.

In that instance, his fears were confirmed. In the face of that child, he saw very clearly the image of a man he'd once known.

Crossing the years, the hurt returned, as sharp and cutting as it had been that long-ago day. He felt the heat of the burning truck. The asphalt digging into his skin. The ghost of a brother long gone but not forgotten stared back at him from that little girl's face.

Anders.

Jack Anders.

Sarah was Jack Anders's widow.

That little girl was Jack Anders's daughter.

Sarah looked up. Across the quad, their eyes met. Sean stood, rooted and motionless in the spot.

Marry me, Sarah.

I can't.

The memory slammed into him, a thousand points of violence penetrating the darkness surrounding his soul.

She swallowed then and looked down at the little girl.

He turned, then, and walked away, the force of the memories driving him away from her.

From the life that could have been that stared back at him from the face of that little girl.

4

"Who's that, Mommy?" Anna asked, holding her Happy Meal to her chest like it was the most precious thing in the world. Which, to be fair, it probably was, since Sarah did her damnedest not to buy the stupid things.

Sarah watched Sean walk away, relieved that he hadn't approached. She wasn't ready to deal with him again today. And she damn sure wasn't about to get into a pissing contest with him in front of her little girl. She didn't want Anna to see what Mommy had to deal with at work. She didn't want her to see that side of her.

Sarah's heart started beating again as she watched his back as he walked away. But it was a long moment before her mouth formed the words she needed. "No one important, baby."

Because he wasn't. Not anymore.

Sarah had never felt like she was being pulled both ends against the middle like she was at that instant. She wasn't actually sure who she was more irritated with as she had driven on post with Anna in tow, but either way, she'd been given an order and, well, she didn't really have the option to say no.

She walked into the battalion headquarters, shoving aside her irritation as she saw another friendly face.

Sergeant First Class Reza Iaconelli. He'd damn near ruined the training exercise before her previous deployment, but he was a close friend of Claire's, which meant she was a friend of his.

Anna ducked into the latrine.

He smiled when he saw her. "Thought you were downrange, ma'am?" he asked by way of greeting.

Sarah's leg ached at the question. "I was. Got sent home early."

"Oh yeah?"

"Brigade commander never really got over the Colorado incident."

His dark skin flushed beneath the fluorescent lights. "Yeah, well, his loss. I thought you were doing a hell of a job."

Sarah waved a hand dismissively. "How have you been?"

"Good. Sober, so that's a win, right?" He looked down at her legs. "What's with the limp?"

"Accident downrange."

He nodded slowly. "So that's what brings you to the Death Dealer battalion?" he said, trying to shift the conversation.

"More or less. I'm in the support battalion."

"I'm sorry, ma'am," he said after a moment. "I know how important command was to you."

"Thank you." She swallowed. "Why are you here?"

"Paperwork for the range next week." Reza shrugged. "What's got you hanging out after duty hours?"

"Investigating a fight between a lieutenant and a sergeant."

"Kearney and Smith, huh? Kind of surprised they've got you investigating that. It's pretty cut and dry."

"That's what I've been saying since I got it. There's nothing to investigate, honestly." She didn't bother to hide her frustration with the case and the entire situation. "LT Smith made some comment about Kearney's wife; they fought. I've literally been in this unit for less than a week, and I'm already getting a feel for how nuts this place is."

He chuckled. "It's got some good things about it. The senior leadership is at least aware that they've got a serious problem on their hands and are at least willing to address it."

Sarah lifted one eyebrow. "From what I hear about some of the lieutenants around here, you'll have to excuse my suspicion on that quarter."

"Yeah, well, there are some bright spots of give-a-damn."

"Surrounded by a sea of incompetence?"

"What's the saying? There are pockets of incompetence in every organization? Well, we're trying to suppress an outbreak of malfeasance."

Sarah laughed as Anna came out of the bathroom. It felt good to laugh. "Ready, honey?"

Anna ignored her and looked up at Reza. "Who are you?"

Reza hunkered down to Anna's level and stuck out his hand. "I'm Reza. I'm a friend of your mommy's."

Anna shook it somberly. "I'm Anna. Do you have any kids?"

Reza's smile darkened just a little. Not so much that Anna would have noticed, but Sarah did. Reza was a man with many demons. Some from the war, some from things Sarah could only guess at. But he responded to her daughter's question with a gentleness that should have been impossible for a warrior like him.

"No, no kids for me," he said to Anna.

"Why not?"

But Sarah didn't have time to stop her daughter's questions. Major Wilson stepped into the hall. "Any time you're ready, captain." Her voice grated down Sarah's spine, then she disappeared back into her office.

Reza met her gaze as he straightened. "If it makes you feel any better, she was probably potty trained at gunpoint." His voice was low.

Sarah bit her lips to suppress the laugh that almost snuck out. "I'll keep that in mind when she's ripping me a new one."

"Enjoy."

Sarah sat Anna down in the command group chairs and prayed she would stay distracted with her dinner. She sucked in a deep breath and held it a moment before she knocked on Wilson's door. The XO looked up over the rim of surprisingly trendy black-rimmed glasses. The elegant frames did nothing to make her less terrifying. She looked like a female version of the Grinch in designer glasses. "You're early."

"Yes, ma'am. Figured it would be bad form to be late twice in one day." She flushed, the words escaping before she had a chance to engage her mute button. Damn it, this situation did not call for sarcasm.

Wilson arched one brow but said nothing. After a waiting long enough for Sarah to fight the urge to fidget, she pointed toward the seat across from her desk.

Sarah sat, her hands resting on her thighs as she waited.

Wilson finally finished whatever she'd been working on, then turned her attention to Sarah. She felt like a hamster caught in the open beneath the gaze of a hungry cat.

"I don't have a written counseling for you, Sarah."

Sarah sat absolutely still. It was kind of like *Jurassic Park*: the T-Rex could only see you if you moved.

"I'm going to be straightforward with you." Wilson removed her glasses, setting them on the desk. "Single mothers do not make good officers."

Sarah's heart was pounding in her ears. Her palms slicked with sweat against her thighs. Still, she did not move. Wilson's words settled around her heart like a vise, squeezing slowly.

Sarah breathed deeply through her nose, trying to figure out the right response. At the moment, her options were completely losing her shit or partially losing her shit. Neither one felt like a particularly viable plan of attack.

Wilson, however, did not seem to recognize Sarah's dilemma.

"Bringing your child to work with you is unprofessional and speaks to a lack of foresight and proper planning on your part." Wilson never blinked or looked away from Sarah. It was like she was trying to make Sarah flip out. Which, to be fair, was starting to look like a likely course of action. "You were fired from command before setting foot in Iraq. You haven't deployed since 2003. You've been hiding out and avoiding your duty while the rest of the Army has been fighting this war."

Sarah couldn't force enough air into her lungs. Denial burned in her lungs. It was a long time before she trusted her voice not to break when she spoke. "Ma'am, I think it's a little unfair that you'll judge me on one, my first day here and two, the one time in the last six months my daughter has gotten sick."

Wilson shook her head slowly. "I've been an officer for nearly ten years. Children are never sick only rarely. This week it's a fever. Next week a school play." Wilson still didn't blink. It was really creepy. "I will not tolerate your childcare issues interfering with your duty performance."

Sarah's skin was clammy.

She and Jack had always talked about how they would manage both of them having military careers if they ever had kids. It was what she'd loved about him—he'd fully supported her need to be a soldier. He hadn't asked her to give it up. Hadn't asked her to choose between the one thing she'd ever been good at and the man she'd fallen in love with. It was heady stuff, leading soldiers.

And for a while, she'd had the love of a good man and had loved her job.

God, but things were so different without him. She'd gotten a taste of what making a difference could do as a commander. And she'd lost it before she'd ever gotten started. Shame burned up her neck at the memory. She almost buckled beneath the pressing sense of loss wrapping around her shoulders.

But Wilson was right. She had been fired. She'd never command again. At this point, she'd be lucky if she got promoted to major. It was a far off dream, out of reach.

"Sarah, the Army isn't meant for officers who are single mothers. You simply cannot give the same as an officer who has no children or who has a wife at home to take care of these things."

Sarah forced herself to speak. To retain some shred of dignity and not just sit there, mute and powerless.

"Ma'am, I've done everything the Army has ever asked of me. Willingly and with everything I am." Sarah choked out the words. Her throat was tight and her lungs burned from not getting enough air.

She would *not* cry in front of this woman.

"Then maybe you should readjust your priorities. Clearly if you've been devoting everything to the Army, your child is suffering."

Sarah pressed her lips together to keep her mouth from falling open. She expected this kind of attitude from a male. Her previous boss had been looking for an excuse to fire her for exactly those reasons. But to hear this from another woman? She'd always had such support from other women, especially since she'd commissioned.

"Mommy?"

They both looked toward the door at the tiny source of the little voice.

Sarah's heart skipped a beat at the little voice that slipped into the office. Anna peeked around the doorframe, a look of urgent distress twisting her adorable features. "What's wrong, honey?"

"I have to go potty."

Any other time, the urgent plea would have been no big deal. "Didn't you just go?"

"Mommy, I have to poop."

Sarah's face flamed red and she was half out of her chair before she realized she hadn't been dismissed. The Army was the only place in the world where she would ever have to ask permission to take her daughter to the bathroom. She turned back to see a smug look on the major's face.

"You're dismissed. I expect you at work as soon as your daughter is well enough to return to daycare."

Sarah stepped from the office, slipping her hand into Anna's as she led her daughter down the hall. The anger was sudden and violent and rose up from a primitive place deep inside her.

She didn't even know how to respond to Wilson's comments.

What could she do? No one would believe her. It was too surreal. Hell, Sarah didn't even believe what she'd just sat through.

Wilson's implication that she wasn't a good mother burned over her skin. Every single minute of her time with Anna was precious to her. She waited for Anna to wash her hands then led her daughter out to the car.

She would be angry later. After Anna was in bed. And the dishes were done. And lunch made.

Maybe by the time she had time to be angry, she'd have forgotten why she was furious to begin with.

SLEEP AND SEAN HADN'T BEEN FRIENDS IN A LONG, LONG TIME. Since before the war, he figured. He lay in bed staring at the overhead fan, wishing there was something he could take, something he could do that would banish the insomnia and finally let him sleep. There was no storm tonight, but that didn't matter because his thoughts were plenty to torment him all on their own.

How the hell had he not known that Sarah had married Jack Anders? Maybe because he'd been busy fighting a war? Not a whole hell of a lot of time to play "show me pictures of your kids" with his fellow lieutenants.

He glanced toward his closet. He knew what was in there. Where the memories lurked. Buried beneath old uniforms no longer authorized for wear was an old shoebox. He didn't actually want to go hopping down memory lane tonight. Not by a long shot.

But since it was approaching midnight, and he clearly wasn't going to be heading to sleep any time soon, what the hell else was he going to do?

And tonight was not a night for ignoring memories.

The shoebox was easy enough to find.

He sat, just looking at the tattered brown lid. It was from the first pair of boots he'd bought as an officer candidate at Benning after his first foot march had nearly crippled him. He flipped open the top and was greeted by a stack of postcards maybe an inch thick. The sum of all of his communication with his parents since he'd joined the Army.

He should be honest with himself. The postcards were since he'd left home. His folks had died on his second tour in Iraq, and because Sean had already had mid-tour leave, he hadn't been allowed to come home for the funeral. Not when they'd been neck deep in the shit in Najaf.

Another one of those choices that his civilian sister just didn't understand. No one believed military folks when they told them they missed funerals and other serious life events because they'd been stuck in Iraq. He could still hear Cynthia calling him a goddamned liar. Yet another reason why they tolerated each other but had rarely spoken since Mom and Dad had died.

He moved the postcards to one side and pulled out a tiny, pocket-sized photo album. He ran his thumb over the dusty cover.

Fear and something else squeezed his throat.

It was a long time before he lifted the cover.

He swallowed hard at the first photo.

Sarah beamed up at him, her arm around a younger Sean's waist. Her face had been rounder then, her smile a little more care-free. God, but he'd been skinny back then.

He turned the page. A picture of them tubing down a river, a cooler of beer between them. Sarah smiling up at him when they'd gone to the field together. They'd been in the same unit once upon a time. She'd been a smart-ass private, and he'd been drawn to her even then.

They'd had a good life together. And then he'd come down on orders for Korea. He'd wanted to marry her. Wanted to take her with him.

And she'd said no.

"I'm not going to be that girl, Sean. The one who runs off and marries the first guy who gets her all hot and bothered."

"Do you realize how fucked up that sounds?" The anger had hidden the hurt that night.

"I don't want kids, Sean," she'd said softly. *"I don't want the white picket fence or the golden retriever. I'm not good at any of those things."*

There were no more pictures in the lonely album. Their life together had ended when she'd said no. He sat for what felt like forever, hand over his mouth.

She'd gotten married within two years of leaving him. He had no idea how old the little girl was that he'd seen her with today, but if he had to guess, he'd say five, maybe.

She hadn't wanted kids. Hadn't wanted to get married. Sean had wanted all of those things. If she hadn't gotten married so soon after telling him no, maybe it wouldn't feel like such a betrayal. Like maybe she'd held on to a small memory of when things had actually been good between them.

They hadn't broken up immediately after she'd said no. They'd tried to keep things going, but the closer he'd gotten to Korea, the worse things got for them. He started going out without her.

And one morning, he'd come home after a particularly bad weekend in Austin, and Sarah had been gone. She'd packed up her stuff—a fact that made him think she'd already been planning on leaving him—and been gone before he'd dragged his ass home.

He'd gone to Korea and tried to forget about her. Then the war started, and he got too busy to wonder what might have been. He'd lost himself in the adrenaline rush of combat and training, then more training and more combat.

He dragged his hand over his face and rolled over, one arm wrapped around the spare pillow. His eyes drifted closed but all he could see were the images of him and Sarah. Memories blended with the present and reminded him of everything that he'd lost.

❀ 5 ❀

Sarah walked out of the morning staff sync meeting unsure if the dread in her stomach was from the realization that she was going to have to see Sean today or from Major Wilson's soul-withering gaze during the meeting.

Today's glare had come because a lieutenant in the ops cell had missed a deadline—a deadline that Sarah had not been aware of, nor had she been aware that the damn lieutenant even worked for her.

Awesome.

And then there'd been a final little jab at the end of the three-hour marathon staff meeting about not having the investigation completed.

This job was going to be just as fun as her last job, working for people who hated their subordinates. By regulation, she had thirty days to conduct the investigation. But no time like the present to get things done. Last night, thanks to field grade officer–induced insomnia and because her leg had been throbbing like a toothache, Sarah had stayed up and gone through the limited paperwork she had on the case, avoiding the obvious reason why she was delaying dealing with Sean and his company as much as possible.

She didn't want to see Sean again but she needed to just bite the pillow and get it over with. Get in, get done, and get as far away from Sean Nichols as she could. She'd moved on once. It was time to do it again. Permanently.

So she braced herself, put on her headgear, and headed toward his company ops. She needed to speak to Kearney and Smith, and then she could close this investigation up, send it to the lawyer for legal review, and be done with everything pertaining to Sean Nichols or his company.

She stepped into his company ops, though, and found the lights off in the front office. Empty but not silent. There was a crowd in the back—doing what, she had no idea.

She debated walking toward the noise, not really wanting to step foot in the middle of whatever chaos was going on.

Thankfully, she didn't have to. Sean stepped into the front of the ops. He paused near the door, his gaze colliding with hers.

Her eyes flicked down his body and wow was that a mistake. He wasn't wearing his uniform jacket. Sweat marked his thin brown T-shirt where it clung to his body, outlining broad shoulders and narrow stomach. His chest rose and fell quickly as he struggled to catch his breath but he stood there, still and silent. She wished she had something smart and witty to say, but her brain was stuck on sweat and heat and a whole lot of thoughts she should not be having about Sean Nichols.

Jesus, the man was sex on a stick. He'd grown into his height and filled out. She remembered the first time she'd seen his chest and the narrow trail of hair that had disappeared down his belly into his pants and her entire body tightened, wondering what he'd look like now beneath that Army T-shirt.

And wow, talk about a mental detour. Nothing like mentally undressing your ex in the office.

"Sounds like you need to call the MPs." Her voice sounded gritty even to her own ears. Damn it. She was going to be professional around this man if it killed her. Which it might, to be honest.

He narrowed his dark eyes, not bothering to hide his suspicion at the carefully neutral statement. She could practically see him calculating his own response.

He hooked his thumbs into his belt loops. "Combatives. Blowing off steam."

Sarah raised her eyebrows. "On cement?" So far so good. They could be civil. They were both adults.

"We put down mats."

"Safety first, right?" She took a deep breath, intensely aware of the weight of his gaze on her. "Look, Sean, about yesterday..."

"I was out of line." He took a few steps closer, stopping just at the edge of her personal space. That he didn't approach spoke volumes about the man he'd become. The boy he'd been would have come too close, come on too strong. She'd loved that about him back then, until she realized that his intensity wasn't limited by anything close to resembling rational thought.

The apology stood between them, sucking the familiar animosity out of the space that separated them. He'd completely disarmed her with that single sentence. She finally looked up, meeting his gaze. There was an unexpected warmth there that threw her off balance.

"So was I," she said simply, when she was certain her voice wouldn't break. "I guess I wasn't prepared to see you again. After...everything."

"Yeah. I get that." A shadow flickered in his eyes, and he looked away, fiddling with a pen that was chained to the counter. He cleared his throat. "So you need to talk to Kearney and Smith, right?"

"That should really take care of it." She set the folder down on the counter and opened it. "I can't honestly figure out why they want a formal investigation here, anyway. It seems like it's a pretty straightforward incident."

Sean nodded and tucked his hands beneath his arms. "I have Smith in the back. We've got to pick Kearney up from his group therapy session in twenty minutes."

She didn't miss how he ignored her comment about the investigation. "Group therapy?" Sarah made a quick note on the yellow legal pad inside her folder.

Sean sighed heavily. "He's in alcohol abuse counseling, among other things."

"Command referred or self?"

"Command." Sean swallowed, his gaze flicking away briefly. "Kearney's got a lot of...issues." There was something off in his expression, a more personal worry than anything she'd ever thought possible. She'd seen that look before.

On Claire when she was acting as Sarn't Iaconelli's shield. Sarah studied the man in front of her, worried that this might be the exact same situation.

"This bothers you."

He met her gaze then. "I've known him a long time. He's a hell of a soldier downrange. It's just his personal life that's a disaster."

She almost smiled. "I know a lot of soldiers like that."

"Don't we all?"

It felt strange talking to him like this. Like they were old friends. He studied her then, and she didn't look away. Not from the past that stood between them. Not from the present that wrapped around them. She simply stood, taking in the changes half a lifetime and war had left on this man. A man she'd loved once upon a time.

He shifted and before her brain could register what he was about to do, he lifted his hand and brushed a strand of hair from her cheek. "It's really good to see you again, Sarah." Soft, hesitant words.

His fingers were warm and rough against her cheek, a shocking sensation. A touch that took her back, way back to when he used to touch her the exact same way. The memory collided with the present.

She stepped back out of pure reflex. Out of his space. Out of range.

"Please don't do that again." Pain and surprise laced those words.

Sean's hand closed where it had still hung in the air, and he dropped it. "I'm sorry. I wasn't thinking."

"It's okay." But her voice wavered, just a little. "I'm...just not...I can't rehash the past with you, Sean."

"I get that." He slipped his hands into his pockets, the muscles in his neck tense. "I'll get Smith for you." But he didn't move, not for a breath, maybe longer. Silence stretched between them. For once, it was not uncomfortable or filled with unsaid things.

It simply was.

She'd wanted to grow old with him. She remembered that now. She missed the comfort she'd had with him. The complete ease and security she'd felt, just knowing he loved her.

Just not enough for her to be a soldier and his wife.

She cleared her throat, needing to focus on her mission.

Needing to put Sean Nichols out of her mind. Because she'd loved him once upon a time and he'd let her down. There was no happily ever after, not in this life.

Not for soldiers like Sarah.

❧

He couldn't say what had possessed him to reach out and touch her. He wanted to blame his lack of sleep, but even that felt like stretching the truth for his momentary insanity.

The truth was he'd simply wanted to see if she still reacted the same way to his touch. Because they'd been good together, once. And though he'd dated and even been marginally serious with a nurse back at Benning, he'd never settled down.

He cleared his throat. "You can, ah, use my first sergeant's office to talk to Smith."

"Your first sergeant won't mind?"

"Nah, he's heading to the motorpool after this so he'll be out of the office for a while." The front door of his orderly room swung open, letting in the bright Texas sun and heat.

In that moment, his total focus on Sarah diverted to the young soldier who walked through that door. The soldier who was only a shadow of the man Sean had once known. Gone was the quick grin and biting intelligence. His civilian T-shirt hung loosely on his thin shoulders. His pants were at least ten sizes too big and a chain ran from his belt loop to his back pocket.

But it was his eyes that shocked Sean the most. There were shadows there, dark and deep and filled with old ghosts and fresh torments.

People always wondered if the kids who came back fucked up from the war had gone downrange fucked up to begin with. Sean knew better.

But that didn't make the shock at Haverson's appearance any easier to mask. Sean tried to play off his surprise but his voice sounded hollow. Empty. "Hasselhoff!"

"Damn it, sir, I told you to stop calling me that. Haverson. Hav. Er. Son." The smile didn't even come close to reaching his eyes. Sean couldn't remember the last time it really had. It had been months since Haverson had been transferred out of their unit and into the Warrior Transition Unit. Guilt wrapped around his throat and squeezed tight. He should have tried harder to get him transferred back to Sean's unit. He'd ask the boss again. He had to try, right?

He threw one arm around Haverson's shoulders and pulled him into a quick one-armed man hug. He felt frail. Far too thin.

"You reenlist yet?" Sean asked, stepping back.

"Nah. I told you, sir, I'm going home." Haverson shook his head, the shadow creeping over his features. "The Warrior Transition Unit is putting my chapter packet on the expressway."

Sarah shifted and the movement caught Sean's eye, reminding him that they were not alone. Sean paused, keenly aware of Sarah watching their exchange. "I thought you were medically on hold?"

Haverson shrugged. "Apparently not. New cadre just took over and apparently, their goal in life is to get rid of us malingering crybaby sissies." He made air quotes around "crybaby sissies."

Sean's mouth moved, but nothing came out. Anger blocked his throat, made it hard to breathe. He hated the fact that Haverson had been transferred to the WTU before Sean had taken command. "I'll try again to get you pulled back over here," he offered.

"Nah, it's fine. I don't think the Army's the right place for me anymore." There was resignation in those words.

Haverson was tired. Burned out from a lifetime at war. The dark slashes beneath his eyes weren't the only signs. There was a gauntness to his cheeks, a hollowness that suggested not enough food or not enough time spent eating. Either way.

Sean needed a break, a space to pull his thoughts back from the edge of what he was afraid he was seeing in Haverson. "Haverson, this is a friend of mine, Captain Anders. Haves was my platoon medic in '03."

"Nice to meet you."

"You too, ma'am." Haverson turned back to Sean when he spoke.

"What's your plan?" Sean asked.

"My dad owns a motorcycle shop. I figure I'll go putter around and work on bikes for a while. Try to get my head straight."

Sarah moved into the first sergeant's office and Sean was at once grateful for the gesture and terrified of being alone with Haverson. He didn't know what to say, how to reach out. How to save the kid from self-destructing.

"You're still not sleeping," Sean said when Sarah was out of earshot. It was not a question.

Haverson shrugged and avoided his gaze. "Few hours here and there."

"No meds?"

Haverson leaned against the counter. "Took too many the last year. Ambien doesn't work for me anymore. They say you're well and truly fucked if that happens. It'll be all right. Have to crash sooner or later, right?"

Sean rubbed his shoulder reflexively. It ached now and again but just then, it flared up, violent and hot and burning. He stretched and tried to shove the pain away. "Just be careful the crash doesn't come when you're driving. Have you talked to a doc?"

"Tried, but the docs in the WTU won't see me anymore because my packet is already in front of the board." There was a crash and a stream of cussing from the back room. "What's going on back there?"

Sean grinned. "Combatives."

"Still using it as group therapy, huh?" Haverson's smile almost reached his eyes. "Anyway, I'm leaving as soon as I get my orders. WTU already cleared me from post." The shadows were back in his eyes now, dark and filled with haunted pain. "I just wanted to stop by and say hi."

Sean pulled a sheet of paper from the printer and scribbled down his phone number. "You ever need anything, you call me. I don't care if it's midnight on Christmas, you call me." Sean gripped Haverson's shoulder and lowered his voice. "Don't... Stay in the fight. Okay? Promise me?"

Haverson swallowed and nodded. "Yeah, man." Haverson stepped away and grinned, trying to shake off the sudden serious-ness of their conversation. The attempt failed, but Sean let it stand. "Keep in touch, though, okay?"

"You too."

Sean said nothing as Haverson stepped out of the life he'd led and into a world outside the Army. He simply stood, watching Haverson walk away.

He felt Sarah watching him from his first sergeant's doorway. "I'm worried about that kid," he said quietly, without looking at her. "The WTUs don't care about their soldiers. I've been trying to get him pulled back into my unit so I can look out for him."

"But?"

"Battalion commander won't even consider it. Says we don't have the resources to look after every wounded soldier's medical needs."

She looked down but not before Sean saw something behind her eyes. Something unspoken, laced with fear and something else. He wanted to push, to ask her about it.

When she said nothing, Sean sighed hard and dropped his hands into his pockets. Found the coins there, comforting and warm.

He tensed when she moved closer and stopped just inside of his personal space. Some part of his brain registered that she walked with a faint limp. He'd have to remember to ask her about that sometime, too.

But when she rested her palm on his forearm, the gesture was both unexpected and unwelcome. The sympathy threatened to destroy the control he was barely holding on to.

He stilled, unable to move. He looked down at her palm, warm and soft against his skin.

"Your commander is right, Sean," she said quietly. "You can't save everyone. No matter how much you might want otherwise."

Sean stared at her, wrestling with a thousand unsaid things twisting and burning beneath his heart. "I know that." The harshest truth.

The kindred spirit of loss wrapped around them. For a moment, the harsh words and breathtaking disappointment were gone, and they were just two soldiers, each with their own scars from the war that had taken those they cared about.

He wanted to tell her. Wanted to tell her he'd known her husband. That Jack had been a friend of his.

That he'd been there when Jack had died. And oh God, he was sorry. Sorry that he hadn't done more to save them. Sorry he hadn't brought her husband back to her.

But he said none of those things. Because he was a coward, and regret sat on his chest like a wet wool blanket.

Finally, he cleared his throat, needing to break the silence and get back onto clear footing with this woman who resurrected far too many things he'd tried to forget. "I'll, ah, round up Smith for you."

He walked away. Because that's what he was so terribly good at when it came to her.

❧ 6 ❧

"You won't make a statement?" Sarah asked, struggling to keep her expression carefully blank.

Across from her, Lieutenant Smith crossed his arms over his chest. "No."

"No, ma'am," she corrected, keeping her voice level. She didn't know who this lieutenant thought he was, but he damn sure had a high opinion of himself.

"No, ma'am. I will not make a statement." There was a hint of sneer there. Just below the surface and yet buried enough that she couldn't call him on it.

Legally, she couldn't ask him why the hell not, now that he was invoking his Article 31 right—the military equivalent of the Fifth Amendment. The interview was over. She couldn't ask him any damn thing about anything.

It was frustrating but it certainly simplified things, that was for sure.

Sarah slid the legal form across Morgan's cluttered desk and handed LT Smith a pen. "I need you to write that in here and sign the front and the back."

She said nothing as Smith made the appropriate marks on the page. He slid the form toward her and stood.

She didn't even look up at him. "Sit down, lieutenant. You are not dismissed." She'd had just about enough of his superior attitude. She waited until he sat, then waited an extra moment, just to prove her point. "You realize that by not making a statement, you're allowing me to draw conclusions based on everyone else's statements."

"Yes, ma'am. I do."

"And you have no issues with that?"

"Ma'am, I did nothing wrong other than drag a drunk and out-of-control sergeant from a bar. I don't have to write anything other than what I already told the police."

The words rolled off his tongue a little too easily. A practiced lie. He wasn't making a statement because he didn't want to contradict himself already. Sarah watched him silently, long enough that he finally shifted uncomfortably in his chair. He couldn't wait to get out of that office.

"You're dismissed." His attitude sucked, and she could see why Kearney—or anyone who knew him, for that matter—was ready to fight him at the drop of a hat.

Smith slid out of the office and barely a moment passed before Sean rapped on the first sergeant's door. "Make any progress?"

She lifted one eyebrow. "He's a charming fella, isn't he?" she said dryly.

"Very much so," Sean said.

Sarah frowned. "Has Kearney gotten back yet?"

"He's on his way. He'll be here in a few minutes."

"Thanks." She looked down at her notes. "I really don't have much to say about this, Sean. They got into a fight. That's really the extent of my findings right now."

He looked over her head at the clock behind her.

"Why does Morgan keep the clock behind him instead of across the room?" she asked.

Sean grinned. "He can tell how much soldiers are squirming by how often they look over his head at the clock."

"That's brilliant." Sarah tapped her pen against the desk. "I'll have to remember that one." She flicked the pen cap off. Back on.

Sean tipped his chin, studying her quietly. "You were in command?"

Sarah looked down at her paperwork, annoyed that she'd allowed that factoid to slip out. "Yes. For about five months."

Silence greeted her private shame. Any commander who was pulled out of command before twelve months had been fired and they both knew that.

"What happened?" he asked finally.

Hell, everyone knew that.

Sarah swallowed. "It's a long story," she said. The truth. From a certain point of view.

There was a question in his eyes now, questions that seemed to surface every time they were around each other. But for once, the tentative truce between them seemed to hold.

"Give me the short version?"

She released a breath slowly. "My boss and I didn't agree about how we were training for the deployment. I had one too many training accidents so when I got hurt in Kuwait, he fired me. Said he'd lost confidence in my ability to lead soldiers."

"Hurt?" She looked up at the intensity in that single word.

"Fire."

Something dark flashed over his face. "Is that why you're limping?" His words were thick now, grating over her skin.

She nodded. "Yeah."

"Jesus, Sarah, I'm sorry." There was no judgment in his eyes. No blame or pity or *I told you so*.

He was so different from the man she remembered.

"Thank you," she said honestly. And she meant it.

Finally, he cleared his throat then looked over his shoulder. "Kearney's here."

"MA'AM, I'D LIKE MY COMMANDER TO BE PRESENT DURING MY interview."

Sarah looked at the sergeant sitting across from her. Too much sun and not enough sleep had chiseled away over the years at what had once been a handsome man, leaving a ragged, haggard man in his place. The black eye and bruises on his face didn't help things.

"Will his being present change your answers?" she asked. Sean was standing in the ops, pretending to read a sheet of paper he'd just pulled off the printer and fooling exactly no one. She remembered exactly how she'd felt when her company had been investigated for the training accident back in Colorado before her last deployment. Protective. Hovering to make sure no one was portrayed inaccurately.

"No, ma'am. My answers will be the same regardless of who's present."

She felt Sean watching her, leaving the silence to stand alone and unafraid. She had the distinct feeling that he really was leaving this decision to her. She looked up at Sean. "If you're okay with that?"

Sean stepped into the office and nudged the door closed behind him. "Sure."

Sarah focused on Kearney. "Please tell me what happened the night you and LT Smith were involved in the fight."

"Haverson and me rolled out to meet up with some of the other guys out at Ropers. We were having a good time, minding our business and all, when the damn XO showed up."

Sarah raised her eyebrows and pressed her lips into a thin line. "Lieutenant Smith?"

Kearney nodded, and she wrote quickly. She'd get this in another sworn statement after she finished going through his original write-up.

"You said in your statement to police that Smith started the argument as soon as he arrived?"

"LT Smith started running his mouth about my wife. Things

got out of control and the next thing I know, we're outside, rolling."

Rolling was slang for combatives. "It sounds like you did a lot more than rolling," she remarked dryly, then frowned. "Why was Lieutenant Smith making remarks about your wife?"

Kearney swallowed and looked down. A flush crept up his neck, and the muscle in his jaw flexed several times. Finally, he cleared his throat. "Just talking shit, ma'am. Our wives had a falling out during the last deployment."

Sarah looked up at the choked words and stared silently at Kearney. "Smith is married?"

"He was. She's a lieutenant over in First Brigade."

"What happened between your wives?"

"Smith's ex, ah, thought Kitty was sleeping with Smith."

Sarah paused, considering her next words carefully. "Was she?"

The silence stretched for an eternity. There was pain and anger written in the lines on Kearney's face. He didn't have to answer for Sarah to see the truth of the situation.

She did not expect Sean's reaction, however.

"You mean to tell me Smith slept with your wife, and you didn't say anything?" There was darkness in Sean's eyes now. Barely restrained fury.

Kearney looked up at Sean, humiliation mixing with defiance in his bruised eyes. "It's none of your business, sir. You've got more important things to worry about."

"One of my lieutenants fucking his soldiers' wives is goddamned good and well my concern." His voice was deadly calm, but even though there had been years between them, Sarah could see him reaching the edge of his control.

"Sean." She spoke softly, highly aware that if she handled this wrong, she could undermine his authority.

He met her gaze, and there was something there, something haunted and twisted and filled with regret. He ground his teeth and took a step back, out of Kearney's line of sight. His presence was a palpable thing.

"What happened after you and Smith fought?"

"Someone pulled me off him. Next thing I know, I'm in hand-cuffs, and he's getting pushed into a car by a couple of his buddies."

"Do you remember who those buddies were?"

"I think McKiernan and Ricks."

Sarah made a quick note. "Why didn't you report the incident between Smith and your spouse to the commander?"

Another long pause. "I didn't want Kitty to get in any trouble, ma'am."

Sarah set her pen down and leaned forward. "Let me get this straight. You went out with buddies, were minding your own business at a bar, and then your company XO picks a fight with you about sleeping with your wife?"

Kearney's jaw pulsed, and he unclenched his fists to rub his palms against his thighs. "Yes, ma'am. That's what's in my statement."

"And you weren't angry that this lieutenant and your wife slept together?" Sarah glanced at Sean then back at Kearney.

"Kitty and I are trying to patch things up," Kearney said. "I'm trying to let the shit—stuff with Smith go. My counselor said something about forgiveness or some crap like that."

Sarah pressed her lips together, watching Kearney closely. Something didn't add up, but short of putting words in his mouth or guessing, she needed to let it go. Hopefully someone else would fill in the blanks and make sense of this madness.

Silence filled the small office as she made more notes. Finally she looked up at him, seeing clearly the broken down warrior trying and failing at being a garrison soldier. Kearney was a man made for war. And after the war, society had no idea what to do with them. "Is there anything else you'd like to add, Sergeant Kearney?"

Kearney shook his head quickly and looked down at his hands. "No, ma'am."

Sarah was alone in the office with Sean. It should have been uncomfortable and filled with unsaid things. Instead, he sat across from her and looked far too at ease in his own skin.

"I take it you didn't know about Kearney's wife and LT Smith?" she said, tucking away Kearney's new sworn statement.

"No. No idea. But it certainly fills in a big piece of the puzzle for me." He leaned back in his chair, resting his hands on the top of his head. "I thought I knew Kearney better than that."

"Because he didn't tell you?"

"Yeah." A single word laced with regret.

She wished she didn't notice. Not the tone in his voice or the span of his shoulders or the easy lines around his mouth. None of them had been there when they'd been younger.

She looked away, unwilling to follow the white rabbit down the trail it was trying to lure her on.

"Why did the previous Chaos commander get relieved?" she asked. "I'm tracking that all the company commanders were relieved recently, right?"

"They were. Captain Rush was removed for incompetence laced with malfeasance."

She almost smiled at that description. "Care to expound?"

"Drunk on duty, caught with porn on his government computer. Basically sat in his office and let the lieutenants and senior NCOs run the unit without any oversight."

She lifted both eyebrows. "Which explains how a lieutenant might have slept with a soldier's wife."

"Rush was certainly an above-average fuckstick," Sean said. "But as far as Smith and Kearney go, the two of them have been nothing but a pain in the ass since I took command. I already tried to fire LT Smith once over his conduct with some of the NCOs."

Sarah leaned back in her chair. "For what?"

"Does being a piece of shit count?"

She lifted one eyebrow.

"I don't trust him. I don't trust his judgment. I think he's arrogant and he doesn't listen."

"None of those are firing offenses," Sarah said.

"Fair enough. I think he lacks integrity. Kearney's statement today is exhibit A." He sighed heavily. "Is it wrong of me to admit that I was hoping the boss wouldn't care and just let me get rid of him in the churn following the changes of command?"

Sarah doodled on the edge of her green notebook. "No. But generally, I tended to avoid taking my boss problems without having solutions to recommend."

He shifted, resting one ankle on the opposite knee. "I know in my bones that Smith is bad news." Sean shook his head. "I wasn't raised to stand by and watch a power-hungry bully ruin those around him. That's what Smith is. I know it. Every NCO in this company knows it. I suspect the sergeant major knows it. But the boss? The boss either can't or won't see it because of Smith's uncle at division headquarters."

"You think his reputation makes him untouchable?"

Sean shook his head slowly. "Not Smith's. His *uncle's* reputation makes Smith untouchable. Some officers get their panties in a knot when someone tells them one of their favorites or their family member is a shithead."

A smile stole across Sarah's mouth. Unexpected and warm. "I can see where that might be a little awkward."

She paused. "You seem awfully focused on Smith and not Kearney. Why?"

He looked down where his hand rested on one bent knee. "I've served with Kearney before." He lifted his gaze to hers. "I trust him. He's going through a really rough time right now, but I trust him to have my back any day of the week."

Sarah said nothing. "What's the deal with his wife?"

"Those two just need to get a damn divorce. They're poison to each other." His voice was flat and laced with judgment.

"I haven't met her, but she seems to be at the heart of this. It doesn't jive that Kearney wouldn't instigate the fight with Smith." She leaned forward, looking at the statements in front of her. None of this made any damn sense. "The guy slept with his wife, and Kearney's not interested in fighting? That doesn't match up with, oh, I don't know, the entire history of masculinity."

Sean studied her quietly for a moment. Long enough that she had to resist the urge to squirm beneath the intensity of his gaze. He shrugged again. "She's trading up from a fire team leader. Happens all the time and if he's letting her go, then better for him."

"That's pretty cynical," she said.

Sean leaned back in his chair. "Nothing surprises me anymore."

Sarah swallowed and made an idle mark on the edge of her notepad. "I'll write up my findings and recommendation then and get them turned in to the commander."

"What are you going to recommend?"

She looked up at the quiet intensity in that single question. "That Smith receive a letter of reprimand for adultery, and Kearney be reprimanded for fighting. I mean, sure, adultery is a court-martialable offense, but there's nothing here worth taking to court-martial, honestly."

"Well," Sean said after a moment, "maybe the boss will finally deal with Smith. Or at least make him someone else's problem."

There was too much emotion in his response for her to ignore. She shifted, folding her arms over her chest, mirroring his. "There's more to your relationship with Kearney than that you two just served together, isn't there?"

He looked at her then, his expression inscrutable. "I'd rather not go into that, if it's all the same to you." Thick, heavy words, weighted down with memories and time.

She wanted to know. Wanted to push him on why he was protecting Kearney so much. She understood that kind of loyalty. She'd just never expected it from Sean.

His loyalty to her hadn't lasted. His loyalty had been to what he wanted her to be, not to who she was.

So what was it about Kearney that had the man bending over backward to protect this NCO?

She was curious now. Curious about the man he'd become.

And she didn't have time for that kind of curiosity. Because that kind of curiosity didn't just kill the cat.

It destroyed her.

❧ 7 ☙

Sean looked at the closed door of his office and winced as he heard the sound of a chair scraping across the floor. Morgan sighed heavily.

"This is bullshit, sir!" Kearney's voice was muffled outside of Sean's office door.

Sean felt Morgan's frustration as he first looked to the ceiling for patience then shouted at the closed door: "Sarn't Kearney, one more tantrum out of you and I'm going to have you in the dying cockroach for the rest of the day."

It would have normally been funny imagining Kearney flat on his back with his arms and legs extended straight up in the air except that Sean's sense of humor was apparently AWOL and had been for some time. "That's cruel."

"Cruel is what I'm going to do to him if he doesn't quit his bitching and moaning." Morgan ran his hand over the three hairs on the top of his head. "So the investigating officer recommended letters of reprimand for both of them? You should just let them take it out on each other on the combatives mat. Get whatever it is between them out of their system."

"If I thought for one second that they wouldn't try to kill each other, I would." Had it not been an enlisted man challenging an officer, Sean might have also considered letting them have a go at it.

Morgan said nothing for a moment. "So which one of them are you going to recommend be moved from the company? I assume you want to keep the XO?"

Sean mulled that over for a minute, considering his response. "Hell no. Just because I'm an officer doesn't mean I'm in the officer protection agency. Smith needs to go. I can deal with Kearney."

Morgan shook his head. "Under normal circumstances, I'd agree with you, but this has been going on a little too long. Kearney's gotten in a lot of trouble, sir. The soldiers are starting to question why he's still wearing his stripes."

"I would hope that those same sergeants would be looking for some compassion and understanding if they ever go through what Kearney's gone through." Sean kicked his feet up on his desk.

"Agreed. But you're going to go to war with the Army you have, not the Army you wish you had, right?"

"I hate that expression," Sean said mildly.

"Got it, sir, but you can't have the NCOs questioning your judgment or thinking you're playing favorites."

There was a knock on the office door. "Excuse me, sir?" The ops clerk Sergeant Sloane stuck his head in the door. "There's a spouse here to see you, sir. Says she won't leave until you talk to her."

Sean sighed and bit back a smart-ass remark. He was not in the mood for some hysterical spouse and he damn sure didn't feel like dealing with demands today. Ninety-nine percent of his soldiers' spouses were awesome but it only took one or two to remind him why he dreaded those phone calls. But part of his duty description was dealing with the spouses and the implied task attached "politely" to that requirement.

He stepped into the ops and saw one very unwelcome spouse standing there.

Face of an angel. Heart of a rabid pit viper. He didn't even know if vipers could get rabies, but if they could, he was sure this woman would be one of them.

Kitty Kearney.

The one spouse Sean wanted absolutely nothing to do with.

Sean deliberately ignored the *I told you so* look Morgan shot in his direction.

"Who do I need to talk to about a restraining order against my husband?"

SARAH STOOD AT PARADE REST IN FRONT OF MAJOR WILSON'S desk for the second time that week. At least she'd just gotten her recommendations back from Major McLean, the brigade lawyer. Too bad he was getting out of the Army. He was damn good at his job.

"You're recommending letters of reprimand?" Wilson sounded incredulous.

"Ma'am, that's the only punishment that passes legal review at this point. There's no evidence of the adultery, only one man's word against another. I also recommend at least one of them be moved to another company."

Wilson studied the paper then looked up at her again. "I'm surprised at these findings, Sarah."

"Ma'am?"

"The recommendation is weak."

Sarah bristled. "The recommendation is legally sufficient, ma'am."

Wilson shook her head. "You should reconsider your recommendations. NCOs cannot be allowed to fight with officers."

"And maybe officers shouldn't be sleeping with their NCOs' wives, ma'am." Damn it, where was her mute button when she needed it?

"Watch your tone, captain." Wilson looked up at her, her expression completely unamused. Then she shifted and pulled out another sheet of paper, one Sarah didn't have to read to recognize. "Talk to me about your profile."

"There's not much to say beyond what's on the paper, ma'am." Sarah ground her teeth. She'd figured this was coming sooner or later. Being on profile was just about the worst sin a soldier could commit. For an officer—well, she might as well drop her release paperwork right then and there.

The only thing in her entire life that Sarah had been good at was being a soldier. It was going to take a hell of a lot more than a cranky major to make her give up the career she loved.

Except that Sarah had problems keeping her mouth shut. Maybe keeping her answers to a minimum would increase Sarah's odds of keeping her foot from sliding all the way down her throat.

"What are you on profile for, captain?"

"Shrapnel and burn recovery, ma'am."

Wilson looked up at her over the edge of her glasses. "Explain?"

"Fire during a fueling operation. I was hurt and removed from command while I recovered."

"That's not the story I'm tracking, Captain Anders." There was no emotion in Wilson's voice but damn if she didn't somehow make Sarah feel two inches tall.

As if she'd gotten hurt on purpose.

Sarah swallowed and said nothing.

"You were removed for being reckless, ignoring your brigade commander's guidance, and failing to follow standard operating procedures."

Sarah breathed in through her nose like her therapist had taught her. It wasn't helping.

"Is that true?"

She counted to five before she answered. "Ma'am, the procedures I violated amounted to letting my soldiers wear eye protection that wasn't authorized but exceeded Army safety specs. I also required they actually test fire *all* of their weapons before leaving the base, as opposed to just the front and rear vehicles. And yes, ma'am, I failed to complete mandatory training as required."

"And you got yourself blown up."

"In a fire that was due to deliberate sabotage by the contractor, ma'am." It wasn't like she was out fucking off down at the market. "That's in the official report, too, ma'am. In case you missed it."

"I don't appreciate your sarcasm, Captain Anders," Wilson said mildly. "You're weak, mentally and physically. How much longer before you can be medically ready?"

And you have the personality of a rabid squirrel. Trying to act tough and fierce but really just a rodent foaming at the mouth.

"Ma'am, I'm prepared to take a PT test tomorrow if need be," Sarah said more sharply than she intended.

"Good. I'll see you at the railhead at 0500 for your record APFT."

Silence dragged on. Sarah watched her, trying to figure out if she was dismissed or not.

"You're dismissed, Captain."

Sarah executed an about-face before her head exploded or her mouth engaged before her brain could stop it.

Perfect. Now she just had to figure out what to do with Anna at four-thirty in the morning. And hope that her leg was strong enough to cash the check her mouth had just written.

Maybe she could ask Jamie Sorren to babysit. She'd been holding off on asking Jamie because her dad was still recovering from a mild heart attack. Maybe Claire. Shit. She retreated to the relative safety of her desk and picked up the phone, hoping that she could pull a childcare hat trick out of her ass.

❧

"I WANT HIM KEPT AWAY FROM THE HOUSE. HE THREATENED TO kill me." Kitty Kearney sat in front of Sean's desk, her eyes wide and innocent. Beside her stood Kearney's platoon leader LT Ricks and his platoon sergeant, SFC Madeira.

Kearney himself, however, was not allowed in the office due to the fact that he'd completely lost his shit the minute his wife had demanded to speak with Sean.

Kitty wore a look of well-practiced terror. And it was complete and total bullshit. Sean felt slightly stabby. He hated people like this – people who abused the system and took resources from people who really needed it.

There was practically a battle drill for this type of thing, and Kitty Kearney knew all the rules. She knew exactly how to ruin her husband's week and potentially his career.

Sean looked at LT Ricks and his platoon sergeant. "LT, you and Sarn't Madeira will escort Sarn't Kearney to his residence to ensure he gets any necessary medication, clothing, and uniforms he needs to function. He will not leave your sight at any point in time. Then, you're to escort him to the corps legal office and make sure he starts an allotment so that Mrs. Kearney has funds." Finally Sean looked down at the future ex-Mrs. Kearney. "Ma'am, I'll order him restricted to the barracks for the next seven days. After that I'll have to reassess the situation. He'll be required to sign in to the CQ every hour. If he contacts you in any way, either directly, through a friend, or through any type of social media, you need to let either LT Ricks or Sarn't Madeira know immediately."

"Can't I just call you?" she asked meekly. Her bottom lip quivered for added effect.

Sean shook his head. The only effect her pathetic look had was to piss him off further. He lashed it back, keeping his words careful and professional. "Ma'am, this is why I have platoon-level leadership."

"Can LT Smith escort me? I trust him." There was something beneath the surface of her words that set Sean's teeth on edge and made his blood turn cold in his veins. The woman was heartless.

Behind her, Morgan choked and coughed into his hand. "Not only no but hell no, ma'am," Morgan said.

Sean shot him a warning look, and Morgan went silent. "Considering I've got sworn statements saying that you and Lieutenant

Smith engaged in an extramarital affair, I'm thinking that's not a good idea. He's receiving a no-contact order for you as well."

A lone tear trickled down her cheek. She sniffed quietly. "I don't mean to make trouble, Captain Nichols. I'm just so afraid."

Sean let her marinate in her words for a moment, unable to find a semblance of credulity anywhere inside him for her bullshit. If he wasn't careful, he'd end up saying something that would have his ass in a sling with the boss. One did not piss off the soldiers' spouses unless one wanted one's ass to spend quality time with the battalion commander's boot. "Have you spoken with a counselor, Mrs. Kearney? Maybe you could stop by and talk with the battalion chaplain?"

Sean was reasonably certain Chaplain Joas was going to kill him for this one.

She swiped beneath her eyes and offered a watery smile. "I'll do that. Thank you so much."

"LT Ricks, Sarn't Madeira, please let me know when everything is accomplished."

"Roger, sir," Ricks said.

They escorted Mrs. Kearney from the office. The door didn't even close before Morgan let out a stream of quite possibly the greatest creative profanity Sean had ever heard.

"She's been threatening Kearney with doing exactly what she did today," Morgan said when he finally stopped swearing.

Sean held up his hands. "Write it in a memorandum, Top. Word for word or as close as you can get to exactly what she said to you." He leaned forward and scrubbed his hands over his face. "Why the hell don't those two get divorced?"

"Because it's expensive," Morgan said. "You ever try getting divorced? Three grand minimum and that's if no one contests it."

Sean left his hand over his mouth. "That explains a lot. You know, part of me was hoping that time might have fixed them."

"You've been around long enough to know better."

"Why can't you be wrong once in a while?"

"It's my superpower," Morgan said wryly.

"Yeah, well, get a marriage counseling superpower," Sean said. "That seems to be the biggest problem we're facing right now."

"War is so much simpler than garrison life." Morgan reached for the door handle.

"On that, brother, we agree."

❦ 8 ❧

Sean's phone vibrated in his pocket. At almost seventeen hundred, it was never a good thing when the phone rang. Hell, it was never good news when his phone rang, no matter what time of day. "Captain Nichols."

"Sir?" Morgan's voice grated on the other end of the line.

"I don't suppose this is you inviting me out to a day of fishing on Stillhouse Hollow?"

"Don't you know me better than that by now?" Morgan snorted. "Kearney's broken restriction. He's at his house."

"Ah hell." Sean sighed. "What's the rest of the story?"

"The MPs are on the way. Apparently, he's on the front porch screaming at his wife to open the door."

"What's the address again?" Sean didn't bother to hide the fatigue in his voice.

"Comanche II, Karankawa Circle. Just follow the MPs. I'll meet you there."

Sean was already in his truck, heading toward the installation. "Get there first. We need to keep the MPs from taking him in, damn it. Kearney cannot get arrested again."

He pulled up to Kearney's house fifteen minutes later and parked behind two MP cars. Kearney was sitting on his front step, and Morgan was squared off with the MPs—four of them in all. One of the cops had the balls to have his hand resting on the butt of his M9.

"Firs' Sarn't, we have to take him in. It's the post commander's policy," the shortest sergeant said. He was built like a bull. A small bull, to be sure, but with a stockiness that did not run to fat. Sean glanced at his nametape. Nelson.

Nelson eyed Sean as he walked up. "I'm sorry, but you'll have to step back, sir."

"I'm his commander. I'll accept responsibility for him," Sean said as he pulled his wallet from his back pocket and flashed Sergeant Nelson his ID card.

"Domestic disturbance—" Nelson started.

"Look, Sarn't Nelson, I appreciate that you're trying to do the right thing. But Kearney's having a real rough time. I'm sure you've got other things to do than take him into custody and file paperwork, only to release him to me in four hours instead of right now." He only hoped it sounded like he was doing the young MP sergeant a favor instead of trying to save Kearney's ass. Again. "Let me take him back to the barracks now, and we'll deal with this in my company. I assure you, I will deal with this."

And he was lying through his teeth, because he knew damn good and well that Kearney was going to be a problem that would not be easily dealt with. But if he got arrested again, Kearney's future in the military was going to be taken out of Sean's hands. And Sean...he needed Kearney next to him when he went downrange again.

Nelson wavered, and Sean pressed his advantage. "He's going to be under guard the rest of this week. He's still on leave. You won't be called back here." *Come on, man, cut me a goddamned break.*

Nelson nodded. "If we come back out here, he's getting taken into custody."

Sean nodded, careful to keep the triumph off his expression and out of his voice. "Done. Thank you, Sarn't." Sean stuck his hand out, and Nelson shook it, then offered a salute. Sean returned the courtesy and waited for the MPs to pull away before turning to his first sergeant and his most troubled squad leader.

Irritation mixed with relief. He'd traded one issue for another because the look on Kearney's face told him he wasn't leaving without a fight. Right then, Sean would be happy to oblige him.

"What happened?" he asked, crossing his arms over his chest.

Kearney stood up, his chin lifted in defiance. "I just want to talk to my wife. She changed the locks."

Sean raised his eyebrows. "What part of a no-contact order did you fail to understand?"

"You are one dumb shit, you know that?" Morgan jabbed his index finger into Kearney's chest. "You're already in trouble and the first thing you do is come here? Real fucking smart."

Kearney sunk back to the step. "She thinks I cheated on her again," he mumbled.

Sean frowned. "And that justifies breaking a no-contact order because...?"

Morgan spat into the dirt. "Yep. Officially the dumbest shit I've ever met. Why are you so strung out over this woman? She left you, man. Get over it."

Maybe Morgan wasn't the right guy to be coaching Kearney through his marital problems.

Kearney shrugged. "Because I did her wrong, too. We both screwed up. She's just still pissed off at me because she thinks I cheated again."

"Did you?" Sean asked. Kearney just looked at him, and Sean took that expression for a yes. "Dumb shit," Sean mumbled. "Why is it so hard for you to keep your damn dick in your pants?"

Kearney grinned, and the expression was like a feral wolf, casting aside the drama for a moment and reveling in past exploits. Exploits that had once more landed him on the wrong side of his wife and the MPs, but apparently fond memories for Kearney nonetheless. "I haven't touched anyone since that contractor in Kuwait. But Kitty just found out about her, and she won't let me explain."

Sean said nothing, letting the silence hang. "I'm not really sure there's anything to explain."

"Kitty just needs to listen to me. She owes me, especially after she shacked up, too. I'll take her back, I really will."

Morgan shook his head. "Dickhead, I don't think you taking her back is the issue here. Get in the truck. You're under twenty-four-hour guard for the rest of the week."

"I just want to see her, Top." Kearney's voice took on a desperate edge.

Morgan put his hand on Kearney's shoulder. "We'll work on that, okay? But no more goddamned screaming matches on the front porch. We'll get the chaplain to talk to her and come in to see you. But you come out here again, and that's your ass. Go wait in the truck."

Kearney didn't argue, but it was a close thing. Sober, he was significantly less belligerent than when he'd been drinking. At least they had that going for them. Morgan waited until Kearney had slammed the door shut on Morgan's ancient F150. "How many chances are you going to give him, sir?"

Sean stared hard at his first sergeant and wished he'd never told Morgan what had happened between him and Kearney all those years ago in that narrow street in western Iraq. But it was too late to close the lid on that box now, and Sean had to deal with the fact that Morgan knew Sean's deepest shame.

"As many as it takes, Top."

Morgan grunted and stalked toward his truck, his silence expressing his disagreement with ample volume.

"As many as it takes," Sean murmured as they drove off. He wasn't going to abandon Kearney. Not now. He was just having a hard time. He'd pull out of it. Sean was sure of it.

But Sean's faith in one man couldn't be explained to LTC Gilliad. Not without revealing a whole lot more that his commander did not want or need to know.

Pulling Kearney back from the brink was the least Sean could do. Because Kearney hadn't just saved Sean's life. He'd saved his soul.

THE DOORBELL RANG AS SARAH WAS PUTTING ANNA'S LUNCH IN the fridge. Claire walked in without waiting for Sarah to let her and set her backpack on the floor near the door.

"I owe you big time for this," Sarah said. Claire was spending the night and going to pack Anna off to daycare in the morning so that Sarah could make it to the PT test. She hadn't even hesitated when Sarah had asked her. Just requested heavy cream for her coffee in the morning if Sarah was running to the store.

Sarah had run to the store.

"Oh, and I plan to collect, but I'm not going to turn down time with my favorite munchkin. Where is she?"

"Legos. She's currently obsessed with Star Wars."

Claire grinned. "A little girl after my own nerdy heart." Claire handed Sarah a bottle of sweet red wine. "In the meantime, you owe me some details. What was it like, seeing Sean again?"

Sarah looked over at her long-time friend. "It's complicated."

"You're going to make me pull this out of you, aren't you?" Claire mumbled.

"Maybe." Sarah smiled. It felt good to break out of the morass of bad memories she'd been wallowing in. Between her run-in with the antichrist in human form and seeing Sean, her entire first week in her new unit had been an epic shit show. "We got off to a very rough start," she said after a moment.

"I hear a 'but' in there." Claire hunted around until she found a bottle opener.

"It's complicated," Sarah repeated. She didn't know what to say. Didn't know how to put into words the emotions that had surfaced when Sean had touched her, when he'd stood a little too close.

Claire poured two glasses, one more full than the other. "Okay, you're going to have to get more articulate than that. Here, maybe some wine will get you talking." She handed Sarah the smaller glass. "Can't have you getting loaded tonight before your PT test, now can we?"

"I don't know how to describe it, Claire," Sarah said honestly.

"Well, I suppose that's better than you still hate him." Cautious words.

Sarah loved her for it. "I don't know how I'm supposed to feel about seeing him." She looked away. "I loved my husband, Claire."

"I'm not sure what Jack has to do with any of this," Claire said gently.

Sarah looked at her friend. "I...I feel disloyal somehow for not still hating Sean."

"Your feelings for Jack weren't predicated on hating Sean. In fact, I distinctly remember you being really reluctant to even go to dinner with Jack when he first asked you because of Sean."

"Breaking up with your boyfriend because he couldn't handle that you didn't want to jump right into being his wife isn't really conducive to wanting to jump back into the dating pool."

"I can see where that might leave some scar tissue," Claire said mildly. "But then why did you marry Jack?"

"Because Jack...Jack treated me like an equal. He never asked me to give up my career for him. Never said his career had to come first. Never made me feel bad for wanting to be a soldier."

"It's part of what he loved about you," Claire said. "It takes a strong man to love women like us; I'll give you that."

"And Sean wasn't that guy."

Claire tipped her head. "Maybe Sean has grown up a little," she said finally.

"And maybe I'm not looking for anything else to do with him. The battalion XO hates me. She's already basically called me a piece of garbage. So yeah, let's start dating one of the company commanders to really make her think highly of me."

"So you've thought about it," Claire said.

"Not until two seconds ago, and no, I'm not dating anyone. Who has time?" Sarah narrowed her eyes. "And speaking of which, I find it somewhat suspicious that you didn't know he was here. You're engaged to the battalion operations officer in his unit."

Claire raised both hands. "I swear to God I didn't know."

"Evan doesn't know him?"

"Evan knows him, but I'd never run into Sean and the fact that we all used to hang out together when we were enlisted never came up." It was Claire's turn to narrow her eyes. "I would have warned you if I'd known."

After a moment, Sarah admitted, "I know you would have." She swirled the wine in her glass, watching the rich burgundy liquid capture the light. "I don't hate him. I hated him for a long, long time, but it's not there anymore." She finally dared to meet Claire's eyes. "Why?"

Silence stretched between them for an impossible duration. "Because you had Jack." Claire reached out, resting her hand on Sarah's forearm before Sarah could tense at her friend's words. "I'm not diminishing the love you had for Jack. Jack...he helped heal the hurt so that it didn't own so much of your heart."

"I miss him." Sarah took a sip of her wine to ease the tightness in her throat. "I think I always will." She tipped the glass up, peering at the wine and wishing she had more. It was one of those nights. "At any rate, my nonexistent love life doesn't matter. I've got to keep my job, and at the rate I'm going, the XO is going to make sure I don't get selected for major."

"Wilson, right?" Claire leaned back in her chair, an odd expression on her lips. "Good luck with that. She's actually had EO complaints filed against her by women before."

"Are you serious?"

"As a heart attack. She's been accused of a hostile work environment, holding women to higher standards and making inappropriate remarks about other females—enlisted and officer."

"You're serious?"

"You already said that. But everything always comes back unfounded because she might be an asshole, but she's a competent asshole. The guys don't have any problems out of her, so it's chalked up as a 'female problem' and ignored."

Sarah scoffed quietly. "Which is exactly why there will be no complaint from me. I've had asshole bosses before. I'll survive her. Especially if I want to save my career."

Claire looked at her intently. "You could consider a life outside the military. You know that, right?"

Something lodged in Sarah's throat at the thought of life without the uniform. "No. The Army is what I know. All my life I wanted to be a soldier. It's what I'm good at, and it's how I'll take care of my daughter."

Claire watched her silently. "What if you die, Sarah? Will Anna's college fund be worth it if she's lost both parents?"

"I won't live in that fear," she said, shutting the argument down. She refused to consider the possibility. "I'm more likely to die crossing Battalion Avenue on Fort Hood than I am in Iraq."

"Yes, but why court trouble?" Claire asked.

Sarah didn't have an answer for that. The remark festered beneath her skin, tormenting her with harsh truths that she'd rather ignore.

Thankfully, Claire let it go, letting Sarah avoid ripping the bandage from those wounds for another day. They talked about nothing and everything before Sarah headed to bed. The ass crack of dawn was going to get there early enough as it was. If she stayed up any later talking to Claire, she'd end up tempted with another glass of wine and that would end badly.

But it was a long time before Sarah fell asleep that night. Claire's words haunted her. She might be determined to paste on a smile and pretend that everything was fine, but things definitely were not fine.

And when she'd found out she was pregnant with Anna a few weeks after Jack died, her whole world had shifted beneath her feet.

She'd lost her husband. But she had his daughter. She'd lost Jack, but she'd survived. She was going to raise their little girl in the life that she knew and loved. She could be a good parent and still be a good soldier.

And that little girl was going to grow up seeing Sarah do something that she cared deeply about, not slaving away in a dull grey cubicle farm.

Because there was no better way to honor the man she'd loved and lost, than to live the life they'd planned on living.

Even if she was doing it alone.

☙❧

"SIR, WE'VE GOT A SMALL PROBLEM," LT MCKIERNAN SAID. HE looked like he was about twelve. Given that his platoon sergeant looked like he was about sixty, they were an odd pair.

"What's up, LT?"

"The support company XO is out back and he's pretty pissed. Apparently, we missed ammo draw for the range next week."

"Where's the XO?"

McKiernan jerked his thumb over his shoulder. "Sick call."

"It's not even six a.m. Fuck me." Sean scrubbed his hand over his face. "Go get the ammo draw unscrewed, LT."

"Roger, sir."

McKiernan wasn't a lost cause, at least not yet. He'd started shaping up the first time Sean had strategically placed his boot on his neck, and seemed to genuinely want to learn how to be a good officer.

Which made Sean suspicious because McKiernan and Smith were classmates and teammates from West Point. That kind of loyalty wasn't broken overnight.

Sean looked up from his computer to find McKiernan hadn't moved. "Is there a reason you're still standing there, lieutenant? Get the ammo fixed, then get to the railhead for the PT test."

McKiernan flushed and looked sixteen shades of guilty. "Roger, sir."

He moved out smartly, leaving Sean wondering at just what was going on with the lieutenants.

The ammo draw wasn't a big deal. McKiernan just needed to go talk to the support company and get it fixed. Sean needed to talk to the ops officer to make sure there weren't any other issues with the upcoming range. He grabbed his headgear and headed to battalion, hoping he could catch Evan before PT. He was not prepared to walk into an old...friend in Evan's office.

Captain Claire Montoya was leaning over Evan's shoulder in a way that suggested an intimacy he'd never imagined Claire possessing. For a moment, the softness in Claire's expression caught him off guard. She was a quintessential warrior. She always had been, even way back when all of them had been a bunch of privates running around doing stupid things that made their NCOs go crazy. She and Sarah had always been close, but where Sarah was a soldier with a sense of duty and obligation, Claire was a fighter, a warrior. Soft wasn't in her vocabulary but that was the only way he could think to describe her right now. Her smile was warm and there was a tenderness in her eyes as if she'd said something only Evan could hear.

The minute she looked up and saw him, though, that smile skittered away, replaced by a cold, hard look that he'd encountered before. Claire had been part of his life that he'd lost when he'd lost Sarah.

Claire was nothing if not loyal. Not to him, of course. Her expression shuttered closed and she straightened. When she smiled at him, it could have fractured glass. "I've heard you were around," she said.

Well, she hadn't threatened to neuter him so there was that. "Nice to see you, too, Claire."

Evan leaned back so he could see both Claire and Sean. "You know each other?"

Sean looked down at his old friend, not sure how he'd missed the fact that his friend had apparently gotten involved—seriously

—with Claire Montoya. "I could ask you the same thing," Sean said dryly.

A slight flush crept up Claire's neck. "Evan managed to convince me to settle down," she said quietly.

"You?" Sean instantly regretted the surprise in his voice. "I've walked into an episode of *The Twilight Zone*," Sean mumbled.

"So is someone going to fill me in?" Evan asked mildly.

Claire looked at Sean, and he felt two inches tall. A thousand bad memories came rushing back, but one stood out against the darkness.

"He and Sarah used to be a thing."

"Anders?" It was Evan's turn to sound surprised.

"Yeah."

"I thought her husband died in Iraq?"

"He did," Claire said. "But before she had Jack, she and Sean were a thing." Claire shifted, tucking her hands into her belt. "They were supposed to get married, but after Sean realized that Sarah really *did* want to be a soldier and wasn't just in the Army looking for a husband, Sean decided he'd rather party with the boys than be man enough to marry a soldier."

Sean flinched. Her statement was the unvarnished truth but that didn't make it hurt any less. And as much as it sucked, she wasn't wrong. He'd been immature. Threatened by the idea of his wife wearing the same boots he did.

Looking back, he hardly recognized the idiot he'd been. How stupid he'd been for letting his fledgling pride get in the way of the goodness he'd had with Sarah.

"The question now, though," Claire arched one brow, "is whether you're man enough now?"

Sean shoved his hands into his pockets. Found the quarters there, resting. "Not sure how that is any of your business, Montoya."

She sobered and there was no threat in her expression any longer. Instead, there was only concern. "Sarah is my best friend, Sean. If you hurt her..."

The first quarter was comforting and warm as it slid over his fingers. "Hurting Sarah is the last thing I intend." He did not look away from her intense inspection.

Finally, she nodded. With a quick squeeze of Evan's shoulder, Claire stepped out of the office, leaving Sean and Evan alone.

"So I need to check on the range for next week," Sean said after she was gone.

Evan tipped his chin. "Anything there I need to worry about?" The simple question was laced with protection and care. Sean couldn't stop the tiny spark of jealousy that twinged against his heart.

"No. Claire's a good friend. Loyal to a fault." Sean looked up at Evan. "She's the reason I still have a career."

✻   9   ✻

There were only a few places on Fort Hood to take a PT test. At least, few places that were officially sanctioned. You could take a PT test anywhere you damn well pleased, but let one soldier fail and every inch of your location would be inspected.

So naturally when there was an approved, flat area, everyone on the installation used it.

Sarah stretched alongside the formation of mostly junior soldiers. She was one of the few officers taking the PT test today. Thank God Claire had come through for her and had dropped Anna off at the daycare so Sarah could sit in her car for an hour and wait to take a PT test that technically, she shouldn't have to take for an executive officer who hadn't even bothered to show up.

But the XO had said be at the railhead at five, so that's what Sarah would do. The fact that the PT test wasn't going to start until six thirty was completely irrelevant. Captains did what majors told them to do. She wasn't going to let Wilson piss her off. At least not until she had her coffee.

She stretched her leg carefully and tried not to worry about the run. She had to run two miles in under twenty-one minutes. She could do that in her sleep.

Except that she hadn't done it, not for a record PT test, since she'd gotten hurt. And while yes, she was in her rights to demand a diagnostic PT test before she took one for the record, she was already on thin ice with Major Wilson. She would be perfectly within her rights to refuse to take the PT test—that's what the profile was designed to do, but in the current environment, giving Wilson any more reasons to target her was only going to cause more trouble. Trouble that Sarah didn't need.

So she'd take the damn PT test.

Sarah stretched and told herself she was fine. She'd been running and stretching and doing everything her doc told her to do. The burns hadn't gone into the muscle.

But the minute the PT test started, she knew she was in trouble. Her shoulders were tight and didn't loosen up until she'd done more than twenty push-ups. And once she started the sit-up event, the skin on her thigh felt stretched too thin. Like it was separating with a thousand tiny tears with each repetition.

Both events went by fairly quickly, though. She'd lost a few push-ups—thirty-eight instead of her normal fifty. She needed to work on that. But she'd passed those two events and that's all that mattered right now. She could work on a better score. Right now, she just needed not to fail.

And failing was starting to feel like it might be a reality. Her left thigh was tight and stiff as she walked to the starting line for the run. She'd be fine. She'd loosen up once she started running.

The whistle blew, and Sarah took off with the rest of the pack. She wasn't sprinting. She needed to pace herself. Her leg remained tight the first quarter mile. It loosened up a little bit on that second quarter mile but not enough.

Her stomach knotted as she rounded her third quarter. Her leg was no longer merely stiff; it felt like it was actively tearing open, like the fire was eating at her flesh once more. She bit back the pain, just focusing on running. As long as she didn't stop, she could finish the run. She wouldn't fail.

She wouldn't fail.

She'd never failed a PT test in her life.

But the second mile was half a world away. Her leg burned. Was weak.

She kept going. Just keep going. One foot in front of the other.

She saw the finish line ahead. Twenty minutes. She could make it. Left. Left. Left Right. She repeated the cadence in her head.

The finish line was farther away now. At the end of a tunnel, getting darker.

"Sarah!"

She heard her name from a far off distance as the fire licked up her leg and consumed her.

⚜

SEAN WAS USED TO FEAR BUT WHEN HE SAW SARAH GO DOWN ON the track, he was hit with a level of panic he hadn't known since the last deployment, when his TOC had gotten blown up.

He raced to her as she stumbled off the asphalt and crashed into the grass surrounding the track. She was already pushing up to her knees by the time he got to her. It didn't escape his notice that the NCO from her unit was *not* rushing over to make sure she was okay. What kind of bullshit unit was she in?

"Don't!" She pushed up to her hands and knees. Both were scraped and bloody. "You can't touch me, or I'll fail the PT test."

"Shit, are you serious? You're fucking bleeding."

"I just tripped and skinned my knees. I'll be fine." She tried to stand and wobbled. "I have to finish."

"Fuck this," he said. He slipped an arm around her shoulder and guided her off the track.

"No, no, no. I have to finish." But her voice was shaking now. She hadn't tripped. No fucking way.

"There's a fine line between *hoah* and stupid, and you just crossed it," Sean snapped. "Sarn't Madeira! I need the combat lifesaver over here."

Sarah finally stopped fighting to get back onto the track and sank into the grass. She started to cover her face with her palms but stopped, finally noticing the blood.

"What happened?" he asked as the company medic started rinsing the scrapes on her knees. Sean took gauze and wiped the gravel from her palms as gently as he could.

"My first PT test since I got hurt." Her voice was limp. Defeated. "Guess I wasn't ready for it."

"It's just a diagnostic," Sean said. "Try again next week."

She looked up at him and shook her head slowly. "It was a record."

"Huh?"

"Major Wilson directed me to take a record. So I did." Her throat moved as she swallowed, trying to blink back tears.

"Jenks, leave this with me?" Sean said to the medic.

"Roger, sir."

Sean took her hand in his. She was small and her hand shook where he held her. "This may sting a little," he said, holding up the bottle of saline solution.

"You guys had a PT test this morning?" she asked.

"Yeah. Good thing, too. Here." He pressed gauze into her palm.

She closed her eyes and rested her forehead on her wrist. "Shit."

"She can't make you take a record PT test if you're on profile, Sarah," he said as he cleaned her other palm.

"She already did. And I failed." She bit her lips together, hard enough that he felt sorry for them.

She sucked in a hissing breath as he squeezed the saline out over her knees a second time. She shifted and her shorts rode up a little on her left thigh.

He paused, taking in the mottled raised skin where she'd been burned. It started halfway up her thigh and disappeared beneath the black shorts. His chest tightened and a thousand emotions ripped through him. She'd been hurt. Badly. The skin was still bright red and hot pink – new wounds, not old. He fought the urge to gather her to him, at once wanting to protect her from something she'd already survived and wanting to offer comfort that she had not asked for.

He looked up to find her watching his quiet inspection of her wound.

"Guess I should expect that I told you so, huh?" She offered a half-assed wry grin and failed.

"I wasn't going to say that," he said quietly.

"What then?" She adjusted the gauze in her hand, checking the ripped skin beneath.

"I was going to say I'm glad you came home." He rested his hand on her calf. Felt the smooth, solid muscle beneath his palm. He had the strongest desire to run his hand down her calf and up her thigh, just to see if she still reacted to his touch.

She swallowed but didn't look away.

"What if you get hurt?" The echo of that fight rose between them, an unwanted memory.

"I'm a supply clerk. We're not exactly front line soldiers," she'd snapped.

God but they'd both been so naïve before the war. Now, long after the war had been going on for years, everyone knew supply soldiers had one of the highest casualty rates from running logistics convoys.

It was a long moment before she responded.

"Thank you," she whispered.

She didn't protest as he cleaned the gravel out of both knees.

The NCO who'd been in charge of the PT test came trotting over now that the last soldier had finished. "Ma'am, you okay?"

Sean bit his tongue to avoid ripping the sergeant a new one. Why the hell had they not sent someone to check on her when she'd first fallen? "Roger, sarn't."

"I'll have to mark you as failed, ma'am," he said, looking down at his clipboard.

"I know."

Sean watched the exchange silently, fighting to keep his temper in check.

She wasn't in his unit. She wasn't his. But the fury he felt at the unfairness of the entire situation burned in his chest. "You have a legitimate complaint, Sarah."

Her smile was flat. "I'm not filing a complaint against my XO. You know how fast that would end any chance I've got of getting out of this unit with a decent evaluation. Officers turn on our own when we call the IG. Wilson would crucify me."

"So instead of fighting for fair treatment, you're going to let her mark you as a PT failure?" He taped a bandage to her knee.

"You don't know what I'm dealing with when it comes to her. She's going to run me out of the Army if she gets her way."

"Try me," he said. He stood and offered her a hand. She winced as he pulled her to her feet.

She studied him quietly. "Since when did you care about what it's like for me in the Army?"

He took a step closer. The field was empty now. It was as if everyone had scattered the minute PT was over.

There was a faint white scar beneath her right eye, extending down toward her cheek. He wanted to ask her where she'd gotten that, but he didn't. She didn't look like she was up for a stroll down memory lane. The concern for her, the old feelings snuck up on him, breaking out of the locked box at the bottom of the well where he kept it buried and restrained and tried to ignore. But now, they broke free and mixed with a powerful storm of new emotions that he had no clue how to process. How to manage. It was too much, too fast.

"Since I lost you for not paying close enough attention the last time."

This was stupid. So stupid. She'd just failed a PT test—a major violation for an officer—and she was standing here, bleeding and sore. And her body was on fire.

But not from the run or from the weakness in her leg.

From the warmth and concern looking back at her from Sean Nichols's eyes.

"You couldn't handle the idea that I wanted to be a soldier when we were younger," she said.

"You're right. I was selfish and immature. Things didn't have to end up the way they did." A pained admission.

"You made your choice. You chose your buddies over me."

"And you chose your career over me." For once, there was no blame in those words. Only a simple statement of fact.

"You're right." She pressed her lips into a flat line. "And look where that got me. Blown up, widowed, and now a single parent too stupid to get out of the Army and find a new job."

"Don't." He cupped her cheek. "Don't take away from everything you've accomplished, Sarah."

She smiled hesitantly. "Who are you and what have you done with Sean Nichols?"

"War has a way of changing people. Making you see what's really important."

He stood too close. Close enough that she could clearly see the lines around his eyes, emphasized by the dark slashes beneath them.

She almost ran her fingers over the dark crease near the corner of his mouth. Almost. But she didn't. Because it was taking too much of a step, too much of a chance. To cross the barriers between them that had become part of the myth her life was built on...it was singularly the most difficult and simplest task in the entire world.

Instead, she chose a dodge. A feint. A hesitant retreat to safer territory. "You don't sleep."

"Not much, no." He cleared his throat, but his eyes never left hers.

"You should see a doc for that." She squeezed her fingers tight around the gauze in her hand. "Not sleeping is bad for your health."

His lips quirked. He said nothing.

"What?" she asked.

"That's the first time anyone has worried about me in a long time." His pulse beat slow and steady against the sunburnt skin of his neck.

It was tempting—far too tempting—to trace her finger over the line of his throat. To see if his skin felt like she remembered, or if it would be new. Different.

For the first time since Jack died, she let herself *feel*. A thousand emotions churned inside her heart, but one beat in constant rhythm with her pulse.

One that terrified her.

She took a single step backward, a full retreat now, thankfully more steady on her feet than she had been. Silence stretched between them.

He'd been the first man she'd ever loved. The first man who'd broken her heart for not loving her enough to let her be her own person.

And yet, he'd been there today when she'd fallen flat on her face. She'd expected an *I told you so*.

She hadn't gotten it. Instead, she'd gotten a glimpse of the man Sean had become in the intervening decade or so since she'd last seen him.

Reminding her that she'd had a life once, before Jack. A life she'd lived just as fully with Sean.

Standing there with him as the sun rose over Fort Hood, she felt something resurrecting deep inside her. Something transforming as it returned to life. Old emotions mixing with new.

"Thank you," she finally said. "For helping me today."

He swallowed, and she tried not to be enthralled by the movement of his throat. Tried to ignore the faint curl of hair at the edge of his t-shirt and the smell of warm male skin.

"I'm glad I was here for you." His gaze traveled down her body where the bandages had soaked through. "You might need to get those looked at."

She grimaced. "You did a good job cleaning them out. I'll put some Neosporin on them, and I'll be fine."

He smiled then. This time when he reached up to brush her cheek with his finger, she didn't pull away. Didn't flinch from the tenderness in that simple gesture. "You were always so damn stubborn, Sar," he murmured.

⁂

HE GAVE IN TO THE URGE TO TOUCH HER. HE LIFTED HIS HAND and slowly brushed his fingers across her cheek. She closed her eyes at his touch and she was there, just there. Far too tempting for him to avoid any longer.

He couldn't lie to himself, not about her. He'd never been very smart where Sarah was concerned.

He skimmed his finger over her skin, until her chin was cradled in his palm. Gently he brushed his thumb across her bottom lip. She was so still, she might have shattered if he moved too quickly. Her lips parted, and he heard the quick, quiet intake of breath.

It stirred a longing inside him that he'd thought he'd buried ages ago. He leaned in, barely brushing his lips against hers. She was still. Infinitely still. She didn't move as he nudged her top lip with his. Hesitant. Questioning. Giving her time and space to back away.

Her breath hitched before she opened for him. Just the barest hint of movement, but it was enough.

It had been almost a decade since he'd tasted her but it was like that time had been only an instance. She tasted the same. Like Sarah. The one woman he'd loved. The one woman who'd devastated him when she'd told him no. He stroked his lips across hers, tasting her, learning how she felt all over again.

Then it happened.

She leaned into him, a gentle sway and the tip of her tongue brushed against his, hesitant. Uncertain.

Long-buried desire burned to life inside him, and he fought the urge to take. To pull her against him and feel his body joined with hers. Her fingers curled against his chest, as though holding herself upright and holding on to him at the same time.

A low groan escaped him before he could rein it in. He felt her still and the distance creep back between them even though neither of them moved.

It was Sarah who stepped back first. She looked at his chest where her hand rested against the bold black letters that spelled ARMY.

Finally she looked up at him. "I can't do this with you, Sean." A tentative admission. He heard the fear underlying those words. Knew the reaction she expected from him.

"Why?" He was terrified he knew the answer already. Terrified that he knew exactly the words that were going to cross her lips next. She lifted her eyes to his, and he saw the sadness mixed with a storm of desire. He hated seeing the conflict within her, and it was somehow worse, knowing that he'd put it there.

She pressed her lips together as she blinked rapidly. Finally, she answered and it was the answer he'd been afraid of. "Because in my heart, I'm still married." Her voice broke and with it, the spell that had bound them together, her words giving voice to the thing he'd feared most.

He let her go, knowing that the truth was going to be the thing that kept them apart. The man she'd loved had died.

And no matter what he did, Sean couldn't compete with a dead man.

❧ I I ☙

Sean walked into the battalion conference room, irritated that he was going to spend the next four hours—after duty—in a marathon staff meeting. And oh joy, his favorite person on the planet was already there. Captain Sal Bello, the Diablo Company commander, was already in his spot on the other side of the conference room table. Which was good because Sean wasn't sure he could occupy the same space as the other man for more than five minutes.

Luckily Teague, one of the other company commanders, walked in right behind him, saving him from having to be alone with Bello.

Sean ran his tongue over his teeth. "Anyone know why we're having this fun fest?"

Teague shrugged and sat in his spot next to Sean. "Chapters, article fifteens. Warrior Transition Unit stuff. You know, the stuff the Army wants to pretend is a distractor from our jobs but is actually our sole purpose in life. Plus, we've got to figure out who is going to be on the rear detachment with Firs' Sarn't Sorren."

"Have they picked the poor dumb bastard who gets to command that shit show?" Sean flipped through his notes, checking off items he'd already completed.

Bello snorted quietly. "Whoever gets the job is going to have their hands full because you poor bastards won't throw your sick, lame, weak, or lazy out of the damn unit."

Teague lifted one eyebrow. "Compassion. It's a thing good leaders do. You should look it up sometime."

Bello shook his head. "Training your soldiers for war is what good leaders do. Compassion gets people killed."

"So does thinking you know everything and ignoring the intelligence briefing," Sean said.

Bello glared at him. "People make mistakes."

"And sometimes those mistakes get people killed."

Bello said nothing and Sean let the old familiar argument go.

Teague swiveled in his chair. "So how's the investigation coming? Anders come up with any interesting findings?" It was amazing how the two of them could carry on a conversation like Bello wasn't even there. Sean was pretty sure that's how Bello preferred it, too.

"Anders?" Bello looked up from his notepad.

Sean closed his eyes. So much for hoping Bello wouldn't get the reference. "Jack's wife."

Bello grunted and leaned back in his chair, absorbing the news silently. "Met her once when we'd convoyed to Baghdad to pick up that equipment for the outpost." It was the closest to civil that he and Bello would probably ever come. He leaned his elbows on the table, turning the lighter he always carried over in his fingers. "Jack was a good dude," he said finally.

The silence stretched into uncomfortable. Sean didn't want to remember a time when he and Bello hadn't hated each other. Didn't want to remember his life as a lieutenant or the friends and soldiers that lieutenant had buried.

I watched his truck fucking burn. He pushed to his feet. He couldn't put a voice to the fury that surfaced every time the memory rose. He couldn't put to words the hate and the violence that he'd wanted to unleash on anything that fucking moved that day.

He'd stepped into the abyss that day. And it had been Kearney who'd pulled him out. And it was something that he could never explain. How could you put words to the need to lash out, to hurt, to kill? To fucking burn the world and laugh as it smoldered?

People would look at him like he was a monster.

And maybe he was. Maybe that urge was still inside him.

He didn't know. Had no idea. But he knew where his loyalty stood—and if that meant protecting the man who'd kept him from becoming a monster, then so be it. There were worse sins to be guilty of.

The battalion commander walked in and the meeting got started. There were eighty-seven slides.

It was going to be a long meeting.

SARAH'S HEART TIGHTENED AS SHE LOOKED IN ON ANNA, WHO was concentrating hard on sticking two silver grey Lego pieces together. It was funny how things changed so much. She'd never wanted kids. It was part of what had damaged things so irreparably with Sean.

But Anna...Anna was a miracle. She hadn't known she was pregnant when they'd notified her of Jack's death. She'd been sent home that same week. Her boss hadn't given her the option of staying in Iraq, even before Sarah had known she was pregnant.

The pregnancy had nearly broken her. She'd wanted Anna. From the minute she'd found out she was pregnant, she'd wanted the baby growing inside her. She'd been sick from the start, throwing up so often that her doctor had worried about her ruining the lining of her esophagus. She'd prayed that her baby would be okay. Prayed that Anna would be born whole and healthy and a reminder of the love she held so close in her heart for her husband.

But the physical discomfort had been nothing compared to the pain and fear wrestling for supremacy in her heart. She'd sobbed when Anna's first cries filled the labor and delivery room. Relief and grief and a thousand other emotions had burned through her in those first moments.

Anna turned around and looked up at her. "What's wrong, Mommy?"

"Nothing, honey. How was school today?" Anna called daycare school for some reason, and Sarah didn't correct her. She'd be starting school in the fall and a piece of Sarah's soul shriveled when she thought about sending her little girl out into the world.

Anna turned back to the Legos. "Good."

Sarah blinked rapidly as her eyes burned, and she stepped out of Anna's room. She tucked her arms around her waist and walked toward her bedroom. Past the wall of pictures that lined the hallway. Pictures she refused to take down for her daughter's sake. For her own.

Jack smiled back at her. She'd gotten to the point where she no longer teared up every time she thought of him. Mostly. It would always hurt. She'd accepted that the pain of losing him would always be with her in a way that Jack would never be again. But tonight? Tonight she was feeling weepy and off balance and not just from the PT test that morning.

Everything was wrong and right and upside down tonight. Old feelings and new. Fresh hurt and long ago forgotten ones. They were twisted things inside her that she couldn't untangle, no matter how much she tried.

Something had slipped out from the box labeled "Sean" that she had locked away and tried to forget years ago. This morning when he'd touched her, things had gone completely off the rails. Part of her had been grateful that he'd been there, that she hadn't had to face the humiliation of falling out of her run alone.

But part of her was glad for other reasons. Dark, primitive reasons that had nothing to do with work or the Army or the life she'd lived since he'd walked away from her all those years ago because he'd wanted a wife, not a soldier.

She stripped off her uniform and turned on the shower. She

needed sleep and she needed to focus. She dropped her head beneath the spray and reveled in the calming heat seeping into her weary muscles. Tonight the scars on her leg ached, a hot burn that coursed over the damaged skin.

The shower did nothing to ease the throbbing pain around her heart. She stood there, letting the water cascade over her body, willing the stress and the tension to leave. But the pain tonight was already beating back the Motrin she'd taken earlier. She needed something stronger.

Something that would make her forget the life she'd lost the day she'd lost Jack.

She stepped out of the shower and reached for the little orange bottle of pills. She didn't need them often.

But tonight, she recognized the signs. There would be no sleep if she didn't wrestle the pain under control.

The tiny white pill wouldn't knock her out. She'd insisted on something that wouldn't get her high, wouldn't make her slur her words in front of her daughter. But it would take the edge off enough, just enough to let her sleep.

Her cell phone vibrated on the nightstand near her bed. It was eighteen hundred, well after the duty day had ended. She groaned when she saw Major Wilson's number. God, but she didn't want to get her ass chewed about failing the PT test.

"Captain Anders, may I help you, sir or ma'am?"

"I need you at the Death Dealer battalion headquarters in twenty minutes."

Sarah frowned. "Ma'am?"

"The battalion commander has questions about your investigation." Wilson paused. "Is this going to be a problem?"

Sarah closed her eyes, hating that her boss consistently put her in situations where she had to bring her daughter to work. "No, ma'am, I'll be there."

She pulled her uniform back on and tied her wet hair back. Popped another Motrin and hoped the pain would subside enough for her to make it through whatever questions LTC Gilliad had for her.

And there went any plans to cook dinner for Anna.

❦

"Captain Nichols, if you bring up Specialist Haverson's warrior transition status one more time, I'm going to shove my size fourteen up your ass."

Sean stood in the command sergeant major's office, an unusual place for a company commander to find himself. But then again, Cox was an unusual sergeant major. There was quite literally no one in the battalion more feared or respected than the CSM.

Which was why when he asked Sean—politely—to step into his office after the three-hour long meeting, Sean didn't refuse.

"Sarn't Major, you know the WTU isn't taking care of our boys."

"And that burns me on a fundamental level, sir, but you can't fix that. Haverson is not going downrange with you next time. You have got to spend your energy focused on the men who are." There was a fatigue in Cox's voice. A long-suffering weariness that came from too much time at war, too many battles lost, too many soldiers memorialized.

And still, the man showed up every single day ready to do it all over again.

"Sarn't Major—"

"Sir, I admire what you want to do, I really do. Keep tabs on your boy if you need to in order to sleep better at night. But stop asking the boss to get him reassigned. We don't have the manpower for it."

The bitter truth, one Sean did not want to hear. "Sarn't Major, I can't just leave him to face this shit alone."

"This isn't a fight you're going to win, son," Cox said roughly. "All you're going to end up doing is shortchanging your credibility with the boss, which is already in short supply after the Kearney and Smith shit show."

Sean pressed his lips together. "Has the boss reviewed the investigating officer's findings and recommendations?"

"He has. She's on her way in here to answer some questions as we speak."

Sean frowned, not sure how Sarah was going to work that with her daughter in tow.

Cox folded his arms over his chest. "You plan on telling me why you're asking?"

"Just wondering if I'm going to get a new XO out of the deal or not."

Cox shook his head. "You're more likely to get a new NCO. Kearney's cashed his last check with that stunt he pulled breaking restriction earlier this week."

Sean shook his head. "Don't move Kearney, Sarn't Major. He'll be fine once he goes downrange again."

"Which isn't for another six months and in the meantime, he keeps hitting the blotter every other week." Cox sank into his chair. "Sir, I admire your loyalty to your men. But this is not leadership. This is favoritism."

Sean met the big sergeant major's eyes and nodded. The truth was an ugly thing, twisted and deformed between them.

He stepped out of the sergeant major's office in time to see Sarah walk in to the command group offices, Anna in tow.

"So much for the end of the duty day," Sarah said, her voice low to keep the colonel from hearing.

"How are you feeling?" Sean asked.

"I'll live." She smiled up at him, and it melted his heart a little more. "I always do." She looked down at Anna, who was tugging at her hand.

"Mommy, who's this?"

Sean simply stared at the little girl who looked so much like her daddy, stunned by the warmth around his heart for this child. Jack's child.

He crouched down to her level, carefully keeping an eye on Sarah in case he crossed any boundaries, and extended his hand. "I'm Sean. I'm a friend of your mommy's."

Anna's hand was impossibly tiny in his. "I'm Anna. Are you and my mommy dating?"

Sean covered his mouth and coughed, barely hiding his shock at the guileless question.

"Anna! Don't be rude."

"What, Mommy? My friend Tiffany's mommy has a friend, and Tiffany says she and her friend go out on dates."

Sarah looked like she wanted to crawl into a hole and die. Sean did his best not to laugh.

She looked at Sean and shook her head and he sobered instantly. "Honey, I need you to sit here and wait for me. Be very quiet, okay?"

"Mommy, I don't want to sit out here and wait."

He could see tension rising up Sarah's neck. He didn't know how parents did it, juggling the demands of parenting with the insane hours the military required. "I can take her to my office, if you'd like. I've got some paperwork to catch up on."

Sarah's mouth moved but no sound came out.

Anna inserted herself into the space. "Can I, Mommy?"

"I don't mean to put you on the spot," he said quietly. "I'm just trying to help."

She swallowed and nodded. A piece of curly brown hair fell from the tie at the base of her neck. "I'll come get her as soon as I'm done."

Sean held out his hand to Anna. "Want to see my office?"

"Sean?"

He paused, relishing the feel of the little girl's fingers wrapped around his. He looked from Anna to her mother, saying nothing, his throat tight with emotion and memories of things he'd wanted in his life before the war.

"Thank you."

❧ 1 2 ❧

Sean led Anna to his office and tried to sort through the range of emotions beating quietly against his heart. Her fingers were small and fragile around his index finger. The top of her head barely came to his hip. Her hair was a glossy, dark brown and puffed out from the hair ties Sarah must have put in that morning.

He couldn't quite wrap his head around the fact that Jack's daughter was there with him. That she was Sarah's.

Part of his heart hurt. She hadn't wanted this with him. It was one of the first things they'd argued about and it was one of the things that had driven him away when she'd said no. And yet, here she was, a small daughter with another man. That was hell on the ego, no matter how long ago it was.

But the other part of his heart ached with something else. Something he couldn't identify. It was a strange emotion. A feeling of...being glad that Anna was in the world. That someone would carry a part of Jack Anders around.

That he wasn't gone forever. At least, not all of him.

He opened the door to his office and flicked on the light with his free hand. "So this is where I work," he told Anna as she stepped into the ops office in front of him.

"Is this where you boss soldiers around?" she asked.

There was something completely innocent and earnest about her question, and he grinned down at her. "Yes, this is where I get to boss soldiers around."

"My mommy did that for a little while. But she got in trouble." Anna looked around his office.

"She did?"

"Her old boss said she didn't follow orders very well. That she wasn't a C – N – O?"

Sean smiled. "NCO?"

"That," Anna said knowingly. "Mommy is good at bossing people around."

Sean didn't resist the smile then, and simply enjoyed watching her check out his space. He wondered what it looked like to little eyes. How did she see the picture frames on the wall? Or the old raggedy couch that he sometimes slept on?

It didn't surprise him that Sarah had trouble with making the transition from enlisted to officer. Hell, he'd been yelled at a time or two that he wasn't an NCO anymore, too.

"Can I draw on your board?" she asked. She was staring at his dry erase board with the next two weeks' training plans written on it in varying states of disarray.

It was chaos, but honestly, it was the only way he really kept track of things.

The company main board in the ops was in no better shape.

"Want to draw on some paper instead?" he asked.

She shook her head, still staring at the fat dry erase markers. There was hope in her little brown eyes. And far be it from him to deny the little girl what she apparently wanted more in the whole wide world.

He handed her the blue marker. "Go wild, kiddo."

He sat back and let her go to town. And wondered how he was going to remember who had been tasked for what tomorrow.

"Whatcha drawing?"

"This is Captain Meow," she said soberly. "He's in charge of all the mice."

"And who is this?" He pointed to a black ball.

"That's Sergeant Bandeet. She's the HIC."

"Don't you mean Bandit?" Sean narrowed his eyes. "HIC?"

"Ban-deet. She's French. And she's the hamster in charge," Anna said. "She's in charge of the rodent airborne division."

Sean laughed out loud. "Are you sure you're only five?"

She scowled at him. "You don't like my drawing?"

"I love it," he said quickly. "I just never thought of hamsters doing airborne operations. What are they doing them for?"

"Because the rats are trying to steal all the strawberries." As though that was the most obvious answer in the world.

"Ah. Makes sense." Sean wondered if she was always this creative and funny. Jack had been a hell of a smart ass. He'd hidden a blow-up sheep in his cot once when the commander had been inspecting their areas out in the field. The commander had not been amused.

Anna turned back to the board and drew a few more hamsters. With parachutes for good measure. Right across his checklist for the range.

And watching the intense fascination on her face as she drew, he realized he didn't care.

She paused, holding the tip of her marker to her mouth, deep in thought. He barely avoided laughing. She looked so much like her mother, it was scary. Right down to the hands on her hips stance that Sean remembered all too well.

"Do you like it?"

"It is fantastic," he said honestly. Because while he had no basis of comparison to judge a five-year-old's art, he loved the story idea about the hamsters protecting the strawberries from the rats.

"Where do you get your ideas?"

"My daddy tells me," she said, looking over her shoulder at him. Sean went very still. "Oh yeah?"

"Sometimes I dream that he's telling me stories. Like normal kids at bedtime." She turned back to the board. "I don't have a daddy, you know. He died in Iraq."

Sean's throat closed off. She said it so matter-of-factly. In some rational part of his brain, he realized that he shouldn't have expected her to have an emotional attachment to a man who died before she was born. At least, he assumed Jack had died before Anna had been born.

Her response wasn't unusual. He'd gone to one of the local schools once on Veterans Day to talk to a class of kindergarteners. A little boy had told him the same thing and in the same matter-of-fact tone.

Still, it was unsettling to hear her say it with so little emotion. It hurt his heart that Jack's kid would never know what a great guy Jack had been.

All these kids growing up without their fathers or mothers. On both sides of the war. No one ever talked about the Iraqi kids growing up without their fathers or their uncles or their mothers. So many kids just like Anna because of actions by men like Sean. What a fucking waste for a stupid war that no one had wanted in the first place.

Sean cleared his throat roughly. "I know. I knew your daddy," he said gently.

Her eyes widened and her little mouth formed a small O. "You did?"

Sean nodded. "He was funny. He used to tell jokes to make us laugh."

He was pretty sure that a five year old wouldn't appreciate the kind of jokes that her daddy used to tell. Maybe someday, but definitely not today. "Do you think he'd like my hamster story?" There it was. The want of a little girl for her father.

It broke something inside him.

Sean had to swallow several times before he could speak. "I think he'd love it."

When he was certain he had his emotions dialed in, he

motioned to the board. "So tell me more about these airborne hamsters. Why do the rats want the strawberries?"

"Because they're dirty, stinking rats," Anna said. She pointed to the board and a few black blobs with long tails and whiskers written over the due dates for the next evaluation reports Sean had been keeping track of. "This is King Simmi. He loves strawberries so much that he doesn't want anyone else to ever have any."

"He's an evil rat king?"

Anna nodded. "And Captain Meow and Sergeant Bandeet are planning a raid to get the strawberries back in time for the Strawberry Festival."

Sean watched and listened intently as she continued to draw. This kid had one creative brain; that was for sure. Her story unfolded with more and more drawings. At one point, she stood on top of the couch, drawing over the phone number for the battalion lawyer's office.

He hoped Morgan had that written down somewhere.

Nothing on that board was irreplaceable. Or at least, nothing had been until that evening. Now he found himself wishing that he'd gotten her to draw this on paper. It was something Sarah would want to keep.

He would. If she were his.

But she wasn't. And neither was her mother.

But that didn't stop the want, beating inside his chest for the life that could have been.

"Sir, you wanted to see me?" She'd held off on knocking on the door until Sean and Anna had disappeared around the corner. She felt strange, letting her daughter leave with him. She knew him. Or at least she was starting to know the man he'd become. And as much as she hated being pulled between her roles as mom and soldier, the worst thing that could have happened right then would have been Anna having a tantrum in the command group offices.

She didn't work for Gilliad, that was true; but damn it, she was a female officer. And it might be unfair, but when she fucked up, she ruined it for all the other female officers out there. She hated that was even remotely in her brain space, but there it was. The harsh truth of trying to be both mom and captain.

So while it went against her instincts to ask for help, she was grateful that Anna had gone willingly with Sean. It would enable her to focus on LTC Gilliad, answer his questions quickly, and then get her daughter home and tucked into bed, hopefully before midnight.

Gilliad motioned for her to enter his office, and she stopped a few feet from his desk, awkward and uncomfortable and distracted while he finished an e-mail.

Finally he turned his attention toward her, and she instantly wished he hadn't. "Talk to me about your investigation, Captain Anders."

His voice was thin and rough.

"Sir, do you have specific questions?"

"I do. I want to know what is the basis for your recommendation when clearly there are other issues in this case that you failed to address."

All righty then.

"Sir, I was tasked to investigate the circumstances surrounding the fight. I identified those and made my recommendations."

He studied her silently. She tried not to squirm beneath his gaze. "You write a recommendation for a lieutenant to receive a letter of reprimand for adultery? Is that standard practice in your battalion?"

It was probably a bad idea to point out that she'd been in the unit a little over a week so she had no idea what the standard practice was in her unit. "Sir, I sought legal review. There is little more I can recommend given the evidence in the case."

"And therein lies the problem. You need to interview Sergeant

Kearney's wife. Get proof that this...allegation happened. I can't accept these findings. This investigation is incomplete."

Sarah pressed her lips together in a flat line but wisely kept her mouth shut. "Roger, sir."

She stomped on her frustration—barely avoiding actual stomping—as she walked out of the battalion headquarters and to the adjacent building where Sean's company headquarters was located.

The light from his office was on while the rest of the ops lights were out. She rounded the corner and was surprised to find him standing in his office alone. Her heart skipped a beat.

"She's in the bathroom," he said quickly. Her reaction must have been written all over her face.

Sarah glanced at the board and the elaborate scene sketched out across all his notes. "Wow."

"She said Jack gives her the story ideas," Sean said quietly.

Sarah swallowed hard. "She mentioned that to me, too."

"Does that worry you?"

"Not really. Little kids are closer to the veil between the worlds, you know? They're more in touch with the spiritual side of life."

Sean tipped his head, studying her quietly. "You never struck me as particularly religious, Sar."

She shrugged. "It's hard to be religious when you're angry with God." In that instance, she deliberately avoided looking at him. She wasn't sure of much but she was pretty damn positive that if she looked at him, if he touched her, her world might shatter into a thousand tiny pieces.

"I wish I didn't understand that," he said. He shifted, stuffing his hands into his pockets.

"Other than destroying your notes, was she okay?"

"She was fine. Cute kid. Bossy as hell," Sean said. "I wonder where she gets it."

"We call it leadership traits now," she said with a smile. "Not bossiness."

Finally, she dared to look over at him. He was watching her, his dark blue eyes intense and filled with a warmth she'd never expected to see from him again. "Thank you for watching her tonight," she said.

"My pleasure." He paused. "She's a lot of fun."

"She is." She hesitated, watching him, unable to look away from the man he'd become. "You never had any kids?" she asked finally.

Sean shrugged and avoided her eyes. "Never really settled down. Tried once, but you know, the war and everything." He lifted his gaze to hers. "She didn't want to be married to a soldier."

"How's that for irony," Sarah said gently.

"You have no idea."

Silence hung on again, stretching between them.

"How're the knees?" he asked.

"Sore. My pride is worse, though."

"Did you talk to the XO yet about the PT test?"

She shook her head. "Didn't have time today. And now that you mention it, I'm actually shocked she didn't pull me into her office and rake me over the coals about it." Sarah leaned out of the office and glanced toward the bathroom door. "How long has she been in there?"

"Just a few minutes. I didn't actually have a good baseline for what normal times in the bathroom look like for little kids, and I figured it was best for me not to check. Didn't know how scandalized she'd be."

Sarah smiled, and a little piece of her heart warmed toward him. "Thank you for watching her."

"Glad to help." His voice changed. Was a little bit rougher, rough enough that she noticed.

"What?" A single word, laced with caution.

"I can't tell you it doesn't hurt that you married someone else." He watched her intently, his dark blue eyes filled with inscrutable emotions. "But I— I'm glad you found someone, Sar."

She rubbed her hands over her upper arms. A chill slithered

over her skin. "Jack never pressured me for kids. Or a family," she whispered, not really sure why she was telling him this.

"I wanted both of those things. With you."

"You knew my past. The shit with my stepfather. I didn't want to bring a child into this world. I didn't want to give up being a soldier just to be your wife. I'm sorry we couldn't make things work, but I'm not sorry I had Jack."

"I was wrong." He stepped closer. "Wrong to ask you to give that up."

She glanced over her shoulder toward the bathroom. "I found out I was pregnant after he died."

"Christ, Sar."

She looked away, blinking hard. "I have her. She's my connection to him forever and always."

She felt, rather than heard, him move, and then he was there, in her space. His fingers were gentle against her cheek, urging her to look at him. "There's no shame in still loving him," Sean whispered. "He was a lucky man."

"Sean—"

"I know you're not ready to move on." He cupped her cheek, his palm warm and rough. "And I won't pressure you. I made that mistake once before." His throat moved as he swallowed, hard. "Just know that...I never stopped caring about you. And if...if you ever reach a place where you'd like to try maybe going to lunch or anything..."

She placed her palm on his chest. Felt his heart beating through the US Army tag on his uniform. There was a warmth circling around her, a warmth she'd never expected to feel for another man ever again. A warmth that snuck beneath her skin and wrapped around her heart and made her want things she'd forgotten how to want.

"It's complicated," she finally whispered.

"It always is."

❧　13　❧

In the end, he hadn't been able to resist touching her. Sarah compelled him like no one else ever had. He dragged his hand over his face and sank into his couch. Wednesday night and please God, no phone calls. He'd like just one night not to involve the MPs or the local police station.

He closed his eyes.

And felt Sarah. So still as he'd touched her. She was so beautiful. So fierce. And so goddamned fragile. She'd stood her ground when he'd moved into her space. She'd felt so good. He shifted as his body tightened at the memory.

He opened his eyes and glanced at the clock. What was she doing right now? He rested one arm across his stomach. Was she thinking about him?

Or was she upset?

He wanted her back, and he had no idea how to get her. If what she said was true, if in her heart of hearts she still thought of herself as married to Anders, then what was he supposed to do?

It was somehow worse that she'd been married to his friend. There were few greater sins than moving in on a dead buddy's widow, but Sarah had been his long before she'd been with Jack.

And what was he, twelve? She was an adult, more than capable of making her own decisions.

He'd screwed up with her. Screamed at her that being a soldier was fucking stupid for a girl. Why couldn't she just be like other women and be his wife?

Shame burned over his skin again at what a childish prick he'd been. He'd crossed the line that night. He'd known it when he'd stormed out of their apartment. Known it the minute he'd woken up in the jail and it had been Claire who had bailed him out, not Sarah.

Sarah had just been gone. Out of his life.

Looking back now, he deserved her leaving. God, but he'd been such an immovable ass. Wanting her to get out of the Army, give up the life she'd worked so hard for.

He'd thrown himself into work after she'd left. He'd devoted himself to the Army, to the life of an infantryman. He'd trained tirelessly and given up on the idea of the family beyond the men he served with. So there had been no one, not like what he'd had with Sarah.

No one had made his pulse beat faster, his blood burn like it had tonight when Sarah hadn't pulled away from his touch, hadn't said no. Was she possibly willing to give him another chance? Maybe not a life together, but maybe something more than the memories that they had.

His cell phone vibrated on the counter.

And his heart sank because he knew, just knew that it was going to be work and he prayed that it wasn't Kearney.

It was a mistake calling him.

She knew it and yet when he answered, she didn't hang up. Sleep, apparently, surrendered the field to latent desire and confusion. Everything circled around to Sean. She'd start thinking about the case, but ended up standing in his office, Sean's scent wrapping around her, urging her close, his lips brushing against hers.

That first aching taste.

Something inside her wanted to hear his voice. She couldn't answer the question of why.

"Captain Nichols."

She smiled warmly as his voice caressed the skin of her ear. "Do you always answer your personal phone with your rank or is this a government phone?"

There was a rustle of fabric in the background. "You don't know how glad I am that you're not my first sergeant."

Settling into her bed, she curled up around her pillow. "Why?"

"Because if it had been Morgan, more than likely I'd be on my way back on post to bail someone, probably Kearney, out of jail."

"How many times has he been arrested?"

His sigh echoed across the line. "A bunch. He's had some real problems since...our first tour."

Sarah's heart caught. "You served with him before?"

A muffled curse. "Yeah. There's a bunch of us from my first tour here. Garrison, Kearney, Haverson. One of the company commanders, Bello, who is my least favorite person in this unit after Lieutenant Smith."

"Why don't you like him?"

"There's a lot of baggage there. Let's just say we've got opposite ideas of what it means to be an officer and leave it at that."

She smiled. "Sounds like you two aren't going to be sharing bedtime stories over a beer."

"Not in this lifetime." He sounded so disgruntled, she had to laugh.

Something warm filled her heart as she realized so many of Sean's current soldiers had been downrange with him before. It spoke to his loyalty to his men. Not all commanders could say that.

She'd pulled away from everyone and everything after she'd lost Jack. She hadn't wanted to be contacted by the Family Readiness

Group. She'd tried to forget that she'd ever been part of the Cav family, even if she'd only been there as Jack's spouse.

"Sarah? Are you still there?"

She rolled onto her back and brushed her hair from her face. "Yeah."

"What are you thinking about?" His voice was low and smooth. The knot around her heart eased back. Just a little. But it was enough.

"Jack," she admitted and felt her face go hot. "I was thinking about how I pulled away from everyone after he died. I never took any phone calls from anyone. Not his commander, not his friends. I couldn't function."

So much hurt in those words. So much truth.

"I don't know what to say," he admitted finally.

The silence stretched between them over the phone line. She heard him blow out a breath.

"Me, either, honestly." The quiet filled with something warm. Something good.

"What do we do now?"

"I don't know." She shifted again, not sure what to do with herself on this phone call. "I know I've got to interview Mrs. Kearney because your boss won't accept my investigation as it stands. Which sounds an awful lot like what Major Wilson told me. I suspect she's trying to fire me or get me to quit."

"Didn't you just get to the brigade?"

"My boss has got a problem with moms in the Army. Told me point blank that I offended her." Sarah sighed and wished that she still worked with friends like Claire instead of with a boss who hated her and everything she represented.

"Really? Can she even do that?"

"Unless it's illegal, immoral, or unethical, she can do whatever she wants. Artificial and arbitrary deadlines don't count under any of those categories."

"That sucks." Silence filled the void. "I'm sorry you have to go through this alone."

"Thank you for saying that." She blinked quickly, and she heard a rustle of blankets. Her mind detoured into a very unprofessional space. "Did you just get into bed?"

He laughed quietly. "Yeah. Are you?"

"Yeah." There was something illicit in that simple agreement. Illicit and enticing all at once.

"So we're in bed together?"

"Ha, ha, ha." She cleared her throat, though, as a fresh heat traced over her skin, warm and needy. "Tell me more about Kearney."

"Damn, and here I thought you were going to ask me what I was wearing to bed."

She hesitated. Only for a moment, not giving herself time to talk herself out of her next words. "What are you wearing to bed?"

A silence that let her mind wander. "Sweats." He paused. When he spoke, his voice was husky and thick. "Tell me what you're wearing."

"Yoga pants and a T-shirt," she said softly, her cheeks turning hot. Was she really having this conversation?

"Sarah?"

"Yeah?"

"This doesn't feel wrong to me. I just wanted you to know that."

She bit her lips. She'd told him when he'd kissed her that she still felt married. But she wasn't being honest with herself because things...things had changed. Because for the first time since Jack died, she felt okay talking to another man. She felt...good. Not unfaithful.

And considering who she was talking to, surprise mixed inside her along with everything else.

"Are you okay?"

"I think so," she whispered. She heard the sleep in his voice now, the sensual awareness tinged with fatigue. "How much sleep do you get on a normal night?" she asked suddenly.

"Define normal night?" he asked through a yawn.

"Someone not getting arrested." Funny how someone not getting arrested could define normal.

"Few hours here and there. I wake up a lot. Bad dreams and all that."

"Yeah. I have them, too, sometimes." She cleared her throat and dared to share her own painful dreams. "I would wake up looking for Jack sometimes."

There was silence on the line. So much so that she didn't know if he was still there. But she was afraid. Afraid to break the silence. Afraid of what she was feeling for this man.

After a moment, she heard his quiet exhale. "It hurts, knowing you married him when you said no to me. I can admit that now." He paused. "But I'm glad you had Jack. I'm glad you were happy."

Her eyes burned and she blinked hard, not trusting herself to speak.

"Did you fall asleep on me?" Soft, gentle words.

"No. I'm here." She pressed her palm into one eye, ignoring the pain in her broken skin. "Thank you for saying that."

"I meant it. And your daughter is beautiful."

She pressed her fingers into her eyes, unable to stop the quiet sob as it escaped.

"I didn't mean to make you cry, honey," he whispered.

"I know." She sniffed, swiping at her eyes. "I loved you and we didn't last. I loved Jack and he died. I'm afraid, Sean." She bit her lips, hoping she hadn't jumped the gun on his intention. "I'm terrified of feeling again." Brutal honesty.

"Try? We'll go really slow. Start with lunch?"

"I—"

"Don't say no. Think about it. Sleep on it. And I'll ask you again tomorrow?"

She nodded and remembered they were on the phone. "Okay."

He didn't say anything for a long moment. "Get some sleep."

"You, too."

"No promises, but I'll try. Good night, Sarah."

"Good night, Sean."

It was a long time before she hung up the phone and rested it on her bedside table. For the first time since Jack died, she felt cared for. That feeling, mixed with a little bit of hope, followed her down into sleep.

As she closed her eyes, she felt Sean's lips press against hers once more. And for once, she did not feel guilty.

❧

SEAN STRETCHED OUT IN HIS BED AND RESTED ONE HAND ON HIS stomach. He stared at his phone for a long time after the line had clicked off, then he pressed the keypad to save her number.

A slow smile spread across his lips. There was an ache in his blood that had nothing to do with fatigue and everything to do with the woman who'd been on the other end of that phone call. He closed his eyes and focused on the memory of her taste. Of her touch. Of the want he'd felt in her body as he'd kissed her.

For the first time he could remember, he drifted to sleep, thinking about Sarah. Soft and warm and welcoming.

He felt hope. Like maybe there was a place for him in this world that did not involve the war.

He closed his eyes, want and need beating through his veins in time with his heart. He had a second chance. One that he absolutely did not deserve.

But he was not going to fuck it up.

❧ 14 ☙

"Ma'am?"

Sarah looked up to see LT Picket peeking in on her. "Yes?"

"Major Wilson needs to see you."

Sarah sighed. "Do you have like a psychic connection to her or something? Or does she just e-mail you to tell me?"

LT Picket laughed and tucked her hair behind her ear. She looked like Jessica Alba but from what Sarah heard, she was a decent shot with an M4 and turning into one hell of an officer.

"No, ma'am. I can hear her in her office from my desk. I'm just giving you a heads up." LT reached into her shoulder pocket. "Oh, and before I forget, here's your ticket to the ball this weekend."

"Ball?"

"Yes, ma'am. The brigade ball. Major Wilson said to make sure you had it."

"Thanks," Sarah said dryly. She'd have to see if Jamie could watch Anna. Sarah stacked her papers neatly and pushed up from her desk. She could use a break from the sworn statements anyway, and if Major Wilson was talking to sergeant major about Sarah, Sarah had a good idea what it was about. She took a deep breath and walked into the hallway.

And collided with LTC Meister, her battalion commander. "Whoa, Sarah. What's the hurry?"

Sarah flushed and stepped away, pulling her arms free from his stabilizing grip. "Sorry, sir. Distracted."

"I can see that. How's that investigation going?"

Sarah grasped for a status. "The lieutenant involved in the fight won't make a statement other than the one he made to the police, and I've got conflicting information from some of the other men involved." She took a step back, out of his personal space. "Shorter version: I still have to interview the wife."

"What's on your mind, Sarah?"

Sarah took a deep breath, bracing for the reality that what she was about to say might very well end her chances at commanding, but what the hell. She wasn't making any progress in that direction anyway. "Sir, why am I investigating a bar fight? Fifteen-six investigations are usually reserved for more serious problems than this."

Meister cleared his throat and jerked his head. Sarah followed him down the hall to his office. "Close the door behind you."

Sarah did and then walked past the conference room table that filled half his office. She stopped about five feet from his desk and stood at parade rest, her feet spread shoulder width apart, her hands resting at the small of her back.

"The purpose of your investigation isn't to dig into a stupid fight. The brigade commander needs to know what's going on in that company specifically. It's the only one in the brigade that continues to have weekly arrests or other misconduct."

Sarah tried to swallow, but her mouth was suddenly dry, her throat thick. "Sir, I'm conducting an investigation under false pretenses?"

"There are a lot of problems in that battalion. Lieutenant Colonel Gilliad has already fired every company commander and first sergeant in the battalion. Hell, I still haven't provided him with a support company commander. But this particular company hasn't managed to get ahead of the curve with the misconduct. This bar fight is only one incident in a string of incidents—and many of them circle around the individuals you're investigating."

Sarah's stomach twisted. "Sir, this fight is about the lieutenant sleeping with the sergeant's wife. It's not more complicated than that."

Meister shook his head. "That's more than complicated enough. That's the other part of this problem. The lieutenant involved has some high-powered friends and family." He paused. "The company commander has already tried to ring the lieutenant up, but he doesn't have any evidence." Sean didn't have an uncle in any of the right places. He didn't have any family—at least not any that would get his ass out of a sling if he got in trouble as a commander.

She tuned back in on Meister's words. "The bottom line is look beyond the fight and figure out what's going on in that company. Get the boss what he needs."

"Roger, sir." She nodded and stepped out of the battalion commander's office. Bracing herself, she knocked on Major Wilson's door. "Ma'am, you needed to see me?"

"Talk to me about your PT test."

"Not much to say, ma'am." The scrapes on her knees started throbbing. God but her life was a cliché.

"Captain Anders, I'm not sure who you think you're talking to, but your tone leaves much to be desired. You have been fired from command, you have failed a record PT test, and you continually fail to do even adequate work."

Sarah ground her teeth and willed her expression to remain blank. Apparently she failed.

"Truth is rarely pleasant," Wilson said.

"Well, since we're talking about the truth, why don't we at least acknowledge that you made your mind up about me before I ever reported." Damn it, she'd been going for tact, not sand paper.

"True enough. But my suspicions have been confirmed." Wilson looked up over her square-framed glasses. "Yes. I need a copy of your family care plan by Friday."

Sarah frowned. "Tomorrow, ma'am?"

Wilson peered at her with something akin to distaste, pressing her lips together. "Yes, tomorrow. If it's current, you shouldn't have any problem with that, should you?"

Considering she needed to update it since she'd moved away from Fort Carson and arrived here at Hood, yeah, it was going to be a problem.

Sarah clung to every ounce of tact she could summon. "Ma'am, by regulation I have thirty days upon arriving to the unit to update my paperwork."

"Don't quote the regulation to me, captain." Wilson leaned back in her chair, the pen slapping down on the desk. Her voice was cold and calm. "Do you have a family care plan or not, captain?"

Sarah straightened and adjusted her hands behind her back. "Yes, ma'am. I need to update it since I moved. But I can turn in the current one and take the authorized time I need after I finish this investigation for the colonel."

Wilson stared. Didn't blink. Didn't move. Just stared. "Don't get cute. You have two weeks. Do. Not. Be. Late."

Sarah ground her teeth. Her tact slipped away. "Ma'am, have I done something to offend you?"

Major Wilson picked up her pen and started writing. She didn't even look at Sarah when she started speaking. "Your mere presence in the Army offends me. You take time off when others have to work. You leave work early when your peers are here late. You play the female card when it's convenient for you, and then you insist you just wanted to be treated equally. I don't play your games, captain. You will be held to the same standard as everyone else. Fairly, without regard to your status as mother."

Sarah couldn't speak. Her throat closed off, squeezing tight the bitterness unleashed with Major Wilson's words. She stood there, mute and shaking. "Am I dismissed, ma'am?" She could barely force the words out.

Wilson nodded and went back to her paperwork.

Sarah walked out of the office, her back rigid, her body radiating fury. It took everything she had to keep from screaming in frustration.

She snatched her headgear off her desk and stalked toward the exit, needing to get away before her composure crumbled and she embarrassed herself at the office. She'd be damned if she was going to cry over that woman.

"Sarah?"

She kept walking, refusing to stop, not trusting herself to be around anyone right then. Some dark corner of her brain recognized Sean's voice, but even then, she kept walking. Humiliation and grief burned behind her eyes.

"Sarah! What happened?" Sean grabbed her arm, stopping her headlong flight from civilization.

"Nothing." She refused to meet his eyes. "I can't talk about it right now, okay? I'm fine."

"You're full of shit, is what you are." He physically blocked her escape path toward her vehicle.

Sarah swallowed and opened her mouth. Closed it.

"Come here."

He guided her to his truck and she climbed in, having nowhere else to go and needing, badly, to unleash the fury storming inside her.

"What happened?" he asked again.

She bit her lips together and shook her head. Finally the words broke free, releasing a flood of anger and hurt. "You know, I've given up a lot for the Army. I gave up a year of my daughter's life when we were getting ready to deploy. I lost my husband. And I'm still here. All because I love the Army, it's the life I know, and it's the only thing that I am really good at. And that... that fucking bitch—" Sarah's voice broke, and with it, her composure crumbled. Hot tears burned down her cheeks. "That bitch has the nerve to tell me that I want special privileges? That I don't belong in the Army because I have a child and no husband?" Her fingers curled into a fist until her nails dug into the flesh of her palm. Her words ripped from her throat. "My husband *died* in this Army."

Sean said nothing for a long while. Then he reached for her, his hand running lightly down her back. A soothing gesture. One that spoke of intimacy and comfort. One that warmed her and chased away the bitter anger and rage.

Sarah ran her hands over her face and sucked in a deep breath. She did not pull away. "I've got to go because if I don't finish this goddamned investigation by tomorrow, I'm sure Wilson will start building my packet and get me a negative evaluation."

After a while he spoke. "She's just unhappy because she found her cat on match.com looking for a new home."

The laugh surprised her. It broke up the furious storm raging inside her. She looked at him then, intensely aware that not only had she just completely lost her shit in front of him, but that he was still there.

Not judging her. Not telling her to give up the life that she loved. Holding her up. Standing with her.

And Sarah fell a little harder.

IT WAS A LONG TIME BEFORE EITHER OF THEM MOVED. THEY SAT in Sean's truck, shielded from prying eyes. For that brief time he simply held her and pretended that they were two normal people without the war and their past standing between them.

"Are you okay?"

She seemed deflated. As though all the energy had run out of her. "I have to be." Hesitant, unsure words.

He looked at her then, taking in the tired lines beneath her eyes, the strain around her mouth. He reached for her, sliding his hand over her neck to cradle her cheek. "You don't have to be strong all the time," he murmured.

Her smile was sadness and grief and the remains of a thousand unspoken emotions and it broke his heart. "Yes, I do," she said. "I don't get to fall apart just because my boss is being an asshole." She paused and he wanted to gather her close again, just to take some of the weight from her shoulders. She was carrying so much, trying to be all things to all people.

Had she been able to lean on anyone since she'd lost Jack?

"This is the first time since I had Anna that someone has made me consider getting out of the Army."

He nudged her chin up. "Don't let one woman take this from you," he said. "This is too important for you to let her win."

She smiled sadly. "You never understood why I wanted to stay," she said.

"Why do you?" He'd never understood that part. Not when she'd told him years ago that being a soldier was important to her. Not when she'd chosen the Army over him. But now? Now he wanted to listen. To understand.

Because she mattered. He could guess, but he wanted to hear her tell him rather than fill in the blanks. Because no matter how many brothers he'd lost, he'd never lost a lover to this war.

"It's the only thing I've ever been really good at." She met his gaze. "I was fat in high school. A mediocre student at best. Figured I'd join the Army and get the hell away from all my mother's drama. Turned out I was good at this whole soldier thing." She looked over at him. "Then I met you and fell in love and the only thing I could see was me becoming my mother." She pressed her lips together, hating the truth of things but needing him to know. "I know that sounds pathetic and sad and all that but it's true. And after I lost Jack, the Army was the only thing that kept me going. I don't know how to do anything else." She licked her lips, hesitating.

"I think I understand that more than you know." He moved then, cupping her cheek with one hand. Offering support. Comfort.

Leaning in close, slowly, so slowly, until his lips brushed against hers.

He'd surprised her. He felt it in the slight hesitation in the heartbeat before she opened for him. She lifted her hand and slid it over his where he cupped her face, and he shifted, twining his fingers with hers.

She kept her eyes closed but she didn't pull away. Silence stretched around them, holding them safe and warm from the outside world.

"Come to lunch with me?" he asked.

"I..." She paused. He could practically see her coming up with reasons to say no. "I think I'd like that."

He tried not to look shocked. "Wow, you said yes."

She smiled up at him and it made her eyes sparkle. "Maybe I'm just hungry."

Her lips twitched and it was good, so good to see her finally relax, even if only for a little while. It transformed her and for a second, he saw a flash of the girl she'd been once upon a time. But that girl wasn't the one he was falling for this time around. No, it was the woman standing in front of him, determined to be strong and independent and in charge of her own fate.

And it was that strength, that woman that made him want to reach for her once more.

And never be stupid enough to lose her again.

They rode in silence to the restaurant. Sarah flipped through papers, trying to get them organized. Sean watched her out of the corner of his eyes. She was so focused that he didn't want to interrupt her, knowing every moment he had with her was stealing time.

When they arrived, though, he broached the subject that had been needling him since the other day. "So is your boss always such a pain in the ass or is today just special? Between this and the PT test, I'd guess she's pretty much using you for target practice."

Sarah sighed heavily. "Basically, she's out to prove a point that I'm not a good officer or soldier because I'm a single parent."

Sean's throat closed off and it was suddenly hard to breathe. "Does she know about Jack?"

"Oh yes. That's actually a big strike against me," Sarah tore at a piece of bread.

"How's that?"

"Because I obviously came into the Army hunting for a husband and clearly, since he died, I no longer belong here," she said dryly.

Revulsion twisted in his belly, souring his mood. He wanted to lash out, to protect her. But that hadn't worked out so well the last time so he opted for a different track. "Want me to vouch for you that that is clearly not the case?"

She laughed and then covered her mouth, looking mildly horrified. "I don't think our history together will convince her." She paused, twirling her straw in her tea. Finally, she lifted her gaze to meet his, her eyes reflecting warmth and confusion. "It feels strange to joke about that."

"It never surprises me the things I can joke about these days. Things that would horrify civilians."

"I wish I didn't understand that but sadly, I do." She twisted the straw wrapper in her hands. "So anyway, changing the subject because I need a distraction"—she leaned across the table, brown eyes intense—"you should know that the brigade commander is watching this investigation closely."

He hesitated for a little too long. "I knew I'd pissed off my battalion commander, but brigade, too?"

"How did you piss off your boss?"

He leaned back against the booth. "I'm too soft on a couple of the guys I was downrange with."

"Kearney?"

"And Haverson," Sean admitted. He wasn't sure how much he should tell her. How much he could reveal and not ruin this fragile truce between them. He swallowed a drink, searching for the right words. "I got into an argument with the battalion commander about Haverson just this week. I want to get him back from the Warrior Transition Unit, and the boss threatened to court-martial me if I bring it up again." He shifted, folding his hands together in front of his mouth, fighting the anger that always drove these conversations. It was part of why he couldn't argue his point cogently with the boss. He got too pissed, too worked up. They sat quietly as the waitress brought their food.

"Why are you trying to get Haverson pulled out of the WTU?"

He dumped ketchup on his fries, squeezing the bottle a little too hard. "Because the cadre over there don't give a damn about the soldiers. They treat them like it's a prison instead of actually checking on them. Haverson stopped taking his medication because he got in trouble for missing formation. It's completely the wrong environment for anyone to get better."

Sarah watched him carefully. "He's had a hard time since your deployment with him."

Sean sighed and pulled a slice of herbed bread from the basket. He began tearing pieces off in random hunks. "Haverson hasn't learned the two rules of combat. One: good men die in war; and, two: docs—or in his case, medics—can't stop that. It haunts him." Sean paused. "It haunts all of us." He met her gaze and for a moment, the world fell away. "Sarah...There's something you need to know." He set the bread down. "And you might not talk to me again after this." He felt her still as she waited silently. "I was there when Jack died," he whispered.

She sank back into the booth with a rush of breath. The noise from the restaurant faded. All he could see was the paleness of her skin, the emotions skittering across her face. She opened her mouth. Closed it.

Said nothing while Sean's heart beat loudly in his ears while he waited...for salvation or damnation, he didn't know.

"I don't know what to say." Quiet, broken words.

"I don't know what I expected." He reached for her hand. Her skin was cold now. "But before this went any further, I needed you to know." He swallowed. "And if you want me to take you back on post now, I...I understand."

She was still as ice beneath his touch. Frozen and immobile.

SHE DELIBERATELY FILLED HER LUNGS, SLOWLY, BREATHING through her nose then released it.

She didn't need to know. She wasn't going to ask how he died. She didn't need to know.

Questions she didn't want to know the answer to burned in her throat but did not break free.

Sarah blinked rapidly and pushed away from the table. "I'll be back in a minute," she said softly.

She walked out the front door to the edge of the building, needing space. Her heart pounded in her ears and there was an ache that wrapped around it, throbbing like a physical wound. Her eyes burned despite her attempts to blink back the tears and she looked up at the sky, praying for composure that was fast slipping away.

She felt Sean lean against the wall next to her, his mere presence a comfort that should not have been. But he was there and she was hurting and she wanted so badly to cling to the comfort he offered in the middle of the maelstrom of her own emotions.

"I didn't know how else to tell you," Sean said quietly.

Their shoulders were touching where they stood together, or rather, her shoulder was pressed into his upper arm. She felt the solid strength in the man next to her but she refused to lean. It felt wrong to want to feel his arms around her when she was crying over her dead husband.

"Too late now," she murmured. The pain eased back just enough for her to draw a deep breath and she greedily sucked in another one.

Silence stretched between them and Sarah struggled to keep her breathing from getting too short, too quick. She swallowed the lump as the feeling of kinship pushed the hurt down a little. "I keep chasing his memory," she admitted. "Even when I know it doesn't do a damn bit of good."

He reached for her then, cupping her chin gently. "You loved him. And he was a lucky man to have you," he murmured.

She closed her eyes and leaned into his touch. Nothing more. A simple, quiet interlude. Taking the strength this man offered to keep herself upright.

It felt strange to lean on anyone.

It felt good to lean on Sean.

Neither of them moved for what seemed like forever. For once, it was the shared silence of loss. Of the impact that war had on each of their lives. And the impact they'd had on one another once upon a time. He brought his gaze back to hers and the echo of the pain she saw in his pale blue eyes nearly brought it all back to the surface again. "Are you okay?"

Her smile was sad and she nodded faintly. "Yeah. I've had a long time to mourn him."

"It still hurts, though." His quiet words were not a question.

Finally, she met his gaze. "I don't want to know how he died, Sean. I don't...I can't go there." Her eyes shimmered with unshed tears. "I lost my whole world when I lost Jack." Finally she moved.

"I can't say that I've lost someone I loved to this war." He wanted so badly to pull her against him. Not just for her sake but for his. "But the losses I've had stay with me."

His heart broke a little in his chest. Fracturing from relief that she was still there. That she hadn't pulled away, hadn't left. He released a shuddering breath. "I lost five men in my platoon that year. Kearney and Haves and the guys who are left...I have to take care of them now." He sucked in a deep breath, scrubbing his hand over his mouth. "They were—they are—my responsibility."

"You couldn't have protected them from everything, Sean." Her gaze dropped to his lips. "Not even from themselves."

THEY WERE IN PUBLIC; THEY COULDN'T BE SEEN EMBRACING OR

kissing. Instead, she threaded her fingers with his and stood silently, resting her head against his shoulder.

He couldn't say who was holding who upright at that point. And he wasn't sure he cared.

He finally spoke, long after he was sure his voice wouldn't break. "I guess...I thought you'd be angry. Thought you'd hate me all over again."

She stroked her thumb over his. "I had Jack in my life for a while. And it was good. I have to be glad for the time we had. I have his daughter. And I will always have good memories of him." She blinked rapidly and cleared her throat. Her fingers tightened in his. "And up until now, as much as I've never thought about having anyone else in my life—but I can't say that anymore now. I don't know what the right answer is. I don't know if I'm supposed to hate you for being there, or if I'm supposed to say I'm glad you made it home. I don't know, Sean."

She rested her cheek against his shoulder, letting the silence hang between them, unable to fill it with anything else. Things were too twisted, too mixed up.

"There are no right answers, Sar. We can only try to do the best we can by each other." He cupped her face, to hell with being in public. "I failed you before. I didn't listen to what you wanted, what you needed." He paused. "I'd like to try and be there for you now. If you can let me."

She met his gaze. Her fingers tightened in his.

And she did not pull away.

＃ 15 ＃

Sarah did not want to interview Mrs. Kearney. From everything she'd been able to gather, the woman was less than pleasant and not too smart. Sarah was honestly shocked that the woman agreed to answer her questions to begin with. As she sat down at Mrs. Kearney's kitchen table and tried not to cringe at the caked-on remnants of food on the surface, she tried really hard not to judge.

She kept things formal. One hundred percent professional. "Ma'am, you need to know you can end this interview at any time. You are not suspected of any crimes."

Mrs. Kearney sucked on a cigarette and blew the smoke out of the side of her mouth. "Why would I be suspected of any crimes?"

"You're not, ma'am. I just have a few questions about your relationship with Lieutenant Smith."

Mrs. Kearney's face broke into a warm smile. It changed her appearance instantly, from someone who had grown up too hard and too fast to something warmer. Approachable, even.

"Paul said he wanted to marry me," she said softly. "He's so... he's good to me."

"Paul? I thought his name was Wilford."

"He goes by Paul because he says Wilford sounds like an old man," Mrs. Kearney said.

"Ah." Sarah made a note on the paper. "How did you and LT Smith meet?"

"Nate brought him home one night for a soft swap. Him and his wife."

"Is that for drinks or something?"

Mrs. Kearney looked at her like she'd grown two heads. "We were trading partners for the night. Just trying each other out to see if we'd want to go further."

Sarah thought she understood what Mrs. Kearney was telling her but she had no idea how to ask for clarification. "So this was all consensual. And your husband knew about you swapping with LT Smith?"

"Of course."

"So then what happened? Why are you and your husband fighting?"

Mrs. Kearney waved her hand with the cigarette. "He just needs to cool off a little bit. He's always blowing off steam and doing stupid shit."

"So you're not afraid for your life from him?"

"Hell no." She looked flabbergasted by the idea. "I just wanted to get him in a little trouble, make him smarten up."

Sarah wrote furiously. "Ma'am, you realize he's in a lot of trouble, right?"

"Because of what happened downrange?"

Sarah looked up sharply. "What happened downrange?"

"With the shooting?" Kitty took a long pull off her cigarette again. Sarah felt the strongest need for a shower. She could feel the smoke permeating her skin.

"Would you be willing to expound on that?"

She shrugged. "Something they were involved with downrange. Some guy died or something. I don't really give a flying fuck. They should have killed more of those fucking savages if you ask me. Turn that entire fucking place into a glass parking lot."

It hurt hearing those words. Sarah wasn't a bleeding heart but the blatant refusal to see the Iraqis as human beings was stunning in its biting clarity, especially for a woman who had never been there. But correcting the other woman was likely to piss her off and Sarah needed to keep her talking.

"Calling them savages isn't really going to help with winning the hearts and minds," Sarah mumbled beneath her breath.

"Fuck the hearts and minds. Why should our boys have to die fighting for their stupid ass country? Kill 'em all, let God sort 'em out."

"Okay, well, thank you for your time," Sarah said. She knew the right thing to do was challenge Mrs. Kearney's rant but that wasn't her purpose. Right now, she needed the woman to initial the form Sarah had just filled out. The war and Mrs. Kearney's politics, such as they were, would have to wait. "Would you review and sign this to make sure I wrote everything down right?"

Mrs. Kearney didn't even read the form, just signed her name where Sarah told her to. Sarah briefly wondered if she ever read anything she had to sign and how much trouble that had caused them over the years with bad credit paperwork.

She left, letting Mrs. Kearney's revelations swirl unchecked in her brain. Shit. The woman had basically just incriminated both her husband and her lover in a potentially illegal shooting downrange.

She needed to talk to Sean. Then she needed to call the police.

❦

HE WAS SKIRTING DANGEROUSLY CLOSE TO THE EDGE WITH Sarah. Touching her. Caring about her. It was all a bad decision, given both their past and their present. But when he touched her and felt her spark to life beneath his fingers... she was amazing and intense and—

She was Jack Anders's widow. He knew guys that did that sort of thing. That went for that twisted kind of sick pleasure from being the rebound guy for these mourning wives. But this...this didn't feel like that. It didn't feel wrong, not like that.

It felt real. And it was hell on his ability to get the job done when all he wanted to do was take her home for a few hours. For a lifetime.

There was a quick knock on his door and then Sarah was walking in, shutting the door behind her.

"Hey. How's the leg?"

"Getting better. Taking lots of Motrin," she said dryly. "That won't do much for my pride, though."

"I still think you need to challenge her making you take that PT test," he said.

"There's no point." She shook her head slowly. "Anyway, do you know anything about an escalation of force incident from last deployment?"

"They happen all the time. Why?" Sean closed out his e-mail, focusing completely on her. Since lunch yesterday, he'd been unable to think of anything but Sarah.

Instead, he focused on her and the concern radiating off her like a live current. "Sarah, what happened?"

"Mrs. Kearney just dropped a couple of bombs in my lap. Said that she and her husband and the Smiths were all having a consensual relationship. Which isn't even the interesting part. The interesting part is that there was something about a shooting that happened downrange. She seemed to think it was no big deal but..."

"Escalation of force incidents are a big deal *now*, but they weren't always," Sean said softly. "The rules of engagement have changed since we've been trying to shift from active combat to nation building."

"Why do you sound bitter about that?" she asked.

He dragged his hands over his face, too close to the ugly truth. "Rules of engagement are designed to make the transition to peace easier. To keep noncombatants safe." His voice thickened with memories. "They don't always work." He cleared his throat. "I've got the old commander's classified laptop in my safe, if you want to look through it. There might be reports on there that could shed some light on things."

She frowned. "Shouldn't that have been wiped before it came home?"

"Probably." Sean shrugged. "But when I took it to the signal guys, they said to just keep it because it kept them from having to load it all over again and I honestly don't have time to tell them how to do their jobs."

Sarah shook her head in amazement. "Are they trying to go to jail?"

"Not wiping a hard drive is the least of the Really Bad Shit I'm worried about from this war," Sean said dryly.

She scoffed quietly. "No kidding." Sarah pulled out her government cell phone and checked something, then slid it back into her shoulder sleeve pocket. "I'd like to read through that computer if you don't mind."

"I've got a room set up where you can read it." Classified information needed to be handled in a certain way. He couldn't just hand her the hard drive and say "have at it". The room needed to be segregated from outside communications. No windows. Cell phones left outside.

He held the door for her and flipped on the light after she walked into the room set up for classified work. He opened the safe and set the classified laptop on the table next to her.

"Thanks. Do you mind if I work here for a while? I don't have a classified space at my office set up yet."

He nodded. "I don't have anywhere to be."

She was already focused on work now, busy hunched over the laptop checking through the files.

He left her to it, needing to pull back, to pull away. To gather his storming emotions and shove them into a box. His skin felt too tight, like his bones were going to tear through with the next hard breath.

He'd skimmed those files once. Just once had been enough.

Reading the daily reports had dredged up too many bad memories, even if they weren't his. Clicking on that first report had been a mistake and he'd shut the computer down, unwilling or unable to read more. It wasn't even his deployment but the sheer aching familiarity raged through him. Every memory came to life in vivid Technicolor brightness. Every radio call. Every MEDEVAC request felt real.

All of it came rushing back and the reports weren't even his own tour. But the names on the report were attached to the faces in his memories. Kearney. Haverson.

He gave himself a mental shake and yanked his thoughts back from the brink of the looming abyss of depression. If he kept up this train of thought, he'd be nursing an Ambien-laced Heineken. Never a good combo on a good night but at least it guaranteed a night of oblivion.

Whoever said sleep was a crutch had obviously not gone days and days and days without a good night's sleep.

When he was alone in his office, he closed the door and simply sat, wrestling with what she might find on that laptop. Hoping she would find nothing. Needing her to find something so he could put this bullshit between Kearney and Smith to bed. He wanted to protect Kearney. She knew that. But she didn't know why. Not all of it anyway.

Some sins needed to stay buried.

He *owed* Kearney. He'd worked too damn long to keep Kearney on the right side to let him fail now. The worst of Sean's sins, though, weren't on a hard drive. But the escalation of force was trading dangerously close to memories better left buried.

Sarah opened up the laptop and logged in because, typically, the username and password were taped to the laptop. And how was *that* for great security.

She surfed through the old commander's files, but there wasn't that much of interest, honestly. Additional duty orders. Daily SITREPs. She opened a folder labeled "Additional Duties" and discovered that Kearney and Smith had been appointed Field Ordering Officer and NCO. That meant they'd been charged with drawing cash from the Army and using it to make local purchases. The program was designed to push money into the local economy.

She found the investigation on the escalation of force incident in another folder. This had occurred six months after Kearney and Smith had been given access to thousands of dollars a month. The incident had taken place on a Sunday morning while Kearney had been on guard duty at the main gate. A car had refused orders to stop, speeding toward the checkpoint. Kearney had ordered the gunner to open fire, disabling the vehicle. To Sarah this seemed perfectly legal, but something felt off: Smith had been appointed the investigating officer to look into the shooting.

And it didn't look like the former company commander had done anything with the report other than file it away. But Smith and Kearney were no longer assigned as pay agents after that.

The whole situation reeked.

She sat at the desk, looking at the computer, wishing she could take notes. But she couldn't because then her entire notebook would be classified and locked away. Then she really wouldn't get the damn investigation done on time.

She hoped she was wrong about the conclusions she was drawing, but not for Kearney or Smith. For Sean.

It was a long time before she summoned the strength to walk back into his office.

"Sean, are you tracking that Kearney and Smith were assigned as the field ordering officer and pay agents prior to the escalation of force incident?"

"So?"

"So that means they were handling money for the battalion, not just this company." She paused, looking up at him. "There have been a lot of investigations around where all the money went in Iraq." She hesitated. "Smith was the investigating officer; he wrote up a report about the escalation of force and they were both removed as pay agents shortly afterward."

It took a minute before her words sunk in. "You don't think…"

"This could explain a lot, especially if they did something dirty and it involves the easy cash that was floating around Iraq."

Sean sank slowly into a chair across from her. "Holy shit."

"Anyone come back with a little extra money?"

He shook his head. "Not that I'm tracking. No more than normal deployment money, at least not from what I've seen."

"Money is a powerful temptation."

He felt sick. Physically ill at the thought of Kearney doing anything so fucking stupid as to steal money from theater.

"I can't believe Kearney would do something like that," he said quietly.

"It's not unheard of. I've seen men ruin their careers over a lot less than money."

He shot her a wry grin that fell flat. "Now if we were talking about Kearney's dick getting him into trouble, I wouldn't even blink. But this?"

"We don't know anything. But I damn sure can ask for an audit of their books."

He frowned. "Isn't it a little late for that? They've been redeployed for months."

"They have to keep receipts for six years." She reached for him then, her palm covering his. "I hope I'm wrong," she whispered. "For your sake."

"Hey sir!"

"Speak of the devil and he appears," Sarah said. She handed Sean the classified laptop as Kearney strode into the ops, a wide grin on his still swollen lip, Haverson in tow. The bruises from the fight had faded, and his lip was still just a little pink. "Look who I found."

Haverson tried to smile but he looked like shit and failed miserably. Deep slashes spread beneath his eyes and there were tired lines etched into his skin. His skin stretched taut over his small frame. His shoulders were hunched and his smile was tense and flat.

Sean fought back the worry. Haverson would just get skittish and run off again if Sean pushed too hard. "Twice in one week? Miss me already, Hasselhoff?"

"Nah. I need you to sign this memo saying I turned my body armor in back in Kuwait," Haverson said, his voice surprisingly steady. He glanced down at Sarah, as if just noticing her. Haverson tipped his chin, his gaze flicking down to her nametape. "You didn't happen to know Lieutenant Jack Anders, did you, ma'am?"

Sarah stilled and Sean braced for her reaction. He'd never seen her talk about Jack with anyone else. He had no idea how she would react to meeting up with some of the men who'd served with Jack. "He was my husband."

"I'm sorry, ma'am," Haverson said softly.

Kearney glanced over at Haverson. "LT was a good man." The rambunctious sergeant was gone, replaced by a sober and respectful Kearney she'd never seen.

"Thank you." She looked over at Sean. "I'm going to finish my report." There were a thousand things left unsaid in that simple sentence.

He nodded because there was nothing more he could say. He couldn't stop this. Couldn't interfere. Because there were limits to what he could do for Kearney.

If Kearney was involved in something like Sarah suspected, the man who'd kept Sean from tripping into the abyss had tumbled headlong into it himself.

And Sean didn't know if he could save him.

Even from himself.

But he had to know. He could not avoid the truth. He looked at Kearney. "I need to talk to you."

Kearney stilled, a thousand emotions flickering over his face. He hesitated, then nodded.

And Sean took another step closer to the edge of the abyss.

৩❀৩

HE STOOD WITH KEARNEY ON THE DOCK BEHIND HIS COMPANY. A formation of soldiers marched by, practicing drill and ceremony. It was an odd sight these days. They were so focused on the war that the basics like marching in formation were often abandoned and ignored.

"Nice to see you sober," he remarked.

Kearney grinned and pulled a can of dip out of his back pocket. "Yeah, well, it's not by choice."

It was a long moment before Sean found the words he needed. Better to get to the heart of it than dance around the issue. He trusted Kearney. Needed to hear the truth from the man who'd pulled him back from the brink of insanity and rage. "Is there anything I should know about an escalation of force incident downrange last deployment?"

Kearney stiffened then, his expression shuttering closed. "That investigation was closed while we were still deployed."

"What happened?"

"Smith wrote up a bullshit report. I didn't kill those civilians. Not on purpose. They didn't fucking stop. We told them to stop." He met Sean's gaze. "You know me, Sean. You know me."

Sean swallowed hard. He thought he did. But now? Now he was starting to doubt. And he felt greasy for not trusting the man who'd kept him on the right side of heaven that awful day. Kearney was a train wreck in garrison, but downrange? He was the man you wanted on your side. "You understand I had to ask."

Kearney shrugged. Just like that, the tension was gone and Sean was transported back to a time when he could hang out with his boys and didn't have the weight of the world on his shoulders.

"Yeah, I know. You having to be all responsible as the commander sucks. You're no fun anymore."

Sean grunted.

"So listen." Kearney twisted the top of his dip can. "Haves is leaving tomorrow. The guys are all going out. I know I'm restricted to the barracks and all but I'd like to send him off with everyone else."

Sean crossed his arms over his chest. "Are you forgetting the no-drinking order I gave you after Sunday night?"

Kearney shook his head and spit onto the pavement. "Hand to God. I won't drink."

Sean snorted. "I doubt that."

"I won't. I promise. This is Haves, man. We've been through a ton of shit together."

"What if you run into LT Smith?" He was going to regret this. He just fucking knew Kearney was going to get into trouble again. But he was right. This was Haverson. And some things were worth taking a risk for.

"We won't. It's a barbecue out at Stillhouse Hollow."

"What about if your wife calls?"

"She won't. She went to her sister's in Kentucky. I'll behave."

Sean frowned. "How do you know she's gone to her sister's in Kentucky?"

Kearney rolled his eyes. "Haverson told me he heard LT Smith talking about it. I didn't break the no-contact order. At least not, a second time." Kearney drew a cross over his heart. "I swear. No trouble. I'll be here bright and smiling tomorrow."

"Sober."

"Sober," Kearney agreed. "I'll be the designated driver."

Sean couldn't really believe he was considering it. But he'd walked through fire with Haverson and Kearney. He was the world's biggest idiot but damn it, Kearney was right. This was Haverson.

He shook his head. "I better not regret this, Kearney."

Kearney grinned triumphantly. "Come on, man, you know me better than that, don't you?"

At one point in his life, he had known Kearney better. But the spiraling-out-of-control sergeant hadn't been acting like his long-time friend for a while. Still, Sean couldn't bring himself to keep him from saying good-bye to their brother.

Haverson walked out from the company and Sean pinned him with a mock glare. "One sip, and I'm court-martialing his ass."

"Thanks, sir." Haverson tried to move past Sean but Sean put a hand on his shoulder. "Hey. Don't fall off the planet now that you're a civilian, okay?"

Haverson nodded and the shadow shuttered back across his face. "Yeah. You coming by tonight? We're grilling out at Stillhouse."

"Yeah. I'll try to make it. Where?"

Haverson rattled off directions as Sean took notes in his little green notebook. Haverson stuck his hand out and Sean took it, glad for the strength still remaining in Haverson's grip. He pulled Haverson into a tight embrace.

"I'll see you tonight," Sean said, his voice thick.

He stood on the back dock of his company for a while. Unable to shake the feeling that he was losing both of them. Frustration burned in his chest that he was a commander, a position with more power and authority over his men's lives, and there was nothing, *nothing* he could do to help either of them.

He felt, rather than heard, Sarah then, moving into his space. It was more a slight disturbance of the air, a faint hint of her scent as she approached, rather than a sound. They were nearly at the end of a duty day that had gone on for way too long and he was tired and irritated.

There was so much he never wanted her to know. Never would want her to live through. Because if he told her, he'd have to relive it all again. He'd have to reveal just what kind of a man he'd become in the minutes after Jack died. It was a nightmare, one he wished had been lived by someone else.

He walked back to his office, felt her by his side. Steadfast. Solid. Unbreakable.

He braced his hips against the edge of his desk and folded his arms across his chest. Saw her gaze flicker to the combat patch on his right shoulder. Saw the sadness and regret and yes, understanding, in her deep brown eyes.

"It's hard, isn't it?"

He rested his hands on the edge of his desk and unlocked his ankles. She stood at the toes of his boots and he wanted to move so that she stood between his knees. He wanted to touch her and pretend that all the history between them didn't exist. That they were starting new and fresh. That the sexual tension between them wasn't tainted with death and old memories.

"We make mistakes downrange, Sarah. Shit happens. We train to do the right thing but when it comes down to it, I want my men to do what it takes to come home."

She shifted then and she *was* standing between his knees. "I know. I wish civilians didn't die but I can't judge men for actions during war. I simply won't do it."

Sean snorted and shook his head. "That's exactly what you have to do. You're investigating why Smith and Kearney hate each other. You have to put the escalation of force incident in your report. You are very much passing judgment, Sarah."

She was so close. The faint hint of her scent wrapped around him, clinging to his senses. His mouth went dry and he swallowed as she rested her hand on his waist. "I might have to assess but I'm not judging you for giving your men the benefit of the doubt," she insisted, her voice like chocolate silk, her gaze dropping to his mouth.

He reached over and swung his door shut. He barely noticed the bang of the thin wood against the frame. Still they didn't move. Their bodies barely touched, except where her hand rested on his waist.

"I don't want to feel these things for you, Sean," she whispered. He shifted so that his mouth was a breath from hers.

"What things?" He slipped his hands up, barely cupping her neck. His thumbs caressed the skin below her jaw and he felt a tremor deep in the muscle beneath his touch.

"Respect. Admiration. Envy." Each word brought their lips closer but still the touch he craved didn't happen.

His lips curled in a smile as he studied her features and lost himself in the depths of her deep brown eyes. "Those weren't the things I was hoping for."

Her tongue flicked over her lips, drawing his gaze down to the glistening moisture. "What were you hoping for?"

"Desire," he whispered, tracing the word across her jaw with a breath of movement. "Need." His breath slid over her ear and she shivered. "Arousal."

She tipped her chin, granting him access to the soft skin on her neck. Relief pulsed through him that she didn't stiffen. Didn't pull away.

"You make me feel," he whispered, skimming his teeth over the edge of her ear. "I can't fight what you make me feel, Sarah."

Her other hand slid up and she was braced against him, her fingers digging into the muscles at his waist.

He scraped his teeth along her jaw, the connection hard between them. Her fingers clenched on his waist and he felt her quick intake of breath. Electricity sparked between them and sent blood pooling in his groin. He hadn't felt a want like this since...

Since Sarah.

He found her lips. Soft. Parted. He pinched her bottom lip between his teeth and watched as her eyes, deep with arousal, slipped closed. He wanted her. Oh God but the want was killing him, slowly, painfully, and with the most erotic pleasure.

He nibbled on her lips, tasting. Teasing. Urged her closer until she leaned against him. She was soft in all the right places. His hand hovered over her back, tracing faint patterns over the rough fabric of her uniform, skimming between her hips and lower. Teasing her, tormenting him. He wanted to touch her. To feel her skin against his and slide inside her. He wanted to lose himself in her. To forget. To feel.

He slipped his hand beneath the edge of her uniform jacket and felt the softness of her t-shirt. A slight tug and his fingertips skimmed over the soft flesh of her waist. She shivered as she angled her mouth against his, deepening the connection. She didn't stiffen as his fingers slid over her skin. Instead, he felt a soft gasp and took it inside him, inhaling her. He slipped higher, brushing the taut cotton of her bra. He cupped the curve of her breast, barely touching her there, losing himself in the sensation of stroking her body.

She was his judge and jury and somewhere deep down, he knew this was wrong. That she might get it twisted after all and confuse what she felt for him with her duty. This could all explode in his face, leaving them both bleeding from the self-inflicted wounds.

But the temptation to caress her skin was too great. Touching her, tasting her, when he'd never thought to see her again. He was in Heaven, tormented with a glimpse of Hell. He wanted her. God but he wanted to be inside her.

He didn't care if they were in his office. He needed to feel her stretched beneath him, around him. He wanted her but he knew that was impossible. Her fingers slipped beneath his jacket, her palms pressed now against the skin of his waist.

It was Sean who finally eased back, creating a semblance of space between them. His lips curled in a smile as he realized he still cupped her breast, their hips still pressed intimately together. He was hard as stone and pressed against the softness of her belly. The heat and the pressure was the most erotic sensation he could remember.

She opened her eyes, meeting his gaze. Hers were dark and heavy lidded. Sexy bedroom eyes.

"I never thought I'd feel anything like this again," Sarah whispered, breaking the silence, still thick with the arousal that wrapped around them.

Sean swallowed and brushed his lips against hers, unable to resist the swollen promise there. "I know."

The problem was, he knew exactly what they were up against. It didn't make her investigation go away. And it didn't take away the fact that once upon a time, they'd destroyed each other.

Sean brushed his fingers over her cheek and didn't speak. How could he tell her he'd been working on being a real man, the kind of man who was there when the shit hit the fan? The kind of man he hadn't been when he'd needed to be, all those years ago?

The kind of man she deserved.

🦋 16 🦋

Lieutenant Colonel Gilliad had more questions than answers after she went to him with her suspicions. Now, he wanted all the facts drawn up so he could brief the boss first thing Monday morning. Which meant that Sarah needed to figure out how to get the work done on a classified laptop on a weekend. Oh, and the brigade ball was tomorrow night, which meant she had even less time.

So she went back to Sean's office. Again. She was spending more time there than at her own desk these days. She found him staring into space behind his computer. For an instance, she was tempted to reach out to him. To put her hand on his arm. Some tangible touch that would reveal too much. Too many things she needed to keep to herself and sort through before she laid them at his feet.

She braced her shoulder against his door. "You're worried about letting Kearney go out tonight, aren't you?"

Sean pressed his lips into a humorless smile but there was a sadness in his eyes. "My relationships with Haves and Kearney are prime examples why distance is good between commanders and subordinates."

She narrowed her eyes and studied him quietly. "You care, Sean. That is a good thing."

"I lost my objectivity a long time ago, Sarah." There was a bitterness there that she didn't understand. He met her gaze and she saw the lines around his eyes, there even when he wasn't smiling. He wasn't the same boy she'd known. The combat patch he wore said it. And the lines of worry around his eyes said it.

"You're still a good leader."

His lips twisted into a wry facsimile of a grin. "We'll see if you still agree after Kearney gets arrested tonight."

She frowned. "You don't—"

Sean shook his head. "No, I think he'll be fine. He's not going to be near his wife; he's away from the LT. And I think it's sinking in that the fact that you're here means he's on his last leg. The sergeant major is tired of hearing about Kearney and his problems." Sean dragged his hand over his face. "Haves will keep him in line tonight. I hope." He paused. "What did the boss say?"

"I have to have complete findings to him by Monday morning. He's not going higher with the information until he's got the complete picture. So since this whole investigation is now classified..."

He looked over at her and jerked his chin toward the classified computer and hard drive. "You need access to that tomorrow, don't you?"

She nodded. "Yeah. But I don't want you to have to come in. I—"

"I'll meet you here at nine thirty."

She cocked her head and looked at him. "I can't ask you to do that."

"You're working on an investigation involving my men. My boss has you working tomorrow. I'll be here." He sighed. "You heading home?"

"Yeah. Have to get munchkin from the daycare."

"I'll walk you out."

"You're not leaving?"

He shook his head slowly. "Clearly you must think I'm a god if you think I've gotten everything done today. My lieutenants are coming back from the range to brief me up on their stats and I've got to get my slides done for command and staff on Tuesday. And that's the easy stuff."

"Sounds like a wild way to spend a Friday evening."

Sarah looked around the office of the man he'd become. Notebooks stood in formation against a bookshelf. His Cav Stetson hung on a rack near the door, his name and rank etched into a plaque below it. And the two all-black picture frames, names etched in silver hanging by the door. She didn't move close enough to read them. One name on that list she knew all too well.

Sarah shouldered her bag and waited for Sean to lock his office. She glanced at her watch. Time was running short but she wanted a few minutes more with him. A few more minutes before work and life interrupted and they were no longer just a man and woman, but instead were "sir" and "ma'am," "mommy" and "commander."

Silence wrapped around them as he walked her to her car. Sean turned to her in the fading sunlight. "It means a lot to me that you can be in the same room with me," he said quietly, standing a little too close. The Army had rules about public displays of affection and while they weren't touching, they might as well be.

Right now, Sarah was too blown away by his statement to even consider rules of proper behavior. She smiled sadly. "I won't lie and say it didn't hurt, seeing you again. And we weren't very professional, even after eight years to heal." She tipped her face up at him, drawn once more to the power and strength he carried with ease. "But part of me is really glad we're getting along." She swallowed and glanced at a pigeon shuffling across the sidewalk.

"Yeah." Sean cleared his throat. "So I'll see you tomorrow?"

She nodded. "Tomorrow." She turned to walk around to the driver's side of her car.

"Sarah?"

She paused near the driver's side door. "Yeah?"

"Think about me tonight?"

Her mouth fell open and she stood frozen for a moment before she laughed and shook her head, even as heat prickled over her skin to settle between her thighs. It was a long time before her lungs started working again. "I'd forgotten about that."

"I did, too. Until just now." His blue eyes glowed in the fading light with a heat that had everything to do with what they'd shared in the office a short while ago and the memory threading between them. Once upon a time, when they'd been separated by a few hundred miles, Sean had been on a training exercise. It had been weeks since he'd seen her and he'd managed to sneak a call on his company commander's tactical phone.

And he'd convinced her to talk dirty to him. It had turned into something of a secret handshake between them.

One that she'd forgotten about. Until now, when the memory of that long ago game warmed her.

One that reminded her that once upon a time, she'd loved a man other than her husband.

And that man was still among the living.

SARAH HAD BEEN HALFWAY HOME WHEN SHE REMEMBERED Major Wilson wanted an update on the investigation. She'd seriously considered sending an e-mail but figured with the way things were trending, she shouldn't risk it.

Twenty minutes later she stood outside Major Wilson's office, listening to her conversation on the phone. She'd made eye contact with Sarah but hadn't waved her into the office.

"No, she hasn't even submitted initial findings," Sarah heard Wilson say. Pause. "No, sir, I was not able to get her initial findings." Pause. "Monday, sir."

Wilson hung up the phone and motioned for her to come in. Sarah stood at attention in front of her desk. "Any progress?"

This new, somber Wilson was unexpected. Damn it, did the woman have any consistent personality traits?

"Ma'am, Kearney and Smith were both tasked to handle a lot of money downrange. They were pay officers. Their problems started after an incident out in sector. I'm writing up the rest of the facts this weekend. I will recommend a complete audit of their receipts. I'm not going to be comfortable closing this investigation without ruling out the possibility that there's more here."

She glanced at the clock on Wilson's desk and Wilson didn't miss the motion.

"You have to go." It was not a question.

"Yes, ma'am. Have to get my daughter from daycare."

Major Wilson nodded. "You'll be at the ball tomorrow night?"

Sarah sucked in a deep breath. She'd forgotten about the damn ball again. "Roger, ma'am." Jamie was already lined up for babysitting Anna. Thank God Jamie's father was doing better.

Wilson let her go, leaving her exactly thirty minutes to get to the daycare. Something was going to have to change. She couldn't keep being one of the first ones to drop their kid off in the morning and the last one to pick up at night. Poor Anna.

She pushed aside her emotions as Anna ran and gave her a hug, a gratifying greeting under any circumstances. Sarah noticed she looked like she'd been crying and bent down to her daughter's level.

"What's wrong, honey?" she asked, brushing her daughter's bangs from her eyes.

Anna sniffed and looked away. "I'm sad, Mommy."

Sarah glanced at the daycare worker, Lisa, who shrugged and looked entirely too helpless. "She wouldn't talk to me."

"Why are you sad?"

"Because Aiden Johnson's daddy came home from Iraq today. He picked him up from school and everyone clapped and cheered."

Sarah's eyes watered instantly as she pulled her daughter into a hug. Guilt slithered in to twine with the sadness. Anna had been missing her daddy while Sarah had been busy fooling around with another man.

Sarah leaned back. "You should be happy for Aiden, honey," Sarah said, desperate to keep her voice from cracking. "He's lucky that his daddy came home."

Anna rested her head against Sarah's shoulder while she thought of something, anything, that would help her five year old understand why her daddy hadn't come home. She cursed her own inability to comfort her daughter.

"Why didn't my daddy come home?" Anna sniffed.

"I wish he did."

"Didn't Daddy love us?"

Sarah's throat tightened and she sucked in a deep breath. "He loved us very much, honey. But he got hurt and he went to Heaven where it didn't hurt anymore."

Anna sniffed. "Daddy's happy in Heaven?"

Sarah twisted and pulled her arm around her daughter. "He'd be happier if he was with us."

"I wish I had a daddy," she said against her neck.

"Me, too, honey." Sarah swallowed hard and simply sat, holding her little girl.

"Mommy?" Anna's voice was just this side of a whine.

"Yeah, honey?"

"Can we have steak for dinner?"

Sarah smiled as Anna pulled out of her hug and sniffed. "I didn't buy steak this week."

Anna's smile shed the last hint of sadness, replaced with mischief. "We could go to Texas Roadhouse," she suggested.

Sarah smiled. "Yeah, baby, we can go to Texas Roadhouse."

She was inclined to indulge her daughter tonight. There was a hole in Anna's life. She'd never known her dad, but as she got older, she was starting to notice the missing piece in her life.

It was only later, after Anna was in bed, that Sarah had time to turn the day's events over in her mind, inspecting them.

She'd kissed Sean today. More, she'd been closer with him than she'd been with any man since her husband. He'd stroked his fingers over her skin; his words brushed over her flesh. And she'd enjoyed it. She'd closed her eyes and granted him access, kissing him, touching him. Wishing for more.

And then her daughter had cried for her father and the rightness she'd felt with Sean was somehow twisted to something less right.

The ache in her chest grew until it felt like she would explode if she didn't let it out. It hurt. Losing Jack still hurt. But for the first time since he'd died, she honestly felt ready. But she knew now it wasn't as simple as what she wanted. Her daughter mattered and she couldn't just drag Sean into her life based on hormones and chemistry.

And what if she and Sean fell apart again, after she'd let him into her daughter's life? Anna would feel the loss of Sean more than she did the lack of her father.

Life was never simple. Not that it ever had been.

Sean had wanted children. It was part of why they'd broken up. He'd wanted kids; she hadn't. She hadn't wanted to get married because she'd wanted to be a soldier. She'd been stupid enough to think you couldn't be a woman and be married and be a good soldier. Marriage and the white picket fence had never been something she'd dreamed of. And Sean had wanted her to get out so she could follow him to Korea. He'd been so pissed when she'd said no.

That she'd married and done all the things she hadn't been ready for with another man? Anna was an unexpected gift, and Sarah cherished her.

Sarah would never wish for things to be different than they were. She'd lived and she'd loved. She'd lost part of her heart not once but three times, and she'd survived. But was she willing to risk her daughter's heart?

Sarah swallowed the lump in her throat and closed the door quietly. She locked up and set the alarm before closing the door to her bedroom. She glanced at her phone before sliding between her sheets. She stretched the tight muscles in her thigh. All the walking she'd been doing was good, strengthening and stretching her more each day. She shivered as the cool cotton kissed her skin, and listened to the silence of her sleeping home.

The home she would have made with Jack.

The home she'd turned into a shrine, hoping beyond hope that she and her daughter would never forget the man who'd been so key to their lives. The silence wrapped around her as she drifted to sleep, wishing things were so much simpler than they were.

Wishing she could trust that her feelings for Sean were real and not a fantasy of the man she wished he'd been, once upon a time.

❧   17   ❧

The scars that ripped down his arm ached. It must be getting ready to storm out. His blood hummed with pain and another ache, long forgotten. He turned on the shower, desperate for a relief from the desire pulsing in his groin.

He dropped his uniform in a pile on the floor and cranked on the shower. He might be working tomorrow but he was going to be wearing civilian clothes. He was willing to bet Sarah would, too. His lips curled. Maybe he should call her and ask. He didn't want to show up in flip-flops and jeans if she was going to be in ACUs.

He ducked his head under the water, his mouth going dry as he thought of the feel of her body against his. God but she was soft. He'd never planned on seeing her again, let alone touching her. Tasting her.

He was hard as stone and wired for her taste. He felt like a damn teenager. He closed his eyes and saw her once more. Her eyes heavy, her lips swollen. She was driving him crazy. His hand slid along his cock, wishing it was Sarah touching him. He closed his eyes, stroking himself faster, imagining it was Sarah beneath him, Sarah's hands on his shoulders. Sarah's body encircling him and driving him closer to the edge. He grunted as he came, bracing one hand against the shower wall to keep from sinking to his knees.

His phone rang, yanking him out of his private fantasy, and he killed the water. He dragged a towel around his waist as he reached for the cell.

"Sir, are you trying to get us both fired?" Morgan growled.

"Your timing sucks," Sean mumbled. No way in hell he was going to tell his first sergeant what he'd interrupted.

"You realize the CSM is going to have my nuts in a vise grip if Kearney gets in trouble tonight?"

Sean imagined Morgan had his feet kicked up on a coffee table and was pulling off his cigar like an old Clint Eastwood movie. "Which is why I'm swinging by to make sure he's obeying my no-drinking order."

Sean heard a *thunk* and he assumed that Morgan had just hit the roof. "Are you serious? You're going to a party with a bunch of junior enlisted guys?"

"No. I'm stopping by a barbecue to say good-bye to one of my former soldiers. I'm going to pop in, make my farewells, and head out. I won't be there more than an hour."

"It'll take that long to get out to Stillhouse."

"Doesn't matter." He swallowed a hard lump that suddenly blocked his throat. "The least I can do is show up for Haverson's farewell."

Silence crackled over the phone. "You're still beating yourself up over not getting his chapter changed, aren't you?" Morgan asked quietly, his voice gruffer than usual.

"He doesn't deserve an Other Than Honorable discharge because he popped hot for heroin. The Army made him an addict." The truth. Enraging and ugly, but there it was.

"It's out of your hands, sir."

Sean cleared his throat and glanced at his watch. "Yeah, well. Either way, I'm going out there. You coming?"

"Can't let my commander do anything without his first sarn't watching his back."

Sean smiled, wishing he'd had this kind of bond with all his enlisted counterparts. "Meet you there?"

"Yeah."

Sean hung up and turned, staring into the still foggy bathroom mirror. The jagged scar running down his forearm was one of many. The faint starburst of white skin stood out against the darker skin on his shoulder. Smalls arms fire had glanced off the edge of his body armor and he'd been lucky the AK-47 round hadn't done more damage.

The visible scars, though, were nothing compared to the ones he carried on his soul. He turned away from the mirror, unable to stand the sight of his own reflection.

Morgan said he'd made hard choices that day. Sean had made bad ones. He'd been young. He'd been dying to charge headlong into battle. Longing for the baptism by fire that he'd believed would make him a man.

He hadn't counted on the fire. He hadn't counted on the memories making themselves permanent bedmates every time he closed his eyes. Hadn't counted on the consequences when innocent people got caught in the crossfire.

He'd lost track of many of the guys from that tour but tonight, he could say good-bye to one of them.

And do his best to put some of the memories to rest.

❦

THE THING SEAN LIKED ABOUT BARBECUES OVER FULL-BLOWN parties was that at barbecues, people stood around and talked. They drank as they talked and they enjoyed good food. But the intent in the late evening as the full moon rose over Stillhouse Hollow Reservoir was to say farewell, not get shitfaced. So far, it looked like everyone was on board with that plan.

The food was good. True to his word, Kearney was drinking Coke and manning the grill, shooting the shit with some of the men from Chaos Company.

Sean glanced around, nursing a single Shiner Bock. For a while it felt like old times, but Sean felt like a piece of himself was missing. Sarah. There was no way he could have convinced her to spend an evening out with him. Not when she was a single mother. Not when she had a child asleep in her home.

But he wanted to. He studied the bonfire, feeling the heat lick his skin. He shunted aside another memory of fire. Fire that burned and seared the hair from his nostrils. This heat was warm. A comfort. A reminder that there was still normalcy in the world.

"Where'd you just go?" Haverson melted out of the crowd to stand next to him by the fire.

Sean glanced over at his now former medic. His lips pressed into a thin line. "Just remembering how many asses you saved over the years. Including mine. Twice."

Haverson's expression drifted far off. "Yeah, well. It was my job."

Sean put his hand on Haverson's shoulder. "It was. You did everything you could and then some. You're the best medic I've ever had." Sean snorted. "I'm going to be sweating bullets the next time I have to go in sector without you."

Haverson sniffed and took a sip from his beer. "Yeah, well, you still got some good guys to patch your ass up the next time you get shot. Sean."

Sean laughed. "Couldn't wait to break out the first name, huh?"

"Shoot, we've been doing that for years. Now, though, I can do it without Firs' Sarn't digging in my ass."

Sean wished that the laugh he heard in Haverson's voice wasn't a shadow of his former smart-assed self. He wished whatever demon was hunting Haves would relent and give him peace. "I hope you find life as a civilian gives you a rest from the war."

Haverson shrugged. "I doubt it. I'm pretty much going to marry my pharmacist so I have a steady supply of Klonopin and Oxy. Sleep is a thing of the past for me. At least for the foreseeable future."

Sean ignored the warning that tingled at the base of his neck.

He no longer had the authority to order Haverson into counseling. Or to see the doc. He opted for a different tactic. "I'm sorry," he said quietly, searching the younger man's scarred face. For what, he wasn't sure. Absolution? Maybe. "For the decisions I forced on you. The men were my responsibility. The decisions were mine alone."

Haverson took a long pull off his beer. "Doesn't change the fact that people died. People in the wrong place at the wrong time."

"You don't get to change that, Haves."

"Then why be a medic? Why bring a medic to the fight at all? I could change it. Sometimes I got lucky. And other times?" The bitterness in Haverson's voice rocketed straight through Sean's chest into his heart. "Other times, we got fucked and there was nothing I could do about it." He held up a hand. "I really don't want to hear about Rule Number Two right now."

"You did your best."

"My best wasn't good enough." Haverson downed the rest of his beer and walked around the fire, melting into the darkness.

Sean watched Haverson fade until he no longer moved in the shadows. He went and found Morgan sticking his finger in Kearney's chest. "If you get arrested tonight..."

Kearney held up his hands. "I won't. I promise."

Morgan pointed at his feet. "Do you see this?"

Kearney frowned. "Your boot?"

"That's right. Before you do anything stupid, I want you to remember one thing. My size thirteen will fit up your ass with the appropriate amount of force."

Sean laughed, hoping that Morgan's good-natured warning to Kearney got through. This really was enough to get him fired if Kearney didn't stay sober tonight. He slapped his hand on Kearney's shoulder. "Keep an eye on Haverson. He's having a harder time leaving than I think he realizes."

"Done."

Sean frowned as Kearney, too, faded into the darkness.

"What's on your mind, sir?" Morgan asked, pulling off his cigar. He wore jeans and a tucked-in, Western-style shirt. The boots he'd referenced were pointed toe Tony Llamas cowboy boots. For a man pushing forty, Morgan had the physique of a professional athlete. Lean and mean and built for punishing acts of physical demand required by the Infantry.

"Worried about Haverson. I'm afraid that leaving his support— his buddies—is going to make things worse for him, not better."

Morgan stayed silent, the cherry on his cigar casting a red shadow across his angular features. "Hope you're wrong. But I'm afraid you might be right."

He lingered at the barbecue far too long, until the fire died down and everyone had left with sober drivers and secure rides home.

As Kearney had promised, there had been no drama tonight. Haverson had been laughing. Talking shit with Kearney who, for once, appeared to be keeping his shit together. But it was a long time before Sean headed back to his place, his heart and his memories a thousand miles away.

His apartment lacked any welcoming committee. No dog. Nothing there to welcome him home but a few empty beer bottles and an old pizza box. He sucked in a deep breath, recognizing the melancholy mood for what it was, but was unable to pull himself out of it. He dragged his hand across his face.

He needed oblivion. He needed an escape from the dull pain in his arm and the potent ache in his heart. He tossed back a single Ambien and washed it down with some water he cupped in his palm from the bathroom sink.

Just tonight. For tonight, he would sink into oblivion and not dream. Not relive the horror and the blood and the smoke. For tonight, he wouldn't hear the screams of the wounded or feel the heat of the fires.

Just for tonight, he would sink into oblivion and sleep. He stripped off everything but his boxers and sank into the mattress that seemed to wrap around him and pull him into the warmth of a puffy cloud, just like the tentacles of the drug reaching into his brain and pulling him down into the darkness. Tomorrow, things would be better. Tomorrow, he'd get to see Sarah.

There was always hope that tomorrow would be better than today. Today was gone forever and no matter how much he might want to change things, they were done, etched into the stone of history.

Forever.

☙❧

"HELLO?"

It was close to midnight. Her phone vibrated on the nightstand near her bed and yanked her out of the fitful sleep she'd barely achieved.

"Sarah."

She sat up, instantly alerted by the muffled sound of Sean's voice. "What's wrong?"

"Nothing. Everything." There was a silence. "I shouldn't have called."

"It's okay." She lay back in the bed, staring into the darkness and listening for the sound of his breathing. "Talk to me, Sean."

"I...I wanted to hear your voice."

She narrowed her eyes in the darkness. "Are you drunk?"

"Not really," he said after a moment. "I took a sleeping pill."

"Oh." She'd had those nights. The nights where her mind would race around corners and through dark alleys, chasing memories that refused to lie dormant. "How was the barbecue?"

A warm sound. "It was good. Sad." He paused. "I'm worried about Haverson," he admitted.

"He's on something."

"A cocktail of things," he said, his voice sounding marginally clearer. "I don't usually take pills."

"I don't, either. But sometimes they help."

"Yeah." A sigh. "You don't realize how important sleep is until you don't get it."

She leaned back in her bed, closing her eyes, listening to the ache in his voice. Trusting that he would get around to talking to her.

Or maybe, he would just fall asleep. It tugged at her heart that he'd called her tonight when he was hurting.

What if he'd been able to do that years ago, before their lives had fallen apart?

"I wanted to hear your voice," he said again.

"You mentioned that." She sighed deeply, her brain slowly waking up from the fitful sleep and keyed in on the sound of his voice. When the silence stretched too long, she stepped slowly into the breach. "Sean?"

"Hmm?"

He was falling asleep. Maybe she should let him. But he'd called and woken her up. Maybe she could be honest with him. For once. "I'm looking forward to seeing you tomorrow."

"Yeah?"

"Yeah."

"Why?" There was an edge to his voice now. A rough tension that sounded like sex.

"Because I liked..." The words caught in her throat. "You told me to think about you tonight."

She left the words hanging there. Wondering if he would piece together what she wasn't quite brave enough to say.

"What did you think about?"

She swallowed the sudden dryness in her throat. "You."

"You'll have to be more descriptive than that." A quiet pause.

"I'm not very creative." A smile teased the edge of her lips.

"I remember you being very creative," he murmured. She heard the mischief in his voice before he'd finished his thought. "I was lying here. Alone in my bed. And I wondered, what's Sarah doing right now?" His voice was low and thick. "Did I wake you?"

Her skin felt hot and the ache between her thighs pulsed with each whisper of his voice over her ear. "No. I was just lying here."

"Hmmm." The sound of his voice caressed her skin. "And you were thinking about me?" he asked softly.

Memories of another time, another phone call, traced through her blood. The time he'd snuck a call on his commander's phone as a young sergeant out in a training exercise. She'd laughed when he'd told her he was lying in the back of a Humvee, alone.

Then the conversation had taken a dark and sensual turn. It was something she'd shared with him that she'd never done since.

She bit her lip and nodded, wishing the ache in her blood wasn't so strong. So demanding. "Yeah."

His laugh was low and quiet. "What were you thinking about?"

Once, it had been a game between them, a sensual game that stimulated her body and her mind. Now, it was a connection. A touch, a caress. A way to be with him despite the distance and the darkness between them.

"You," she whispered. "You'd been gone for weeks." An ache bloomed in her belly, spreading like slow fire through her veins. "I wanted you to touch me." She slipped her hand beneath her tank top, her own fingers familiar and foreign against her skin. Her stomach clenched even as her nipples pearled into tight buds and she imagined his tongue on her flesh, tasting her, stroking her pleasure. She heard his breath in the phone and imagined his lips on her ear. She closed her eyes and ran her fingers beneath the waist of her sleep pants. The wickedness of what she was doing pulsed through her body, inciting the arousal to fevered levels. A need that demanded satisfaction only his touch would provide.

There had been sensual heat in his question and she imagined him lying with her, the rough strength of his body scraping against hers even as his lips trailed wet and hot down her belly to her core with that relentless ache.

"Where? Where did you want me to touch you, Sarah?"

"My neck. Like you did the other day." Arousal, slick and hot. "I used to like it when you licked me there."

"When I scraped my teeth over your pulse."

She closed her eyes, letting her imagination take over. Her skin ached where his teeth had been. She traced her fingers over the spot, imagining they were his. "Yes."

"I'd lick your neck," he whispered roughly. "I'd kiss that space between your shoulder and your throat. Nibble on you there."

Her breath stopped. "What else?"

"What else do you want me to do?"

"My back." Her words were thick, the ache between her thighs demanding. Potent and powerful. "I'd want you to kiss my back."

"You were always sensitive there," he said. "What are you doing right now?"

"Lying in bed," she murmured. "Imagining you're here."

"Are..." He cleared his throat roughly. It sounded pained. "Would you touch yourself?"

"Shit." A gasp, laced with pleasure.

"What?"

"That's...really hot."

A warm laugh. Like liquid heat. "You should try it from my end." His voice was clearer now. "Are you?" he asked. Heavy anticipation. She whimpered as she slid her fingers lower, over the mound of her heat where she throbbed, still covered by her sensible cotton panties. They were no longer sensible. They were a barrier to pleasure but still she hesitated, the pressure of her own palm creating a wicked sensation made more erotic by his words.

"Are you aroused?"

"Mmm."

"Wet?"

"Mmm hmm." She flushed, her skin hot—nervous and aroused all at once. There was anticipation in his words that mixed in her belly, creating more need that slid through her veins.

"Are...are you touching yourself?"

She swallowed, unable to move and slip her fingers beneath her panties into her own slick heat. She lied, enjoying the tease of his words that built into the need inside her. "Yes."

The memory of his fingers sliding against her aching swollen center was beyond foreign, a teasing mix of erotic and forbidden made all the more arousing by his voice against her ear. She arched her back and inched her thighs apart, opening to the soft caress of his words. Almost, she stroked herself there. Almost gave in to the pleasure his words and her touch would bring.

"What do you want?" His voice was barely a thick whisper now and she had a visual of him, naked and rough, the hair on his chest scraping against her nipples.

❧

HE WAS NAKED AND AROUSED AND IMAGINING HER OPEN AND spread before him like a beautiful, erotic canvas. In some dark corner of his mind, the fact that he was on the phone might have been disturbing, but the quiet gasps she didn't even know she was making were driving him crazy. He ached to the point of pain but still he whispered in her ear and tasted her on his lips.

❧

SHE THOUGHT ABOUT IT. ABOUT SLIDING HER HAND DOWN OVER the softness of her belly. Beneath the edge of her panties.

Into the heat that ached for his touch.

She was wet. It surprised her that she was. Swollen and slick—her fingers slid through the moist heat and she gasped.

"Sarah." Her name was a plea. "Tell me what it feels like."

"Warm." She bit her lips as her fingers found that most sacred place. "Wet." Too long. Far too long since she'd felt this sensual arousal. Since she'd felt whole and real and infinitely female. The scars on her leg were tight and stiff but tonight, they were secondary, the heat between them hotter than the memory of the pain. "I want your fingers there," she whispered. "Stroking me."

"I want to kiss you there," he said. "I want to taste you. I want your knees over my shoulders." She closed her eyes, letting the visual take over. Imagined the feel of his skin beneath her fingers, the sweep of his tongue over her most sensitive flesh.

She moaned quietly as her fingers sought the pleasure his words promised. "Yes," he urged. "Come for me."

A small noise. "Harder," he urged. "I'm right here. It's my mouth on you. My fingers inside you. I want to feel you all around me."

Her body tightened. Tensed. "Sean."

"Say it again." A rough demand. "Say my name."

"Sean." Close, so close. Her thighs clenched. It was there, just there. Tighter. Higher. Until...Her breath locked in her throat. A tiny noise escaped her as the orgasm washed over her, her breath shuddering from her lungs.

"Come with me," he whispered, hearing her gasps thrusting his own pleasure tighter. He stiffened, growing harder with each stroke of his palm, a vision of her hips rising beneath him, open and offering her sweet darkness.

Sarah couldn't remember the last time she'd felt anything so complete and erotic all at once. Once, she'd given up any hope of intimacy, but as Sean's words slid across her skin her pleasure increased and she slid her fingers into her own slick heat. Heat and wet slicked over her fingers and she felt cherished and safe and amazed that it was Sean's quiet urges stirring her arousal on. Tracing pleasure down her spine and spiraling out even as she stroked the beginnings of her release to sparkle in her blood.

She trusted him. It was novel and exciting as he breathed words that sent her staggering closer to the edge. If he was here, it would be his fingers circling her swollen center. His tongue pressing against her aching opening. His erection filling her. But now it was his voice, describing in dark erotic words what he wanted her to do. What she did under the warmth of his urging.

"God that's sexy," he said in her ear. "I...That's fucking beautiful, Sarah."

When she could speak, she said, "You can't even see me."

"I've got a pretty good imagination."

"Apparently," she said. "But you didn't..."

"Says who?" A sensual edge to his voice. A dark arousal.

She smiled. "I'm glad you called."

"I'm sorry I woke you."

"No you're not."

◈

"STILL THERE?"

Sean stretched one arm over his head and arched his back, feeling his spine pop and crack. Sleep licked at him with black-tipped fingers, urging him down into the darkness.

"Yeah." He heard the satisfied smile in her voice. "I can't believe we just did that."

He smiled in response, his own body still humming with the buzz of his own release. "Brings back memories," he said quietly.

"Yeah."

He closed his eyes and imagined her lips sliding against his in a soft good night kiss. "Sleep well."

"Sean?"

"Hmm?"

"Tonight, if the nightmares come? Call me."

He swallowed and glanced toward the small bathroom mirror where the Ambien sat in neat formation with a myriad of other pill bottles. He didn't want to take more. Regretted that he had to take the one but things were too twisted tonight. Too raw.

"Thank you," he mumbled, not quite sure how she'd known or if she'd merely suspected.

She remained silent long enough that Sean caught himself wondering if she'd fallen asleep. "See you tomorrow," she whispered, her voice thick with sleep.

"Good night."

He flipped his phone shut and dragged the comforter over his shoulders as he curled on his side. He'd thought that life was simpler before Sarah had reappeared in it but that was a lie. He closed his eyes, realizing that if he did not receive a phone call tonight, it would be the first weekend since he'd taken command that he hadn't had to bail somebody's ass out of jail or pick them up from the hospital.

His breathing slowed and he hoped the fluke was actually part of a trend.

❦ 18 ❧

The sun was too bright as Sarah walked out of her house. Thank God for Jamie Sorren. She was hoping to be done with things at Sean's office by lunch and leave herself enough time to get ready for the ball.

She hadn't been planning on the ball but these things were pretty much mandatory. Plus she'd talked to Claire, who was going as Evan's date. She promised not to leave Sarah alone.

She pulled in next to Sean's truck, not at all surprised that he was already there. If she'd learned one thing about him, it was that he was punctual. She hated being late but Sean took timeliness to new heights.

Her blood warmed at the thought of seeing him. A quick walk down the path seemed to take forever. So why did she pause outside his orderly room, a sudden jolt of nerves twisting in her belly? She deliberately filled her lungs and pushed into the orderly room. Light radiated from Sean's office. He was already there.

Deep breaths. Last night...last night had changed a lot of things.

She knocked quietly on his door and tried to smother the worried expression that crossed her face the minute she saw him.

He looked like hell. Like he'd spent all night drinking or worse. "What happened?"

His eyes were bleary and bloodshot, the dark purple shadows beneath them accentuating the depth of his fatigue. He hadn't shaved and if his hair hadn't been wet, she might have wondered if he hadn't showered. "Is Kearney—"

Sean shook his head and scrubbed one hand over his face. Peeking out from the short-sleeved shirt he wore was a deep, nasty-looking purple scar that bisected the muscles in his forearm. No hair grew around the scar, making it more obvious.

"Kearney's fine." He flipped over some paperwork and looked like he wished she wasn't here.

"What's wrong?"

Sean closed his eyes and for a moment, the strain in his jaw relaxed. He looked as if he might have fallen asleep if she hadn't been standing there. "That sleeping pill last night? Apparently, I've developed a tolerance because I was up all damn night, half awake, half asleep. And now I feel hung over."

Sarah smiled, her lips quivering as she attempted to smother her reaction. He glanced up at her and glared. "I'm glad this is funny for you. I feel like I've been hit by a truck and you're laughing."

"You look like you've been hit by a truck." She leaned against the doorway, the irritation dissipating like a cloud of CS gas on the breeze. "Look, go home. I'll work on this some other time."

"Did your boss cut you a break?"

"No. I have to turn in my report Monday." She frowned, remembering the conversation she'd overheard from Major Wilson's office. "I think the whole purpose of getting me to turn this in early is to make the investigation go away."

Sean frowned. "What are you talking about?"

"I overheard my boss talking last night. Someone who outranked her called and asked her about my investigation."

"That's what you overheard?"

"I'm assuming as I only heard half the conversation. I can't imagine that there are too many open investigations in the support battalion right now."

"So your battalion XO wants you to make a shitty, half-assed recommendation." He pushed away from his desk and came around it to flop onto the couch. His legs spread wide before him and Sarah tried not to notice the way the jeans hugged his muscles. "It's probably brigade pushing to have this done and over with."

Sarah frowned. The only person who could be looking out for LT Smith with any kind of pull would be Sarah's former boss—Smith's uncle.

Sean's smile was brittle and he remained silent, tipping his head back and closing his eyes. "It wouldn't be unheard of for his uncle to inquire about his nephew." He sighed. "I've done that with Kearney."

"Why do you keep protecting him?" Sarah asked, suddenly realizing that Sean had been doing exactly that.

Sean didn't budge. "I owe him," he said simply. "More than I can ever repay."

"*Why*, Sean?"

He glanced at her then, his expression unreadable. "The combination to my safe is 32, 14, 12. You can get the hard drive and the laptop out."

He walked out before she could say anything else, brushing past her without a glance.

She understood. She'd been there. She'd breathed in the smoke and felt the confusion as she'd tried to secure her formation as the world burned around her. She'd felt the sting of enemy shrapnel entering her skin and the struggle to maintain control in the confusion and the smoke of a firefight.

She remembered with aching, burning clarity the desire to burn the fucking world down around them. The rage. The hate. Oh yes, she remembered those feelings before the pain took over and blocked out everything else.

Was that why he was protecting Kearney?

She debated for one hot second just getting into his safe and ignoring his pissy mood. Her internal argument lasted barely a single breath before she followed him outside.

He hadn't gone far. He sat on the front step of his orderly room, his elbows braced on his knees, his gaze distant.

"I'm not in the mood, Sarah." His voice still had that low, feral edge—the warning of a cornered beast. Ready to fight.

"Tough. This is an investigation and if you don't want to tell me the whole truth—now, without any more lies or half truths—then we can do this the hard way."

Sean narrowed his eyes at her, the muscle in his jaw pulsing in time with his heartbeat. "The only thing that you need to know about Sergeant Kearney is that he's dealing with some psychiatric issues from Iraq and I refuse to let him be prosecuted while he's undergoing treatment," Sean said stiffly.

Sarah crossed her arms over her chest. "Bullshit, Sean. Why let him go out last night? Why assume that risk? What aren't you telling me?"

"I'm not going to give you ammunition to use against him." He pinned her with a hard look. "I fucking owe him, Sarah. I owe him more than my life."

She took a deep breath, searching for a way to diffuse the anger between them. "I'm not the enemy, Sean, and you need recognize that. There's something else going on here and just because you want to wish that fact away doesn't make it true."

He rounded on her, stepping right into her space, his expression contorted with anger and something she wasn't sure she wanted to name but she recognized it nonetheless.

Self-loathing.

The realization nailed her in the gut and forced the air from her lungs, the anger from her blood. Sean's breathing was deep and hard, his pulse visible in his neck. His fists were knotted by his sides. If she were on the outside looking in, she'd guess he was about to strike her.

But he wouldn't. Not Sean. No matter that she no longer knew the man in front of her—in the dark part of her heart, she knew he'd never strike her. He might be furious. He might yell and tear down the walls but he'd never hurt her. But it still took a massive leap of faith to step into the space of his anger. It pulsed off him in waves, hot and feral and dangerous. She reminded herself that she didn't know him anymore. That this temper was more than she'd ever seen from him.

It didn't stop her from feeling the tiny shard of hurt when he stepped back. "Not now, Sarah."

"Yes, now, Sean." She stepped closer to him once more and lifted her hand to settle in the center of his chest. Above where his rank might have been, had they both been in uniform.

"You don't know what this feels like," he whispered, his voice thick and rough as gravel.

"I can guess just by looking at you." She slid her hand up until it rested over the pulse in his neck. "Trust me, Sean. Trust me to do the right thing."

She saw him swallow before his arms slid around her waist and he pulled her close. She buried her face in his neck, breathing in the scent of anger and fatigue, soap and man. She felt his pulse beat against her cheek and felt his breathing return to normal. Slowly, so slowly, she felt the tension ease from him, like it was sliding down his back to the floor.

His face was pressed into her neck, buried in her hair, his hands fisted in her shirt at the back. She was his lifeline, his oasis in the middle of the desert of blame and regret. He held tight to her while the anger passed— more angry words gone into the history of their lives.

"I'm sorry."

THE STROKE OF HER PALMS AGAINST THE SMALL OF HIS BACK SENT a shiver skittering down his spine. "Ambien makes me bitchy."

"I can see that."

Sean eased back so he could see her face. Her eyes were shadowed and dark, wary from his explosion of temper. "Maybe you shouldn't take it, then."

He pressed his lips together in a bitter line. "Have to sleep some time."

"Try yoga."

Sean smiled and lowered his forehead to hers. The fact that she didn't pull away warmed his blood. The simple intimacy of the gesture touched something deep inside him. A yearning. "Sometimes I just need to shut my brain off."

She skimmed her fingers over his cheekbones. The closeness of their contact warmed his blood. They'd just had a major argument and now they stood, their bodies nearly touching, their souls connected by a shared past tainted with blood and loss.

"I've been there." He felt her tense beneath his palms. Tightened his arms around her in a silent offer of comfort and support. "I had to find a different way of dealing with it because I was alone with Anna."

Sean smiled sadly even as his fingers loosened their grip on her blouse. He didn't release her, didn't let her go, instead pulling her up and into his arms once more. She didn't resist but she also didn't fully relax. He rested his cheek on the top of her head. "How did you snap out of it?"

"Mostly, it was Anna. I couldn't be a zombie, zoned out on drugs to get by without Jack. I had to get my shit fixed to be there for her."

She tipped her face back and Sean looked down at her, at the honesty in her eyes. "I loved my husband, Sean. That's what makes what I feel for you so confusing. I had a good marriage and a good life with him."

He swallowed hard. "You loved me once, too."

She cupped his cheek, her palm soft and smooth against the roughness of his stubble. "If I can forgive you, you should be able to forgive yourself. We all do stupid things when we're young."

He blinked rapidly, unable to speak. They stood together for a moment—Sean's eyes closed, their foreheads touching. One of his thumbs stroked an absent rhythm against her back and the silence no longer snapped with anger. Instead, the air around them was comforting. Quiet. Familiar and needy all at once.

Sean swayed against her. She shifted and brushed her fingers on the edge of his jaw. "Don't fall on me," she whispered.

He smiled but didn't open his eyes. "I'm just imagining falling asleep with you pressed against me." His voice was thick, and he felt like he was half asleep already.

"Why don't you crash on your couch while I finish this up? You can catch a nap before the ball tonight."

He pressed his lips to her forehead. "Will you tuck me in?"

She shook her head and smiled, urging him toward the small couch in his office. His feet extended over the edge when he lay back. "Can I convince you to lie with me a minute?" he asked, looking at her with a combination of hope and something more.

She glanced at the small couch that barely fit him. "Not likely." But she pulled the blanket down and tucked it around his body, then turned off the light and left him to sleep.

He felt like an asshole, but not enough to push away the consideration of her gesture. He was exhausted. Once upon a time, going twenty-four hours without sleep wouldn't have bothered him. But that was before he turned thirty. Suddenly, he felt every ache and pain, every hour of lost sleep. He wasn't old but he felt older than his thirty-two years.

He threw one arm over his eyes as she clicked off the light and peeked out after her as she left. He'd taken a shitty mood out on her and she'd fought back and refused to put up with his crap. When they'd been younger, she would have walked away, coming back only when things had settled down between them. His lips curled with a smile that was both tender and bitter.

She didn't know the worst of it. And he was so fucking pathetic that he wanted to keep her from finding out the worst of his sins. He wanted the tenderness, the caring she revealed bit by bit. He wanted the freedom to touch her, to kiss her. He wanted to feel her curled into him at night.

He was lying to her. He hadn't told her everything. He was building any chance of a future they had on a lie.

He frowned even as he closed his eyes, wishing for at least an hour of sleep. Then he'd do some work. Then he'd figure out his way forward with Sarah and everything else. Just an hour and he'd be back on his feet.

The darkness of sleep stole over him, pulling him down. But the dreams and the nightmares were there, licking at the edge of his consciousness. He slid further into the darkness, unable to escape the fire that burned his memory.

SARAH RESTED HER FOREHEAD ON ONE PALM AS SHE READ THE after action reports. One after another, relentless days of enemy contact. Day after day of IEDs, small arms fire and rocks mixed in with grenades. It was amazing there weren't more escalation of force incidents than the four she'd read about in early August. The height of the summer heat in Baghdad and the civilians had shown their restlessness. Some neighborhoods were friendly. Others, not so much.

She felt the frustration in the previous commander's reports at his inability to end the attacks on his men. In the entries for the days that led up to the incident with Kearney and Smith, his notes were short and curt. She could fill in the blanks with swearing in her mind.

He'd been frustrated. She figured his men had to have been more so. Sent into the same streets day after day when they'd seen their buddies injured or killed. She noted that there was no confusion over the escalation of force. The rules of engagement had been clarified by the chain of command each time they'd gone into sector out on patrol.

August 15th turned out to be the date that things had officially turned to shit between Kearney and Smith. They'd been heading into a neighborhood, where they'd lost a soldier two weeks prior to a grenade attack. There were kids throwing rocks.

Sarah frowned. Someone had opened fire over the crowd's head. Then the report got confusing. Someone had called weapons free at the same time someone else had called cease-fire. There was an explosion consistent with a grenade.

It took three minutes for the shooting to stop, according to the commander's report. Another two had passed before Smith was able to establish a secure perimeter, and by the time the commander had finished calling in the troops in contact, he had three wounded and a vehicle disabled.

The previous commander concluded in his after action report that he was unclear about exactly what had happened in what sequence of events so he ordered the platoon leader—Smith—to investigate. "See Attached" was all Sarah had regarding Smith's investigation.

The key now, then, was Smith's report. She glanced into Sean's office where he hadn't moved since she'd sat down, almost two hours ago. She wondered if Ambien always made him act the way he had this morning. She wondered how often he took a sleeping pill.

And she wondered what haunted his dreams to make him crave the oblivion of a sleeping pill in the first place. She looked back at her notes.

She'd been charged with finding out what was behind Kearney and Smith's hostility to each other. Without Smith's report and Kearney's rebuttal, she wasn't going to be able to finalize her report.

She frowned. She was missing something. The whole thing felt off. Like it was entirely too easy for her to point to a single incident. She leaned back, kicking her feet up on Sean's conference room table, and began sorting through the sworn statements.

She landed on Smith's statement, remembering how he'd refused to make another one. She tapped her pen against her lips. If he had nothing to hide, why not make another statement? She needed to talk to him again. He had the right to remain silent but she had every right to ask about the escalation of force incident.

She made a note. *Interview Smith.*

Monday. Major Wilson wasn't going to like it because she was going to be late but tough crap.

Since she couldn't come right out and ask Major Wilson, she had to go with what she knew. Jansen was Smith's uncle and he was assigned to the Cav. Jansen was in a position to call in favors to look out for his nephew. Sarah wished she'd been part of the Cav for a lot longer than she was now. She'd know who had been whose aide, or who had worked with whom before. Not understanding the relationships made things treacherous for Sarah, especially considering what Lieutenant Colonel Meister had told her.

She had a ton of questions and no answers.

"He's gone. Haves, you can't help him anymore."

She jumped at Sean's sudden outburst and glanced in his office, expecting to see him sitting up. Instead he looked braced for battle.

And he was dead asleep.

There was never a question in her mind that she would approach but she did so cautiously, aware that as a combat veteran, he could react violently. That was assuming she could wake him. That was assuming he knew where he was before he did any real harm.

She moved around the couch to the small space between the wall and Sean's head. His face was turned into his arm, his brows drawn into a frown. He was breathing hard, his lips parted.

"I don't give a fuck about them. *Listen* to me." He flinched and Sarah wondered what he'd just seen in his nightmare. "Goddamn it, Kearney!"

She knelt and jostled his shoulder. "Sean. Sean wake up."

She thought of the night terrors Anna used to have. The nightmares where she would cry and scream inconsolably, refusing comfort until Sarah managed to wake her. Only upon waking would Anna curl her little body into Sarah and allow herself to be comforted back to sleep. "Sean." She leaned down, speaking his name sharply near his ear.

He jerked upright with a shout. His hands dug into the fabric of the couch as he sucked in hard breaths, gauging his surroundings. The ragged edge of the nightmare eased back and she saw realization spread across his features. Saw his breathing slow. His fingers relax.

He smiled wryly. "So much for my pride."

She moved then and sat next to him. Sean nodded and she tried not to be hurt when she dragged her fingers down the scar on his forearm. "Where did you get this?"

"Can't you guess?" he asked, leaning forward to brace his elbows on his knees.

"Fallujah?"

He swallowed and nodded once more, the muscles in his arms clenching tightly as he worked his fingers open and closed. As though he was trying to release the tension in his entire body through his fingers.

"Do you have nightmares a lot?"

His lips pressed together, flat and humorless. "Almost every night. Sometimes worse, sometimes not. Most nights I just deal with it."

She refused to glance at the clock on his wall. She knew the time today was ticking by. She had so much to do before the ball. But she sat and threaded her fingers with his. He tensed, then turned their twined fingers until her palm rested on top of his.

"Make any progress?" he asked. She didn't object to his changing the subject, but she had the distinct feeling that they might have this conversation again.

"Some. I need to get a copy of Smith's investigation from downrange."

Sean shook his head. "I can see if Evan or anyone else has copies from downrange, though. Maybe it's still on the SharePoint portal."

"That would help, especially since I don't think Smith is going to cooperate if I try to interview him about downrange." Now she did glance at the clock on the wall. Thirteen hundred. She was running out of time. "I've still got to set up my Dress Blues for tonight and feed my babysitter before cocktail hour."

He smiled and this time his eyes crinkled with warmth. "Can I be your date?"

She bumped his shoulder and shook her head. "Yeah, there's a fast track to getting thrown off the case and possibly out of the brigade."

He smelled good. Warm and sleepy, mixed with the edge of adrenaline from his dream. It might not have been real, but his body had reacted like it might as well have been. He leaned into her suddenly, twisting his upper body to reach across and cup her cheek. He bussed her nose with his, brushing his lips over hers in the barest hint of a kiss. "Will you at least save me a dance?"

She smiled against his lips, enjoying the sensation as his scent wrapped around her, heating her blood. "Yes, Sean, I'll dance with you."

He didn't kiss her but he didn't release her. "Things are only complicated until you finalize your investigation," he said softly.

His lips were parted, his breath warm and mingling with hers. She knew she was destined to disappoint him. "Things only get more complicated after that."

"They don't have to be."

She smiled against his mouth. "Will you stop talking and kiss me?"

His tongue traced her top lip, tempting her with a promise of more. "Not until you answer me. Why are things complicated?"

She sighed at the faint contact. "Because of my daughter."

He pulled her bottom lip between his teeth, sucking gently. Fire sparked in her blood and set her skin alive. "I can live with that," he murmured.

She leaned back. "You can?"

"Yes." He traced his tongue over her bottom lip where his teeth had scraped. He kissed her then. The kind of kiss that bolted through her as his tongue slid into her mouth. She wanted him. She couldn't deny that. She wanted Sean. Not just someone to satisfy the need she'd denied since she'd last said good-bye to Jack. This wasn't about the physical. It was so much more with Sean.

This was Sean. And his touch meant so much more because of who he was. Of the past they shared. The love, once upon a time. The loss that had touched them both so deeply.

Sean broke away, his breath ragged. "I want...God, I want to touch you."

"Sean." A jagged whisper. Torture in a single breathless word.

Sarah pulled on the deep navy blue skirt but it hung open in the back, her panty hose holding in the worst of her dietary sins. She wore a beige lace bra, knowing the neutral color would blend beneath her white dress shirt if she removed her jacket later.

She wished for one hot second that she had something slightly less functional to wear beneath her uniform. Her body hummed with awareness that Sean would be there tonight. She had Jamie staying the night, even though Sarah had no intention of staying out all night. She'd given herself time, though, time to take a chance and let herself feel.

She'd managed to get her hair restrained in a stylish bun and pulled her bangs down to a side swoop that she never would have attempted during duty hours. If she'd been a spouse, she would have gone to the ball decked out in a formal gown or at least a more formal cocktail dress. But she was part of the unit so her outfit tonight was dictated by Army customs and uniform regulations.

She wore her uniform like every other soldier. Captain's bars rested on her shoulders. Her medals and awards were pinned straight above her left breast. The Purple Heart next to her Army Commendation Medal.

Sean would know that award for what it was. He would ask. And she wouldn't be able to hide the real reason she'd been sent home from Iraq and removed from command early.

She didn't really think she'd earned the Purple Heart. She'd only taken a few scraps of shrapnel. It didn't really compare with folks who'd taken a bullet or lost a limb.

Or their lives.

She had Jack's award and medals tucked away in a velvet-lined box. She'd give them to Anna someday. Her father's medals. Her father's Bronze Star with V device. Her father's Purple Heart for giving his life in service to his nation.

She swallowed and shrugged into her white dress shirt, buttoning it and tucking it into her skirt. She had thirty minutes to make it out of the house and on post. Thank God Anna was obsessed with Jamie Sorren.

She glanced over as Jamie padded into her bathroom carrying Anna in her arms. Anna looked at her in awe. "You look pretty, Mommy."

"Thank you, baby." She leaned over and kissed her daughter's head.

She finished tucking in her shirt and fastened the black neck tab beneath her white collar, adjusting it until it was centered.

She put the essentials in a small night-out purse that she reserved for occasions such as this and set it by the door near her keys and her Stetson. Another reason why she didn't opt for a bouffant hairdo. The mandatory Stetson required for all Cav officers would surely crush any efforts at a prom queen hairdo.

"Anna, come give me a kiss." In a flash, Sarah had small arms wrapped around her neck and her daughter's small head pressed to her heart. Things might be complicated with her and Sean but she wouldn't change a thing in her life that had given Anna to her. "Be good tonight, okay?"

Jamie laughed. "We're going to drink beer and smoke cigarettes and keep her up watching *The Exorcist*."

"Ha, ha, ha," Sarah said with a smile. Jamie was a good kid who'd gone through some pretty rough stuff in her young life. But she was working on things and Sarah figured the best thing she could do was help by providing some stability and a job. Her mother, Melanie, had pledged her eternal gratitude for Sarah hiring Jamie.

She hadn't wanted to admit that she was looking forward to seeing Sean tonight. She didn't want to allow the tease of his touch to draw her to the ball with any more excitement than it might have been otherwise. The temptation of a simple dance sent a nervous edge through her veins like she hadn't felt since she'd been a nervous teenager.

She pulled up outside the Civic center and sat in the car for a moment, watching soldiers and their wives, men and women walking into the great hall, all in their Dress Blue formal uniforms. She smiled. Wives were on display tonight and many of them took the opportunity to go all out.

She swallowed and grabbed her Stetson, wondering if Claire was there yet or if Sarah would be standing alone in a corner, waiting for a friendly face to bail her out.

She didn't have to wonder long. Within minutes of scoping out a small corner of the main hall near the door so she could watch the entrance, she spotted a familiar face weaving toward her through the crowd. She groaned, though, as Major Wilson appeared in her line of sight, looking somewhat cartoonish under heavy amounts of uncharacteristic makeup.

"Sarah, nice to see you tonight," Wilson said, taking a sip from a glass of red wine. Sarah refrained from asking her if it was the blood of innocent staff officers. "Glad you were able to find suitable childcare arrangements." She paused. "How's the leg?"

Sarah bit her lip at the backhanded compliment and smiled thinly. "Fine, ma'am." As much as she wanted to slap back at the major, she felt that in this case, discretion was probably the better part of valor. And her leg was back to normal. Or at least what passed for Sarah's new normal. A little stiff. Sometimes sore. She'd managed to camouflage the worst of the scrapes on her knees for tonight and her palms were healing quickly.

But she was reasonably certain that Wilson didn't give two shits about whether she was actually hurt.

"The investigation is still not complete, I take it." A statement, laced with venom.

"Correct, ma'am. I've got to re-interview the LT and discuss an incident downrange."

Wilson peered at her over the edge of her glass. "You're slipping up, captain. There's no place for you in this unit."

Sarah opened her mouth to speak, to tell this woman exactly where she could get off when a familiar voice stopped her.

"Sarah, nice to see you."

Sarah turned at a familiar male voice and smiled, relief at her rescue. "Colonel Jansen, sir. Good to see you."

Jansen smiled warmly down at her and she remembered why she'd loved serving with him. He made her feel like she belonged, like what she did mattered. It was a rare talent for a leader. "I thought you were deployed," he said.

"I was, sir. It's a long story."

"You'll have to tell me about it sometime. Now you're slumming down in Fifth Brigade? Need a job? I could use your sense of humor on my staff."

"I'd love to, sir, but I think I've got my hands full at the moment. Speaking of which, Colonel Jansen, may I introduce my boss, Major Christine Wilson."

"Oh, I already know Christine. She was my aide de camp a few years ago. You need to take good care of my girl here," he said to Wilson. "She's an incredible officer."

Wilson's smile could have cracked glass. "Yes, sir. She's diving right into work. I'm sure she'll be nothing but successful in the support battalion once she passes a PT test and fixes her childcare issues. If you'll excuse me, sir? Sarah."

Sarah fumed as Wilson melted away into the crowd.

"I take it you and Christine are getting along well?" Jansen asked dryly.

She shot him a baleful look. "We're besties, sir."

"Christine is tough but she's good. Don't let her get to you. Just do your job and she'll back off. Eventually."

"Thanks for the encouragement, sir." It gave her hope, though, that she could handle Major Wilson. If she couldn't, she didn't deserve the rank on her shoulders. She might seek out Colonel Jansen for mentorship but she damn sure wasn't going to piss on his leg about her boss being mean to her. "So I hear your nephew is in my brigade, sir," she said, hoping her comment wasn't as glaring a probe for information as it felt like it was.

Jansen's mouth pressed into a flat line, the only hint of emotion at the mention of his nephew. "He is. He'd be a better officer if he wasn't associated with me."

"Sir? I'm not sure I follow."

"You know, one of the things I liked about you, Sarah, was your no-bullshit way of telling me what I needed to hear, not what I wanted to hear. Some people don't like that but once you make full colonel, everyone wants to kiss your ass and no one wants to tell you the truth." Jansen sighed. "My nephew seems to like dropping my name when he gets his ass in a sling and sadly, I can't seem to get the message across that I'm not going to protect his little ass. He needs to do his job and stop pretending he's already a full bird."

"I wish I didn't understand that, sir," she said. She had no idea how to read between the lines there. If he was telling her to stick it to his nephew or if he was telling her to do her job and let the cards fall where they may. Damn it. So much for that idea.

Jansen clapped her on the shoulder and wandered off even as Sarah deserted her post to meet Claire halfway in the middle of the hall. It was shaping up to be an interesting evening; that was for sure.

“Will you quit fidgeting?” Morgan asked, taking a sip from his short glass of Crown and Coke. “You’re acting more nervous than a virgin on prom night.”

Sean grunted and said nothing. Morgan looked out of place without his index finger curled around a cigar but he cleaned up better than most. He still looked just as mean and ornery as ever, only now he wore a Stetson and Dress Blues. The lighter pants the men wore were a tribute to the days when soldiers’ pants were bleached a lighter color than the jacket from the sun.

They stood near the bar but Sean deliberately kept his back to the wall and his eye on the door. One was an old habit he’d started back when a local national had walked into a chow hall and killed twenty-two people. Sean had never sat with his back to the door since Iraq.

Tonight, though, he wasn’t looking for a suicide vest. He was looking for Sarah and of course Morgan had noticed and called him on it. Sean didn’t deny it but it was humbling to think that he was acting like an eighth grader at his first dance.

He saw her, and from across the room he felt a warmth slide through his veins like a drug when their eyes met. Her lips, lush and red, drew his gaze instantly when they curled into a slight smile. A hint of a nod and she started in his direction. He watched her while trying not to look like he was watching her and thought of their argument that afternoon.

Once upon a time, she might have run from him. From the anger between them. But something had changed her over the years and she stood and fought now. Sean felt the stir of arousal in his blood once more. There was so much drawing him toward her.

“Suppose we need to go pay our respects to the commander?” Morgan asked, glancing toward where the brigade commanders were standing around shooting the breeze. As the group of full bird colonels broke up, they began holding court for officers in their units. Ambitious ass-kissing began in earnest, disguising people who genuinely wanted to ask questions of the senior leaders in the division from those who were more interested in face time. It was a shame that some of the country's best and most brilliant minds were surrounded by sycophantic yes men.

He lost sight of Sarah as the crowd shifted and he scanned the faces, looking for the woman he'd dreamt of last night. He'd jerked awake and for the first time in a long time, his heart had been pounding through his veins with arousal and need, not fear and helplessness. He'd lain back and closed his eyes and imagined her lips on his neck, his chest, her fingers sliding over his belly.

He took a long sip of his drink, trying to pull his mind from the erotic and decidedly inappropriate thoughts. He wanted her. He didn't deny that. And despite everything that had happened between them, despite the investigation and the soldiers she had yet to judge, he was certain she felt the same.

He caught a glimpse of her in the crowd of black Stetsons, talking with a big infantry officer. The big man turned and Sean frowned as recognition cooled his previous thoughts. Why was Sarah talking with Colonel Jansen? He scanned the crowd and found his XO standing with a bunch of the other LTs from Sean's battalion.

Sean watched his LT and his buddies circle a group of female lieutenants. It was like they were at a frat party. The females were giggling and laughing while the guys preened. It was so damn juvenile.

"When did we get so old?"

Sean barely avoided jerking and glanced over to see Sarah looking at the same group. "I don't know but I feel like I was never that young."

She nodded. "I don't know that we ever were." She angled her body toward him and he caught a scent of vanilla. His body tightened. "You clean up pretty good," she said with a warm smile.

He leaned back and let his eyes sweep over her body. Her eyes glowed like melted chocolate and they looked like they were lit by candles. He frowned.

"What?" she asked quietly. She was standing close, under the pretense that she couldn't hear him. She tipped her neck at him and he saw tiny diamonds sparkle in her ears.

"I was just thinking that you looked beautiful tonight," he murmured as he leaned in closer than he probably should have. Just being near her overwhelmed his sense of decorum. It made him want to take risks just to see her reaction. "You wear your uniform really well."

She frowned but a teasing smile bit at her lips. "That does it. Who are you?"

Sean laughed. "I'm a different man than I was," he said.

He swallowed, wishing they could have more time alone before they moved into the ballroom. He wanted to sit near her. Maybe he could slip his hand beneath the tablecloth to her thigh. Maybe a little higher.

It was a thought he should avoid if he wanted to avoid looking like a sexual deviant in the receiving line.

He did not resist the temptation to lean closer to her ear. He loved how she tipped her neck up toward him. The brim of his Stetson created a barrier and he had the strongest urge to nip her earlobe. It would be an unbelievably stupid thing to do in a crowded hall full of senior officers.

Sean opened his mouth to speak, the words just there, to ask her to come home with him tonight. "Don't forget you saved me a dance." He blew on her ear beneath her own Stetson before she leaned away, his voice low. "Where are you sitting?"

"I have no idea." There was a rough edge to her voice that hadn't been there a moment before.

"Sit with me." He brushed his hand against hers. "You won't be alone."

"Don't you have commander-type things to do tonight?"

He nodded. "Won't stop me from having dinner with a beautiful woman."

"Serious cliché," she said with a smile. "You can do better than that."

"Sadly, all my finesse is gone when it comes to you. It's all I can do to get myself dressed when you're around."

She smiled and shook her head, sipping her wine.

But she didn't move away.

❦ 20 ❧

Sarah followed Claire to their table and stood behind her chair. She scanned the massive ballroom, decorated with yellow roses in the centers of white tablecloths, waiting for Sean to come through the receiving line.

"This is stupid," she murmured to Claire.

"Not really. You're sitting with me and Evan. Sean just happens to be at the same table."

Sarah grinned over at Evan. "Good, maybe I can use this as an excuse to find out if you have any of the reports from last deployment hiding out in the ops office or the intel shop."

Evan took a pull off his beer. "Actually we do. We've got a mirror image of the classified share drive that's been declassified since we came back because the last brigade commander wants to write a book about his tour." He frowned at her, his eyes shadowed beneath the wide rim of his Stetson. "Why?"

Sarah filled him in quickly on the reports of the escalation of force incident and how she suspected it might tie in. "I can send you the report on that," he said. "Can it wait until Sunday morning, though? I'd really rather not go back to work tonight after the ball."

She could not actually believe her luck. This kind of thing just didn't happen, but thanks to a colonel's desire to be the next Hemingway, she was finally catching a break. She'd be damned if she was going to look this gift horse in the mouth.

"That would be awesome, Evan. Thank you."

"What are you thanking Captain America for?" Sean appeared by her side then, melting out of the sea of ball gowns and Dress Blue formal uniforms.

He might have been wearing the exact same outfit as everyone else but Sean wore it better than most. His uniform hugged his shoulders, accenting his strength. Not just physical strength. There was so much more to this man than the boy she'd left. He'd pushed himself into a new mold. The mold of a leader. A man his men could trust. It wasn't a stretch to envision him on the battlefield, in a cloud of smoke and fire, giving orders and directing the fight. Before she could stop herself, she brushed her fingers across the Bronze Star Medal on his chest and the tiny V in the center. He hadn't simply been awarded a Bronze Star, one of the highest combat awards for serving in Iraq. He'd been awarded one for valor.

And she didn't know what to call the feeling that tumbled through her stomach when she'd first seen it. Pride mixed with a lingering sense of fear. Sean was a warrior. A true warrior. He was an infantryman.

Why couldn't she find a nice military intelligence officer to fall for? One that would sit in a TOC somewhere and stay safe and unharmed on the base?

No; she had to find her ex and fall for him, knowing damn good and well he was going back into harm's way. She didn't want to think of Sean dying, alone on some God forsaken street, half a world away from anyone who cared for him. But he'd gone through two tours already. He'd survived. Fate could not be so cruel as to send him back into her life only to take him away again. Could it?

The speaker called the room to attention. The toasts rang out, the answering cries from the crowd supporting the president, the colors, and finally the First Cavalry Division. Sarah smiled. The speaker had a good voice. Deep—it resonated through the banquet hall across the shoulders of the men and women who'd served the Cav in a far off land.

"As you entered the banquet hall, you may have noticed a small table here, in a place of honor, near our head table."

Sarah swallowed and caught Claire's sidelong glance at her. Claire squeezed her hand quickly. This was the toast to the POWs. The men who'd never returned from Vietnam, not even in a casket.

"This table set for one is small, symbolizing the frailty of one prisoner alone against his oppressors. The tablecloth is white, symbolizing the purity of their intentions to respond to their country's call to arms. Remember."

Sarah remembered. Her own father had been touched by Vietnam, a war he rarely spoke of. She'd worshiped him. Wanted nothing more than to make him proud of her by being a soldier, too. Just like her dad. Sarah blinked rapidly, the symbolism of the yellow rose, calling for remembrance of the families who waited, keeping faith for their safe return. And she saw Jack's flag once more as it had been folded and handed to her at his funeral.

Jack wasn't coming home. The speaker called for the toast to be made with water, instead of wine. "Out of respect for our former Vietnam Prisoners of War, this toast is made with water." There was solemn silence as every person present raised their glass in toast to their comrades who'd gone off to fight in a foreign land and had never returned.

"Mr. Speaker, I propose a final toast. Let us raise our glasses in silence to honor our fallen comrades, who have ridden their final ride and gone ahead to wait for us at the Fiddler's Green."

Every arm in the hall raised in silent tribute. There was an absolute silence. The kind of remembrance that only soldiers, who stood in mourning for lost brothers and sisters, could understand.

Sarah's hand trembled as she held her glass high, her throat tight. She blinked rapidly, pushing back the sudden memory of the day she'd laid her husband to his final rest.

She blinked back the burn behind her eyes that surprised her with its intensity. In the silence of the banquet hall, that seemed to go on forever, she felt it.

The brush of his fingers against hers. Seeking her out. Twining with hers in a silent offer of comfort and support.

And in his gaze, she saw understanding and genuine pain. A pain they shared. A pain that still hurt and would always hurt.

Somehow, holding Sean's hand, the pain eased back a tiny bit, salved by the compassion and understanding she saw gazing back at her.

And her heart, once full of love for one man and one daughter, shifted, making room again for a man she'd loved, long ago.

Sean turned and leaned against the bar, looking down at the woman who'd occupied his thoughts all evening. She smiled up at the man in front of her and licked the corner of her lips.

Sean had long ago rested his Stetson in his chair and relaxed, enjoying the company of this beautiful woman.

"Are you drunk?" he asked quietly, leaning in close just for a hint of her scent.

"You wish," she said with a laugh.

"Damn." He was standing too close. All evening, he'd tried not to stare in her direction like a moonstruck puppy but he hadn't succeeded. He'd watched her move. Watched her laugh with Claire. He knew it but since all of the power players in the brigade had long ago given up holding court and abandoned the field, he didn't care. The evening was winding down or winding up, depending on how he looked at it. Couples had moved from the tables to the dance floor. The excuse to have his hands on Sarah's body was pulsing through his blood.

He didn't move when her fingers brushed across the awards over the left side of his dress uniform. Over the Bronze Star with V device that he'd tried to refuse.

As much as he'd tried to avoid talking about what was quite possibly the worst day of his life, he prayed she wouldn't ask. He saw the questions in her eyes, simmering below the surface. If he wanted to get closer to her, if he wanted to move forward with her, he'd have to answer those questions. If she asked.

Please don't.

Only Haverson and Kearney knew the true extent of the darkness Sean had proven himself capable of. But as much as he knew that, he couldn't bring himself to lay his soul at her feet.

The thought of losing her again, of seeing that same disappointment and betrayal on her features, made his heart ache. She brushed her fingers over the awards again and his eyes were drawn to the awards she wore. The purple and white medal struck him. How had he not noticed that before?

"Purple Heart?" he asked.

Her lips pressed into a tight line as she nodded. "My reason for no longer being in command," she admitted flatly.

"You were shot?" He barely grasped the reins of the panic that twisted through him at the thought of her bleeding in the dirty, dusty streets of Baghdad.

"No. Shrapnel. The contractor had deliberately tried to sabotage the fuel point."

Sean swallowed and leaned down near her ear. "Can I see your scars?"

He'd wanted to change the subject. He wanted to enjoy the night with her instead of standing around, recounting the blood and sweat lost in Iraq's dirt.

He didn't count on her reaction. Her eyes were suddenly darker. Her lips parted and he saw the edge of her tongue dart across the inside of her bottom lip. She blinked rapidly and he saw her pulse hitch beneath her ear.

"Only if you show me yours." She bit her lip as soon as the words were out, as though she'd tried to capture them back.

Sean's mouth went dry. "Guess I'll have to take a rain check on that dance," he murmured.

She lifted one shoulder, feigning a carelessness she couldn't possibly feel. Everything in Sean's world just went tight and hard. There was nothing careless about the pounding of his heart in his throat.

He didn't know how they made it to his apartment. Neither of them were drunk and Sarah had insisted on following him in her own vehicle. Through the drive he'd watched her headlights in his rearview mirror, afraid that she would turn toward her home instead of toward his. He practically held his breath as they passed the turn off to his apartment, exhaling with relief when he saw her car stay behind his.

She didn't touch him as he led her up the stairs. Anticipation crawled over his skin in sliding, slipping waves of warmth. Her cheeks were flushed. He didn't think. Didn't want to talk himself out of this.

He wanted her. There was no way around it. What had once been inconceivable was now a want, beating through his veins in time with his heart. Hot and thick, and demanding the feel of Sarah's skin against his.

He unlocked the door and turned to her. He'd loosened his tie at some point on the ride home. "I'm not going to ask you if you're sure," he said softly, brushing his fingertips across her cheek.

He held his breath while he waited for her answer. Her gaze dropped to his mouth for a long moment and then she moved.

She took the single step into his space. The distance between them dissolved in that simple action and Sean was a goner. Her hands ran up his chest and twisted around his neck until her lips were pressed against his ear and she offered the only response he wanted to hear.

"I'm sure."

That was the only answer Sean needed. He crushed her against him, pouring his soul into the kiss that this time would lead somewhere other than a cold shower. Her tongue slid against his, driving the heat in his veins to a flash point.

He lost himself in that kiss and when he opened his eyes, she stood pressed against him in his bedroom. He groaned when he saw the room through her eyes. His bed was unmade. There were dirty clothes crumpled in the corner, somewhat near the collapsible hamper.

He looked back at her and saw a smile painting her lips. "You are such a cliché," she said against his mouth as she molded her body to his.

He cupped her neck, dragging his thumbs across the soft skin beneath her ears. His fingers slipped into her hair, tugging until the pins gave up their tenuous hold. Her long dark curls tumbled free from the soft twist and Sean buried his face in her neck, simply holding her until the ache in his heart faded to something manageable. She tensed in his embrace, her back stiffening.

"What's wrong?" he asked, nuzzling her neck.

"I was going to ask you that."

He stroked her jaw with one thumb as he leaned away and looked at her. "I don't want to screw this up."

She smiled. Lit only by moonlight slipping through his small bedroom window, her skin practically glowed. Her lips were darker. Fuller.

"Me, either."

He laughed suddenly and pulled her against him, some of the tension easing out of the vise around his chest. "At this rate, I think we might end up talking rather than doing."

She tipped her chin at him. "I turn into a pumpkin at three."

Sean glanced at his watch. "Then I've got five hours to do this right." He brushed his lips against her ear. "It should be enough time."

Her soft laugh vibrated through her body and Sean felt it against the full length of his own. He let his fingers drift down the front of her jacket, releasing each gold eagle Sta-Bright button one at a time until he slipped the dark blue coat from her shoulders.

He saw the mirror over his desk—a silver plate framed in simple black—and urged her in front of it, standing behind her. He wrapped his arms around her waist and simply stood, looking at the image they created together. Her hands came to rest atop his and she tipped her head back on his shoulder.

"I want you to watch." He needed her to see who she was with. He didn't want there to be a hint of confusion in her mind as to the man she stood with. He would not compete with her dead husband. Not tonight, at least. Tonight, he was going to make sure she knew. She was his.

❧

THE PROSPECT OF UNDRESSING—OF SEAN UNDRESSING HER—IN A mirror was both erotic and unnerving. She opened her mouth to speak but he silenced her with a quick brush of his lips, tilting her face and cradling her neck until the wet heat of his mouth covered hers.

His fingers worked her collar until the small black neck tab was gone, lying on top of her jacket. One by one, he worked to free the buttons on her blouse. He watched her in the mirror. Unsure what to do with her hands, she finally reached behind them to twine around his neck. The effect caused her to arch her back against his. An offering of the simplest form. Inch by inch, he parted her dress shirt, tugging the tails free from her skirt. In the pale silver of the moonlight, her skin glowed in the mirror, the darkness of his skin a stark contrast against hers.

He released her arms from around his neck and slid the blouse down her arms until it snagged at her wrists. He left it and left her arms trapped behind her.

He stood behind her, completely clothed in his dress uniform. The contrast between her nearly naked skin and the dark blue uniform struck her even as he surrounded her, his heat, his scent. This was his place. His home. She twisted and moved, trying to free her wrists from the confines of her blouse.

Her breath hitched as his hands settled on her shoulders, a feather light touch. She closed her eyes as his fingers kneaded the soft skin just there at the edge of her bra. She hadn't thought of seduction as a possible outcome to the night's activities. At least, she hadn't actively considered it.

But Sean's hands skimmed over her shoulders and down her arms in a teasing light caress. He barely brushed his fingers over her waist and she shivered, sucking in a shallow breath that didn't even come close to satisfying the need in her. For air.

For Sean. Just Sean.

HE TIPPED HIS HEAD AND SCRAPED HIS TEETH OVER HER shoulder, near the strap of her bra, and smiled as she bit her lips together. He was already hard, already entirely too aroused to maintain this breathtakingly slow pace for long.

He traced his fingers around the band of her skirt where it hugged the soft curve of her hips. Found the delicate snap and the fragile zipper. He wanted to feel her skin slide beneath his touch as he dragged the skirt down her legs.

Her eyes, dark as pools of midnight, fluttered closed as he stroked her stomach, her ribs, drifting higher until his touch encountered the softest satin barrier. He was suddenly aware of the rough skin on his hands, made hard from years at war.

She smelled so good. Clean and warm and heat all bundled into one delicious flavor begging for him to taste.

He nipped at her earlobe as he freed the hooks at the arch of her back and felt a pulse of satisfaction at her tiny gasp. This. This was what he wanted. Her. Naked. Aroused.

His.

He could claim her tonight. Mark her as his own. He wanted her to remember tonight. Despite anything that might happen still between them, he wanted her to know that tonight, she was his. His to care for. His to cherish.

His to love.

The thought struck him with the force of a fifty cal striking a still-beating heart. He loved her. He slid his hand around her ribs, toward the soft curve of her breasts, all the while watching her in the mirror. Watching the soft rise and fall of her breasts with each quick breath she took.

Her lips parted as his palms cradled her curves, still not completely cupping her. She shifted, her arms still trapped behind her and her bra lifted, barely covering her. The image in the mirror was incredibly erotic. Those beautiful curves filling his dark hands. Her head tipped back and resting on his shoulder.

Desire bolted through him as he cupped her, stroking his thumbs over her nipples in one smooth movement. Another soft gasp as he touched her, finally caressing her sensitive peaks.

He shifted and forced her back, arching her body against his. The bra fell away and she was exposed and vulnerable. Erotic with the curves of a woman now.

❧

"Perfect," he whispered before suckling her earlobe. Sensations rocked through her, whipping her pulse to a fevered pitch. Liquid arousal slid through her veins, making her soft and pliant beneath his touch. "I want to taste you."

The promise held in those words shivered over her skin. She closed her eyes against the image of herself and him in the mirror. Never in her entire life had she done something so erotic.

His eyes went dark as he pushed the bra down so that it hung across her stomach, draped on her arms. She wanted to be free from the confines of her clothes. She wanted to feel his chest against hers. The contrast of his thighs against hers.

She felt like a woman. Not a mom. Not just a wife. A woman. A woman with need making her soft and silky and shockingly wet. She clamped her thighs together, hoping to make the ache ease back. She whimpered at her frustration. She wanted...

He teased one of her nipples as he slipped one hand beneath the loosened fabric of her skirt. Beneath the edge of her panties.

He cupped her heat and the ache exploded like brilliant stars as his touch gave her what she craved. She couldn't move as he stroked her to pleasure, deep and dark, never parting her slick heat but giving her a taste of what he could do.

HE FELT HER THROBBING AGAINST HIS PALM, ALREADY WET, slick with her arousal, and the urge to taste her pleasure nearly undid him. He rocked against her even as he stroked her heat, her gasps and whimpers sending erotic hunger through his blood.

He shifted then and parted her heat with a single finger beneath her panties. She cried out in surprise and something more. She was swollen and hot and unbearably wet.

"Naked," he whispered near her ear, watching her, always watching her in the mirror. "I want you naked."

God but the picture they made was stunning. Her eyes were barely open, dark with pleasure. Her arms caught behind her, her back arched, thrusting her breast into his palm. One arm dipped into the waist of her skirt, stroking her.

He didn't know how she would react to what he wanted. He didn't want to ask and risk her denying him. He moved and peeled the remainder of her clothing from her body until she was naked and beautiful in front of him.

The scar stood out against her thigh. He laid her on his unmade bed, slid his palms over her skin. Cradled her. Watched her, his eyes locked with hers, as he pressed his lips to her wound. "I'm so glad you're okay." Soft words brushed against her mouth.

Her curves were softer, her thighs stronger. And the scars she wore on her skin were nothing compared to scars on her soul. He covered her with his body, his uniform scraping against her sensitive skin. He kissed her and she surrendered to his weight. Her wet heat pressed against his still-clothed hips and he rocked against her, reveling in the feel of her lifting her hips in a silent offering.

THE SOLID WEIGHT OF HIM BETWEEN HER THIGHS DROVE THE desire inside her higher. Hotter. She wanted him. Wanted the ache satisfied.

He moved before she could react. One moment he'd been kissing her, his taste deep and smooth and utterly arousing. The next he'd draped her thighs over shoulders still covered by his uniform and parted her heat and licked slow and deep. The heat from his tongue speared her and she surged up, her surprise tearing from her throat. She pushed at his shoulder but he wrapped his arms around her thighs. He suckled her and she thought she might die.

His hand slid up her belly, urging her to lie back. She watched him taste her before her pleasure coiled tighter and she closed her eyes. He nuzzled her thigh before a deep, slow lick drove her closer to that dazzling edge.

She fisted her hands in his short hair, not sure if she was pushing him away or pulling him closer. "Sean. Please."

He paused, caressing her swollen opening with his fingertip. "Come for me," he murmured before he slipped his finger inside her.

Sensations burst like a rainbow as he stroked her. As she shattered beneath his touch and he tasted her pleasure exploding all around him.

She barely opened her eyes to watch him undress. Awareness returned as she noticed again the jagged scar on his forearm. The puckered silver pale hole on his shoulder. And the changes that nearly a decade had made on his body. His shoulders were wider, stronger. The hair on his chest darker.

He covered himself without her asking and she watched as he rolled their protection into place. He was bigger than she remembered. Thicker. And when he knelt on the bed and his erection stroked against her heat, she realized that he was not the same man at all. There was a care to his touch now, a deliberate search for her pleasure.

He sought her hand, threading his fingers with hers. The intimacy of the gesture sparked tears in her closed eyes as she felt him near her. Just at the entrance of her aching sex.

"Open your eyes." He dragged his teeth over her neck. "Sarah." He whispered her name against her lips. "Say my name," he urged as the tip of his erection pressed against her.

She gasped at the sensation and shifted, lifting her hips. "Sean."

He nudged a little further inside her, nibbling at her lips. "Mmmm, that sounds good. Say it again."

"Sean." A gasp.

His fingers twisted in hers as he slid inside the sweetest, tightest heat. He felt her pulse around him even as his own reaction was close to sending him over the edge. He thrust deep, slow and smooth inside her and knew he was lost.

Nothing had felt as sweet. Nothing had felt as right as this exact moment, on the edge of pleasure, complete and filling. His blood pounded in his ears as he lost his rhythm and when she shattered beneath him, she took him with her. Her orgasm quaked around him even as she cried his name softly in his ear. Her thighs tightened around his waist and she met his strokes even as she continued the sweetest movements beneath him.

His release stunned him, slamming from the depths of his soul with a force that destroyed him.

He rested his forehead against hers, listening to the sound of their racing heartbeats and ragged breathing.

In the silence, she whispered his name again, pressing the softest kiss against his shoulder.

And he was lost.

                        ❧ 2 1 ❧

"Your apartment is quiet," she said, holding the comforter against her stomach as Sean lay wrapped around her. His body surrounded her now in ways it never had when they'd been young. One arm was draped over her ribs, holding her against him. She felt the rough hair on his chest and thighs against her back and rear and wriggled closer until he nuzzled her neck.

"No it's not. You can hear cars at all hours of the night." His breath teased her skin and she shivered. A moment later, he dragged the thick comforter over her shoulder and pressed closer.

"That's not it. It's just...no kid sounds. It reminds me of Iraq in the CHUs when you could hear people walking by on the gravel."

"Hmmm. Let's not talk about Iraq," he said, brushing her hair from her face and kissing her ear.

"I have to go soon," she said, her words breaking the silence.

He wanted her to stay. She knew that. And if she'd been single, she might have. She twisted until she faced him. Her nipples tightened as his chest hair brushed against her. She brushed her lips against his, wanting to put voice to everything that was churning against her heart.

Not once since she'd lost her husband had she thought of

another man. Not once had she considered sleeping with anyone else. She dragged her fingers against his cheek and already felt the scrape of his beard against her fingertips.

"I—"

He kissed her. Deep and hard and with everything that matched those things unsaid within her. He brushed his thumb over her lips and shook his head. "This wasn't a one-night stand for me, Sarah." He slipped his thumb aside to brush her cheek as he kissed her tenderly.

Sean pressed his lips to her forehead and pulled her against him, wrapping her tight and strong in his arms. She breathed in his scent and felt the strength that surrounded her. Protected her.

And she had no idea what to do with those feelings.

Time passed too quickly. Too soon, she found herself standing in Sean's doorway, wearing her skirt with no stockings, her blouse with no jacket. Her hair was down and she'd tried not to see the image she made in the mirror.

She looked like she was coming from a man's bed. Her entire body throbbed with awareness of Sean. With the memory of Sean's touch.

He'd walked her to the door wearing nothing but a pair of old Army sweats. They hung low on his hips and her gaze kept traveling down his muscled stomach to where the trail of hair disappeared beneath the waistband.

"Keep looking at me like that and I won't let you leave," he murmured, backing her up against the door and pressing the lean hard length of his body against hers.

"Then you should put on some clothes and stop distracting me." She was stunned by the intensity of the emotions rolling through her. By the pure pleasure she felt from his touch. By the ache in her heart at the thought of not seeing him until Monday.

She looked into those pale blue eyes and for the first time, honestly believed him. Truly felt like they might have a second chance.

Pretty stupid of her to sleep with him before she'd come to that realization, she thought, curling her fingers into his skin as she kissed him goodnight for the final time. He kissed her, deep and smooth, and she was stunned when her blood filled with renewed longing. Oh, but the man could kiss.

"Good night." He brushed his nose against hers.

"Night."

And she left, closing the door quietly behind her before she was tempted to stay any longer.

☙❧

He lay in bed, his body humming with a desire still coursing through his blood like the remnants of a drug. Her taste lingered on his lips, her scent still filled him. His bed smelled like her now, like warm vanilla and oh-so-hot sex.

Her response had been uninhibited. Not awkward. Not like they were strangers but like old lovers, reunited.

For the first time, the years of animosity and hurt had felt like a distant memory. For the first time, Sean felt hope. Hope that they might be able to make this work. Hope that his life might once more feel complete, the way he'd felt with her once before and never again since.

He closed his eyes and listened to the overhead fan hum through the silence. The room felt empty without her.

He rubbed his stomach and rested his other arm behind his head, stretching the tight tendons beneath the scar tissue.

The scars hadn't freaked her out. Then again, he'd had more than a few women ask him about the ones they could see beneath the edge of a T-shirt.

He glanced toward the side of the bed and made sure his phone was in arm's reach out of habit. He hoped tonight might continue to buck the trend of the constant arrests and phone calls. Maybe with Kearney at the barracks, Sean would actually be able to sleep.

When sleep finally did reach up to pull him down, he went willingly into the dark depths, for once not fearing the memories and nightmares of war. For once, he fell asleep dreaming of soft sighs and warm arms wrapped around him, holding the nightmares at bay.

✣ 22 ✣

His phone rang, jarring Sean from a dream of a soft and willing Sarah moving her hips beneath his, her fingers gripping his. He opened his eyes to the still dark bedroom and swore into the darkness even as he reached for the phone. His body throbbed; his cock was achingly hard and unless it was Sarah on the other end, he was pretty much guaranteed to need a cold shower after this one.

"Yeah?"

"Sir?"

"Kearney?" Sean sat up in his bed, his comforter wrapped around his hips, instantly alert to the fatigue in his sergeant's voice. Thoughts of Sarah faded fast until Sean was focused only on the trouble he heard brewing beneath what Kearney didn't say.

"Yeah."

"You okay? What time is it?"

"Four thirty. Listen, I just wanted to, you know, thank you. For not throwing me under the bus."

Sean frowned and scrubbed his hand across his face. Maybe he'd been imagining something there when in reality, he'd just been otherwise distracted. "Is there a really good reason why we're having this conversation at four thirty in the morning?"

Kearney's laugh eased some of Sean's irritation, but not nearly enough. "Yeah. Haverson dropped by tonight and we were talking about you."

"Again with you not answering my question. What's wrong?"

Sean heard Kearney snort. "Caught that, huh? Just thinking about everyone we lost that day. Haves is the last one out of our platoon still around."

Technically, Haverson and Kearney weren't the last. Garrison was still around. So were a bunch of the officers, but they were spread out around the division. But as far as the men, the soldiers, were concerned? Yeah, Kearney and Haves were it. The other men in Sean's original platoon were scattered, both around the US and around the Army.

"I'm sure he's just glad to get out of here," Sean said quietly.

"Yeah. Do you think he'll be all right?"

The million-dollar question. What could Sean say? If he said yes, he was flat out lying. If he said no, it could send Kearney off the five days of not fucking up that he'd just had. "I don't know. I wish I did."

Silence ticked by with the counter on Sean's clock, sending worry skittering over Sean's spine. Something was wrong. Kearney didn't just call for a chat at four-thirty in the morning. Ever. "You okay?"

Kearney didn't answer. And didn't answer. There was no sound on the other end. Not the rustle of cloth. Not the other man's breathing. "Have to be, don't I?"

This time there was the silence of the dead line. He looked at the phone and saw the call had disconnected. Sean swore and flopped back onto his pillow, dragging the comforter over his stomach against the cold air of the A/C.

There was more to this late night phone call but Sean was too tired to riddle it out.

His brain, however, wasn't in the mood to cooperate. He closed his eyes but failed to push the worry about Kearney from his brain. There was something there just at the edge of his thoughts. Something that he was missing. Something had started in Iraq between Kearney and Smith and had just kept growing until they'd gotten to where they were last Sunday.

Kearney had been wrong for fighting with Smith, but Sean had too much loyalty to the man who'd bled on the streets of Fallujah with him than to the officer who was supposed to have Sean's loyalty. He'd spent too long as an enlisted man to be blindly loyal to the officers he served with. In Sean's world, loyalty was earned, not a given.

Sean dragged his hands over his face and rolled onto his side, staring into silence.

What had he missed? It felt like it was staring back at him from the edge of the darkness like a pair of cat eyes lighting the back of a Kevlar in front of him. It teased at his consciousness until he slipped into sleep.

And it was no longer Sarah in his dreams. Once more, death's hand wrapped around him, pulling him back to that street. To the casualties. To the horrible choices he'd made and had to live with.

To the choices he had made and would have kept making had Kearney not pulled him back from the brink.

"Mommy?"

Sarah glanced at her bedroom door, which had parted just a crack to reveal a small dark head, still wet from the bath over an hour ago. She set the laptop next to her on her bed and patted the comforter near her hip. "What's wrong, honey?"

Anna shuffled into her bedroom and climbed up next to Sarah, immediately curling her small body into the crook of her mother's arm. "I had a bad dream."

Her voice cracked at the end of *dream* and Sarah brushed her hair from her face and kissed her forehead. "What was your dream about?"

She always worried about what the impact of not having Jack

had on Anna. Sarah's heart pounded a little faster as she recalled the night terrors Anna had after she'd been born. She'd wake up screaming and crying. She'd arch her back and refuse comfort and Sarah had felt beyond helpless until she figured out that she needed to wake Anna up, then comfort her.

Sarah dreaded hearing about Anna's dream, afraid she already knew what had upset her daughter.

"I dreamed that I was a dog," Anna said in a small voice. "And I had a really great house. But then another dog came and took my house."

Sarah fought the urge to laugh. Anna was really upset, but Sarah had this visual of her daughter as a basset hound and choked on a small laugh. She cleared her throat instead. "Why did the other dog take your house?" she asked, stroking Anna's hair.

"Because he liked it better than I liked it."

The complexity of a five year old's dreams was amazing stuff. "How did he know whether he liked it more than you?"

"He was bigger, so he got to tell me what to do."

Ah. Reality dawned with a bright light and Sarah squeezed Anna close, any thoughts of laughter chased from her heart, now heavy with a host of confusing emotions. "I'm scared you're going to go away, Mommy," she whispered. "Like Daddy."

Again a silent nod against Sarah's cheek. Sarah cupped Anna's face and tipped her chin up, stroking the hair at her temples. "Honey, no one will ever take me from you. You will always be first in my life."

"But what about the Army, Mommy? The Army might take you away like it took Daddy."

Sarah bit her lips hard to fight back the tears that welled up. She didn't know what to say. She couldn't lie to Anna but right now, she just wanted to reassure her.

And she couldn't. She couldn't promise that the Army wouldn't take her away.

For one bitter moment, Sarah regretted the decision to stay in the Army after Jack died. How could she have thought that her life as a soldier would be compatible with her life as a widowed mother?

She breathed in deeply and waited until the wave of emotion passed. "Sometimes. Sometimes I might have to go away for a little while because of the Army. But my heart will always be right here with you. No matter where I am in the world, I'll always love you and I'll always take care of you."

"What if you get married again? My friend Shelby's mommy got married and Shelby says her mommy loves Shelby's new daddy more than she loves Shelby."

She'd always done her best to keep pictures up and talk about him, knowing that it wasn't fair that Anna had never known her father. She'd been torn by what to do and how to handle it and in the end, she'd made the best decision she could, never guessing that she would someday question the wisdom of that decision.

It was a terrible thing the day a mother regretted keeping her daughter's father alive in her young memory.

Because at that moment, Sarah realized that this wasn't about Jack. This was about Sarah, and Anna's claim on the only stable thing in her life.

"Mommy?"

"Yeah, baby?"

"Will you always love me best?"

Sarah smiled and pulled her daughter close, cherishing this quiet interlude, knowing they would lessen and then finally stop as her daughter grew up. "Yeah, baby."

Work fell away and Sarah pulled the comforter over their shoulders and just savored the time with her little girl.

❀ 23 ❀

Thanks to Evan, Sarah finally got her hands on Smith's investigation from the previous year in her inbox Sunday morning. It was even unclassified, so she wasn't breaking any rules. Evan had found it on the SharePoint server. She scanned Smith's inquiry.

"Facts: The platoon, under SGT Kearney's direction, fired randomly, using no positive target identification. Witnesses (see appendix A for statements) state that they heard orders to 'kill everything that moves' in the midst of the firefight. The militia we engaged strategically placed women and children at the front of the formation moving down the street, effectively creating human shields for the advancing forces.

SGT Kearney was out of control during the firefight, urging his men to lock their sectors down through alternating fire and ensure that nothing moved in their perimeter.

As the platoon leader, I was unable to stand SGT Kearney down, despite multiple attempts to stop the bloodshed. He completely disregarded my orders. As the platoon sergeant, SGT Kearney should have been focused on the wounded at the casualty collection point but instead was running around the inside of the perimeter to ensure that no one stopped firing.

After approximately fifteen minutes of constant fire, all weapons abruptly ceased. Multiple witnesses reported hearing SGT Kearney ordering the cease-fire but that conflicts with earlier witness reports stating he ordered weapons free.

Conclusions: The wounding of four men set off a panicked reaction in SGT Kearney. In his fear for the safety of his men, SGT Kearney ordered the escalation of force without proper target identification, the result of which was 15 dead civilians, including six children. Despite the militiamen's use of the children as human shields, SGT Kearney made no attempt to order his men to shoot over their heads at the armed men or to try to disperse through the use of warning shots.

Recommendations: SGT Kearney should be formally tried for his actions, which were clearly outside the rules of engagement. His failure as a leader resulted in chaos within the platoon and did not save lives that day."

Sarah frowned. Despite the legal rhetoric, Smith's inquiry was one-sided at best.

Despite sleeping well, she felt a dark frustration burning in her heart for the lack of progress she'd made on the fifteen six and the competing pressure to get the damn thing finished. Everything looked cut and dry, if she believed the reports. Smith had placed all responsibility on SGT Kearney and Kearney was holding a grudge. She found the endorsement memo from the previous commander, closing the investigation and taking no action against anyone.

Sean would be out with his formation, conducting mainte-nance. She sent him a note, asking him to meet at the company. Heat snaked between her thighs at the thought of seeing him and she tucked her hair behind one ear, even though there were no hairs out of place.

She'd slept with him. Sarah had let the man completely back in her life and with him had come an awareness of herself as more than a soldier and a mom. It was awareness of herself as a woman. She didn't want to feel that kind of intense passion again. She didn't want to become accustomed to feeling him next to her even when he wasn't. Didn't want to depend on the sound of his voice and the craving curling through her veins. He warmed her and comforted her, and at the same stroked a need inside her that she'd tried to forget.

She glanced at her phone before she tucked it into her pocket. She needed to finish this today. She wanted to turn in her report to the brigade legal office and be done with it. She wanted to be free to see where this thing between her and Sean would lead.

Something ached inside her near her heart, but part of her was glad, too. An incredible guilt wrapped around her chest for being glad that Sean had come home when her husband and the father of her daughter had not. She frowned, wondering how she could feel the two mutually exclusive emotions at the same time.

She met Sean at his company ops. His eyes warmed when he saw her but otherwise, his expression was carefully professional. She mirrored his expression, not wanting to broadcast what had happened between them to the entire company.

"Smith is in the back." His voice was subdued. Professional. "I've cleared space for you. You won't be interrupted."

"Thank you," she said, keenly aware that they were being watched by the soldiers in the company ops.

Lieutenant Smith sat at the conference room table, his hands folded in front of him, his uniform neat and fresh. Sarah cleared her throat and retrieved her notepad, setting the flustered feeling behind a barrier of calm composure as she sat down across from Smith.

As she read him his rights once more, she refused to glance toward the door where Sean had disappeared. And she was terri-fied of what she might find. Not for herself. But for Sean and what it meant for the loyalty he had toward his men.

"Tell me about the Iraqi civilian who died on August 15th."

There it was. The flicker of surprise in Smith's eyes. A quick flash of white terror before the mask shuttered down. "Ma'am?"

"The local national. One of the civilians who died in that esca-lation of force incident. He was your biggest contracting contact.

Must have made life difficult when you accidentally shot your contractor."

Smith shifted, gripping his hands together in front of him. "It was a pretty fucked up day," was all he managed.

"I read through the reports. You purchased a lot of expendable supplies from him. Did you really go through that many batteries?" She kept her voice calm. Level.

This was a dangerous game she was playing. She had very little to go on other than a hunch and a name.

But something more than an escalation of force was driving the wedge between Smith and Kearney. And if she was right, that wedge involved money. Large sums.

"I think I need a lawyer, ma'am."

"That's a very good idea," Sarah said, having all she needed in that simple statement. "But I'm going to recommend to the brigade commander that this investigation be turned over to CID. I suspect that you and Kearney had a scheme going where you were getting bogus receipts from the man who died that day. He was giving you the receipts and you were keeping the money. But one of you got greedy."

"You're so fucking full of shit." Smith leaned forward, his face twisted with anger and bitterness. "You think you know what combat is like? You think you know what it feels like to patrol streets knowing that the men lining it would rather gut you than talk to you." Smith's eyes held hers but there was something about the frozen set of his features that had the hair on the back of her neck standing up. "You know nothing about war."

"I know that war asks good men to do terrible things," she said quietly.

"I did nothing wrong. I protected my platoon. Yeah, we got bogus receipts. But we were putting most of that money back into the local Iraqis pockets. We were paying them. The powers that be down at Camp Victory wouldn't let us use the money for bribes but that's what they were. So we lied. And we bought our boys' lives with that money," Smith spat.

"Why are you and Kearney fighting?" Sarah asked.

"Because that little fucking weasel felt bad that our contractor got himself killed. That rat fuck contractor wanted more money. We couldn't get any more money. He threatened to go to the commander with the proof that we'd been buying him off. He was in the wrong place at the wrong time."

Sarah's throat went dry. Smith had just admitted to being party to what could easily be construed as a murder. It explained why he and Kearney were falling apart.

A man was dead, and while they might not have outright murdered him, it certainly was on the edge of being justified under the rules of war. "Lieutenant Smith, I'm going to advise you to seek advice from a lawyer. Our interview is over."

Smith went still. The kind of still that had fear crawling over Sarah's spine like a live thing.

Then he leaned forward, covering a ragged sound with his hands. "You don't know what it's like, ma'am." When he looked at her then, she saw grief and regret looking back at her. Not contrived. Raw.

Real.

"We didn't mean to kill him. It...he...we just panicked. I panicked. When they changed the rules of engagement, I thought if I sent up the report we'd all get court-martialed. I couldn't leave my team, ma'am. Not where we were. We were getting hit every day and they changed the rules of engagement and it made us more vulnerable." He met her gaze, then. "Everything has just gone to shit since then."

"Why did you blame Kearney for the escalation of force?"

"Because he told me to. Said he'd take the fall because they wouldn't punish him. They overlook that stuff when it's an NCO. Said it had happened before. That it wasn't a big deal." He rubbed his hand over his mouth. "Then everything got complicated with Kitty and...fuck. I don't expect you to believe me, ma'am."

Sarah did not miss the crumbling of LT Smith's expression. The ragged grief that ripped across his features, making him look at once vulnerable and young. Too young to have made the kind of choices he'd made.

Too young to have dealt with everything the war had thrown at him.

Her sympathy for the man surprised her. But it did not outweigh her duty to do this right.

"You need a lawyer, LT."

SEAN PAUSED OUTSIDE THE DOOR TO SARAH'S OFFICE. HE'D never been to her space before. It felt like her. Organized and neat and focused. Her head was bowed, her fingers flying over the keyboard. She was entirely focused on her work. He admired her intensity, her drive. He could see that now. Regretted being the young man who'd been unable to accept her for who she was.

But he wouldn't change anything. Because she'd had Jack. He still couldn't believe he'd never run into her. But Jack had joined the unit late and she'd been on another base. They'd been so damn overwhelmed with the war—the fighting and the absolute fucking chaos.

He shifted and she looked up, her expression softening when she saw him. "So things are pretty fucked up, huh?" he asked.

"I'm meeting with the battalion commander in an hour." She sighed and moved around the desk to stand close to him, nudging the door closed with her toe. "For what it's worth, I don't think Kearney is a murderer."

"Some people would be hard pressed to see the distinction between killing and murder," he said after a moment.

"Some people haven't been to war. There is a difference between defending your men and killing someone outright in cold blood." She rested her palm over the US Army nametape covering his heart. "I don't know what the boss will say," she said. "But I think you gave your man the benefit of the doubt. Far too many leaders can't say they've done the same thing."

He nodded, his heart tight in his chest. "That means a lot to me. More than you know."

She leaned up, brushing her lips against his. "So once I'm done, I wanted to see if you'd like to have dinner with us tonight."

"Us?" He knew what she was asking. Needed her to say it.

"Me and Anna." She finally dared to meet his gaze. "I'd like you to come home with me." He slid his hand up, covering hers where it rested on his chest.

"Sarah."

"It's not a marriage proposal," she said with a quiet smile. "It's just dinner."

But it was so much more than that. It was an offering. A taste of a slice of her personal life that she held apart from her life in the Army.

Such a simple thing. That overwhelmed him in its magnitude.

❧

SARAH KNOCKED ON LTC GILLIAD'S DOOR AND HE MOTIONED her in. She handed him the file and stood silently as he read through her findings and recommendations.

Finally he looked up at her. "Looks like we need to get CID down here."

"Sir, I think that's the best course of action at this point. We can't know if the killing was within the rules of engagement or not. Given the tie-in with the contractor, I think it's best to dig deeper into this."

"So much for a simple bar fight," he said dryly.

Sarah said nothing.

"I appreciate you digging into this, Sarah. You've been thorough and persistent in hunting this down."

"Roger, sir." She didn't need the compliment. She just wanted to do her job.

"If you were investigating this as CID, what would you recommend?"

She paused, thinking through her options carefully. "Sir, this is really tough. I think both Smith and Kearney have bigger issues than just this. Kearney...I think Kearney needs counseling. Lots of it, or he's going to end up on the streets. Smith? I can't get a read on him, sir. I don't know if he's telling me the truth or not. I can't say, honestly."

It hurt her to recommend even this. Hated that men might have made decisions during war that would haunt them—legally and morally—for the rest of their lives.

Gilliad nodded. "Thank you, Sarah. I appreciate your candor."

She left then, not sure what the outcome would be but glad to be passing off the case to someone more qualified to pass judgment on the actions men took during war.

❧ 24 ☙

Sean was more nervous tonight than he'd been in a long, long time. He wasn't sure what it was. Whether it was the fact that he was terrified of stepping into the domain of a five-year-old girl or the fact that he was going home with Sarah. Maybe it was both. He was terrified. Fear pitched in his belly and he wasn't sure he was actually going to be able to eat. So much was on the line tonight. This was her daughter. This was *Jack's* daughter.

He could not fuck this up.

He took a deep breath then went to knock on the front door.

He heard tiny feet slap toward the door. "I'll get it, Mommy!"

He held his breath as the door swung wide.

A small face peered up at him. God, but she looked like Jack from the tip of her dark head to the light brown of her eyes. "Hi Sean!"

Sean managed to catch her as she launched herself into his arms, nearly crushing the flowers he'd hidden behind his back. His shoulder protested the move, the old wound tight because he'd been ignoring it for far too long.

"Mommy said we were having friends over for dinner tonight." She frowned and looked so much like Sarah that Sean forced himself not to laugh. "She didn't mention that she was the only one having friends over."

"I can be your friend, too," he said cautiously.

Anna folded her arms across her chest. "I don't think so," she said.

"Why not?"

"Because I'm not allowed to have boy friends until I'm at least twenty-three and out of college."

Sean choked. He covered his mouth with his hand and tried not to die of laughter. "How about we leave it at I'm your mommy's friend, then?" He pulled the small bouquet of spring flowers from behind his back. "I brought these for you," he said carefully, watching her expression.

Her eyes lit up and her mouth dropped open. "For me?"

"Can you put them in water?"

Sarah came to the door, her hair loose from the bun she typically wore at work. "Come in. Don't let the gatekeeper scare you away."

He looked down at Anna, who was still wide-eyed at the flowers. "Can I?"

Anna nodded eagerly then remembered her manners. Or her job—Sean wasn't quite sure which. "Yes. But take your shoes off at the door."

With those final instructions, Anna bolted from the room into the kitchen. He could see her little head buried beneath a cabinet, banging things around.

Sean slid his arm around Sarah's waist and kissed her quickly. "Hi."

"Hi."

"What did the boss say?" he asked.

"CID is taking over. It's out of our hands now. The whole thing is a mess. If this happened under different rules of engagement, we wouldn't even have had an investigation done on it, let alone be investigating it as a potential criminal act." She nuzzled his neck. "Can we please talk about something else?" She glanced over her shoulder at a noise in the kitchen and saw Anna trying to arrange the flowers.

"That was really sweet," she said against his mouth.

"I figured I probably need to do a little flagrant sucking up to the other woman in the house." He smiled against her lips.

"It worked." Her fingers were warm against his cheek and he nuzzled her palm. She made a warm sound in her throat.

"Ugh, Mommy!" Anna burst back into the room and stood near the door, her eyes curious and questioning. "Why are you kissing him? Is he a prince?"

"Not quite, honey." Sarah laughed at Sean's confused expression. "She's got a small princess obsession going on. I can't beat it out of her with a stick. I caught her trying to kiss the neighbor's cat."

Sean choked back a laugh. "That's terrible."

"It's true." She threaded her fingers with his. "Anna, I'm kissing Sean because I like him. When two adults like one another a whole lot, that's how they show affection."

Anna studied them quietly. "So does this mean you're going to marry him? Can I wear a pretty dress?"

Sean squeezed her fingers but said nothing.

Sarah crouched in front of her daughter, her hand slipping free of his. "Sean is going to be around a little. Like for dinner and stuff."

Anna was listening carefully. "Does that mean he'll play with me?"

Sean's brain took a sharp detour and he imagined saying *no but I'll play with Mommy*. He managed to keep the remark from escaping. It wasn't exactly a G-rated comment to begin with. "Let's not scare him off on the first day," Sarah said instead.

"Okay. So he's here for dinner?" Anna asked. "What are we having?"

"Spaghetti."

"Yay!" Anna sprinted toward the kitchen, leaving Sean and Sarah in the living room.

She stood just there, inside his space.

"That went...well?" he said cautiously.

"I think so. She's little and she's a pretty easygoing kid." Sarah released a quiet breath. "This is terrifying," she whispered.

He cupped her cheek. "I know." He brushed his lips against hers.

She smiled and Sean felt it warm the dark center of his heart. "Hungry?"

"Starving."

But he didn't move. He held her there, a warm contentment wrapping around his heart. For now, he was here and she was allowing him to find a place in the fabric of her world. She'd brought him here, near her daughter. She'd brought him to her table.

He followed her into the living room, decorated in warm wood tones and jewel-colored throw pillows. There was a picture of her and Jack on their wedding day resting on a small table behind her sofa. He picked up the picture, absorbing the happiness and youth in both her and Jack's faces. He finally looked up to find her watching him closely. "You looked happy."

"I was."

Sean set the picture down and took a step closer to her. Until he was close enough to slip his arms around her waist and tug her to him. "I'm so glad you were, Sarah," he whispered into her neck.

The truth. Simple. Honest.

And for once, not laced with sadness and regret.

"Anna, honey, go get ready to get in the tub," Sarah called from the kitchen.

Sean snuck up behind her, wrapped his arms around her waist. She leaned back into him, loving the feel of him pressed against her back. He was solid and strong and oh so real. She ached for more. Wanted so badly to ask him to stay.

Needed so much more to take this slow. Not just for her sake. But for Anna's.

He tugged on her earlobe with his teeth. "Tease," she whispered.

"I'm trying to figure out how to thank you for dinner." His voice was low and warm against her skin.

"'Thank you' usually works." But she was smiling and she did not pull away.

He traced his tongue over the edge of her ear and she shivered, pressing closer against his chest. "Thank you."

She turned in his arms. "This was nice," she said finally. She toyed with the buttons on his shirt, wishing they were alone so she could slide them open one by one.

He cupped her cheek, his fingers warm and strong and firm against her skin. Nudged her face up until she met his dark eyes. "We can take it slow, Sarah."

She smiled then, her heart swelling a little more, shifting around and making room for him. "I don't remember you being a patient man," she said after a moment.

"Maybe I'm working on it." He brushed his lips against hers but she slipped her arms around his neck, threading her fingers in his hair and pulling him close, opening for him. Taking a little taste of pleasure before he left.

His breath mingled with hers. Time stopped and all she could do was feel. His mouth on hers. His body pressing hers against the cabinet. The want aching inside her for this man.

It was forever and a day before he leaned back. Brushed his thumb against her lip. "I'll see you at work," he whispered.

"Good night."

She walked with him to the door, wanting him to stay. Terrified to ask, to cross that line so soon after bringing him back into her life.

"Sean!"

Anna shot out of her bedroom, wrapped in her fluffy pink robe.

Sean crouched down to her level. "Yeah, honey?"

"I made you something." She thrust it toward him then followed it, pushing herself into his arms. He froze, uncertainty written in the tension in his neck, the rigid set of his body. "Will you come back?" she asked after his arms came around her.

"Yeah, baby, I'll come back."

"Anna, Sean's got to go," Sarah said, deeply curious about what her daughter had made.

Sean looked up at her and then down at the folded piece of paper. Sarah shifted so she could see.

And her heart stopped in her chest.

A drawing. Three stick figures.

"That's Mommy," Anna said, pointing to the one with the anatomically correct boobs. "And that's me." She pointed to the square man with the oversized hands that were holding the stick figure Anna and stick figure Mommy's hands. "And that's you."

Sarah rested her hand on his shoulder. Felt him tense as he continued to study the drawing.

"Do you like it?"

His throat moved as he swallowed. "I love it. I'll put it on my fridge." His voice was thick, his expression closed off as he stood.

He ruffled Anna's hair. "Good night, kiddo." But the words, the gesture—they were stiff now. Distant.

"Night." Anna skipped back to her bedroom, leaving them alone.

"Sean?"

He looked at her then and she couldn't recognize the myriad of emotions swirling in his eyes. He cupped her cheek, brushing his thumb over her skin. "I'll see you at work," he said softly.

And then she was alone, unable to determine if things had just ended before they'd ever really begun.

🎕 25 🎕

Sean sat at his desk, looking at the drawing Anna had given him. Her artwork still covered his dry erase board.

His throat was thick, his heart tight. Everything was raw and burning today.

He headed out of his office, needing space and air and distance from the memories that were cascading inside him. He shoved his hands into his uniform pockets, ignoring the regulation that forbade the practice and walked through the warm sun and cool breeze. He wasn't even sure where he was going but as he realized he'd crossed the First Cav's parade field, his throat went dry and threatened to close off the already limited air.

First Cav Operation Iraqi Freedom Memorial. Twice now the monument had been rededicated—each time adding new names to the gleaming granite monument. It would be dedicated again after the next deployment, more names added to it. He blinked rapidly, the same crushing sadness that had overcome him the first time he'd stood before the black granite nearly consuming him now.

He circled the memorial until he found the panel that had those brothers he'd lost. He found Jack's name on the wall easily and knelt as the sadness and the guilt warred for supremacy inside him, both attempting to crush the life from his lungs.

He was a soldier. He was an officer. He'd made the best decisions he'd been able to at the moment they'd been required. It was only now, years after the facts, that guilt consumed him. That doubt made him question the very basis of his entire existence.

Haverson had always talked about the guilt, about the intense wish that he could have done more. Something, anything other than stand there while the world burned.

"I'm sorry, Jack," he mumbled, his voice barely able to escape the thick blockage. "I don't know if this is okay." He dug his index finger and his thumb into his eyes, trying and failing to stop the burning behind his eyelids. Anna's picture was so fragile in his hand. "She's a great kid, man. Sarah's done so damn good with her." He looked at his friend's name. "I don't want to fuck this up." His eyes burned and he blinked hard, swiping at the wetness on his cheeks. "I...I'll do the best I can for her. For both of them."

"It doesn't get any easier, does it?"

Sean jerked roughly to his feet at the voice behind him. He dragged his forearm over his face and shoved his sunglasses on.

"Don't worry, I won't tell," Claire said as she walked up, her expression immobile. She stopped when she was shoulder to shoulder with him. For a moment, they just stood silently, staring at the names of friends they'd lost. "You okay?" she asked finally.

He took a long time before he answered. "Not sure." It was as honest as he could get. He shook his head. "No. I guess maybe I'm not."

He handed Claire the picture Anna had drawn. She took it silently then handed it back a minute later. "I wouldn't give up your day job. Your drawing sucks."

The laugh surprised him. It broke free, shattering the tight band around his heart. "You're an asshole," he said with a grin when he could speak. "Anna drew it for me."

"Kind of figured that out," Claire said. "Why is it freaking you out?"

He looked down at the picture again, then back to Jack's name.

Claire spoke when the silence hung on for too long. "You don't feel like you deserve a second chance, do you?"

The lump was back, blocking his throat. "No. Not really."

"With Sarah or with life?"

"Both. Either." He dragged his thumb over the image of Sarah. "He had a good life with her. A good one. Better than anything I could have given her. He didn't make it home. His daughter never had a chance to know him." He pinned Claire with a hard look. "How do I do this with Sarah and Anna, knowing I'm going back? Knowing I might leave them alone, too?"

"I don't have an answer for that." Her voice was thick and tight. "I wish I did."

He looked at Claire, the warrior standing strong and steady next to him. "Is Evan okay with you going back?"

Claire shook her head, her lips pressed into a tight line. "I wouldn't use the word okay." She swallowed, though, and her voice thickened just a little more. "I just hope it's not my time, you know?"

"Sarah's a soldier." A truth that had come between them before. "I don't know how—what I'd do if something happened to her."

"Ask her," Claire said. "She's already lived your worst fear. But that's part of this. She's a soldier, just like you. She'll make the same sacrifice, do the same job." Claire looked at Sean. "But this isn't about Sarah. This is about you."

Sean closed his eyes, thinking back to the night of the ball, when Sarah had slept in his arms for a few hours. There had been no sense of her holding back, no reticence in her touch.

But the thought of leaving her to go to war. The thought of losing her when he'd just found her again.

The thought of her hurting all over again if something happened to him.

He looked at Claire. "What do I do? How do I go into their lives knowing I might not make it back?"

Claire gripped his shoulder hard. "I can't answer that for you.

But I know we only have a little bit of time in this world. And I would rather spend that time with the other half of my heart than alone, being afraid of when it might end."

She left him there, alone with Jack and the picture that Jack's daughter had drawn for him.

And then his phone rang, dragging him away from the past and back to work.

❧

"Ah, fuck," he mumbled when he saw Morgan standing in the foyer of a shitty apartment complex on Rancier. Kearney sat on the stoop next to him, his head down, a bottle of Jack nestled between his thighs. "This is why you called me? Has he been arrested again?"

Morgan shook his head. "Nope. Kearney's got something to tell you."

"Smith and me, we did something really fucking stupid." Kearney cleared his throat and stared at the hands he'd twisted into a tight ball on his lap. "We had this really great fucking idea to buy off the local militia. But things got all fucked up." Kearney took a long pull off the bottle between his knees. Neither Morgan nor Sean stopped him. "Smith twisted everything in the report around. He's the one who lost control. He's the one who fired into the crowd and refused the orders to stop firing." He looked up at Sean. "You know me better than that."

Sean stared for a long moment, feeling Morgan's expectant gaze on him and knowing he should react. Because he did know better than that. Kearney was the reason Sean was standing there. The reason Sean wasn't in jail right now.

"You're better off without her." Words he never should have said. Not as a commander. Not as a friend.

"I love her."

"Then why do you keep fucking around on her?"

Kearney offered a limp shrug. "I'm trying. I'm still trying. But it's the only time I feel alive. Fucking is the only thing that feels worth doing. Fucking and fighting."

"Smith said I told him to blame me. I didn't. He just wants Kitty."

"I can't protect you from this." It was a bitter truth, a truth Sean hated. "Don't you fucking get it? It's your word against an officer's word."

"Haverson knows," Kearney said quietly.

"Then why isn't he saying anything?"

"Because I asked him not to. Because I was trying to work things out with Kitty and if he spilled, Smith would have told the WTU commander that Haverson was using heroin." Kearney closed his eyes and tipped his head back on the wall behind him. "Again."

Sean finally looked at Morgan as the fire inside him banked to a manageable blaze. "Is Haves still in town?" he asked, looking at Kearney, who was deflated and beaten down.

"He didn't answer his phone when I called him earlier." Kearney shrugged. "We can swing by his hotel room. He was supposed to leave tomorrow night but he said he might be checking out sooner."

Morgan palmed his keys. "I'm driving."

It was barely fifteen minutes before they pulled into the hotel parking lot. It was a dive, the kind that had doors that open to the outside and a flashing Vacancy sign in the window. Sean wondered just how big the roaches were, rather than whether or not the joint had them.

Kearney led the way to Haverson's room, on the backside of the building, facing the wooded lot behind the dumpster. The curtain split, allowed a sliver of light to pierce the darkness inside the room. Morgan pounded on the door but only silence greeted them.

"I'll go see if he checked out," Kearney mumbled.

Sean pressed his face to the window, blocking out the light with his hands, trying to see inside.

His heart caught in his throat. "Ah, Christ no."

But he knew. Even as he kicked the door in, he knew. Even as he tried to revive the troubled medic, he knew. As the wail of the ambulance grew closer, he knew.

And when Morgan and Kearney finally pulled him off and let the EMTs take Haverson's body, reality sank in.

Haverson was gone. By his own hand and with a needle in his arm, Haverson was gone.

Sean went through the motions. Made sure Morgan got the chaplain down to the unit for the guys who knew Haverson. Made sure Morgan took Kearney home and didn't leave him alone. He locked away the grief and the rage and the injustice of the whole goddamned world. He locked it down and his statement to the police about how he'd discovered Haverson's body.

He didn't go back to work. Powered down the Blackberry and turned off his personal phone. Haverson wasn't even the first suicide Sean had dealt with. But his was the worst.

It burned. In the blackest part of his soul, it burned that Haves was gone. He'd made it. He'd survived combat twice. He'd brought good men home. But the pain hadn't stopped when they'd landed on American soil. There was no amount of drug that could ease it for him.

Tonight, he would drown the pain. His mouth was thick and swollen and he washed away the taste with a splash of Jack Daniels, immediately feeling the warming sensation curl down his throat and through his blood. Retreat from the war, the ugliness of command, the bitter failure of not being able to get Haverson the help he'd needed.

It didn't work. It never did. But he tried anyway. The nightmares came tonight, just like they always did. All at once. The dead staring eyes. The mutilated bodies. The severed heads with drill bits in them. The dying man and his crying wife in the burned-out sedan.

Tonight, he wanted to forget. Wanted to sink into oblivion and hope that tomorrow, he would find the strength to get back up again.

$\mathscr{H}$ 26 $\mathscr{H}$

Sarah finished typing up her report and e-mailed it to the battalion lawyer for legal review. There was little chance this shit show was going to go away any time soon. Smith's admission and Kearney's meant that the fight was about significantly more than an extramarital affair. Despite the infidelity and the false investigations from downrange, Sarah had managed to untangle the threads and did the official hand off to CID.

Kearney and Smith had lied about a man's death. Everything else was fallout from that one bad decision.

There was a sudden flurry of movement in the ops. Sarah stuck her head out of her cubicle. LT Picket stood near one of Sean's lieutenants, her hand on his chest, her expression filled with sympathy. Tears shimmered in the young man's eyes. "What happened?" Sarah asked.

"We lost a soldier, ma'am." McKiernan paused, clearing his throat and swiping at his eyes. "Haverson—"

All the blood flushed out of Sarah's face a moment before she grabbed her keys, heading to her car.

"Captain Anders."

Sarah paused as Major Wilson's voice raked down her spine. "Ma'am?"

"You have a meeting with the battalion commander in fifteen minutes," she said.

Sarah turned and shook her head. "Please tell the boss I've had an emergency."

"Your daughter sick again?" Wilson asked.

Sarah's mouth engaged before her brain even considered taking over. "You know what, ma'am, I don't know what your problem is with me and I don't really give a flying fuck at this point. One of my friends just lost a soldier and I'm going to sit with him. I'll sign my counseling statement when I get back."

She left to the sound of Wilson's voice screaming at her from down the hallway. She'd worry about that later. Right then, all that mattered was Sean. Finding him. Making sure he was okay.

Because she wasn't sure that he would be. And that fucking terrified her.

The door to his apartment wasn't locked. Sarah eased it open to find the space cloaked in darkness. The fading light from outside did nothing to light the dim interior. The absolute silence added to her fear, making it too big for her to contain.

"Sean?"

She heard the sound of glass clinking against metal and she frowned, walking slowly toward the bedroom. Fear curled around the base of her spine, squeezing tight.

He was sitting on the floor, leaning somewhat to the left, his back pressed to his bed. One arm rested on a bent knee and a half empty bottle of Jack dangled from one finger. His eyes were glazed as he looked up at her, his handsome features blurred and twisted with grief.

"Haves is gone," he mumbled, his speech thick and slurred.

Sarah knelt by his side and pulled the bottle from his fingers. He held tight, resisting her attempt to remove it, then he released it.

Then she saw them. The pills in the orange bottle resting by his hip rattled and shifted as she picked up the container. Ambien.

"Did you take any?" she asked quietly, fear blocking her throat. Would she be able to get an ambulance here fast enough to pump his stomach?

He shook his head and relief crawled over her skin like goose bumps. "Was just going to try and sleep. Couldn't get the damn bottle open."

He doubled over then lunged for the bathroom, slamming the door in her face. She heard him empty his stomach and was glad his system had purged itself.

It was a long while before she heard the faucet turn on. Even longer before the bathroom door opened, flooding the dark bedroom with artificial light. He staggered to the bed and sank onto the edge, cradling his head in his hands.

It was even longer before Sarah moved to sit beside him. An eternity before she rested her hand on his back. There was strength there. And warmth. But right now, all that escaped her as she simply sat, her hand on his shoulder, offering her silent support in the dark that surrounded them.

"We both know you shouldn't be here," he mumbled behind his hands.

She didn't answer. Instead she rested her cheek against his shoulder, wrapping her arms around his waist. "This is exactly where I'm supposed to be," she said quietly, when she finally trusted her voice.

"No really, you shouldn't." He dropped his head back against the wall, hard enough that she winced in sympathy. "You know why I'm protective of Kearney?" His smile was bitter and cold, so unlike the man she'd come to know.

"I don't care about that, Sean." But fear crept in and brought doubt along for the ride.

"You should. Because that escalation of force that Kearny is being crucified for? I did the same fucking thing my soldier is about to be nailed to a cross over and nothing, *nothing* happened to me."

Her skin went cold but she stayed still. Not moving. Frozen to the space.

"I snapped. Jack's vehicle was burning. We couldn't get a MEDEVAC bird so we had to hold our position. We set up a perimeter. There was a barricade. A vehicle was screaming toward us. I gave the order to blow the engine block. And we did. And it was a husband, trying to get his wife to the hospital in the middle of one of the worst battles of Iraq." He scrubbed his hands over his face. "I was so far gone, so pissed. I wanted to leave them. I wanted to burn the whole fucking country to the ground." He didn't see her. He was staring at a scene only he could see. "Her husband died. Haves delivered her daughter right next to the body of her husband." He looked at her then, really seeing her. "I would have let them die, Sarah. I didn't care."

When she was sure her voice wouldn't break. "Sean..."

"Don't make an excuse for me." He shoved away from her, prowling the dark space. "I *wanted* them to die. I wanted to kill everything that moved. I didn't care. War didn't demand anything I wasn't willing to do." He snorted. "The only fucking reason Kearney is being investigated and I'm not is because the rules of engagement were different on his tour than on mine."

She stepped into his space, stopping him. "So what do you want me to do? Judge you based on something you wanted to do? You were at war, Sean. And no matter how much you beat yourself up over what you might have done, I'll judge you for what you *have* done." She placed both hands on his chest. "Somewhere in Iraq, there's a little girl who is alive because of you. You didn't have to listen to Kearney but you did. *That* is what matters."

"How can you just brush it aside like it was nothing?"

"It's not nothing. It's a very big deal. But you came home. And you brought your men home. And you're still a good man."

"I didn't bring Jack home. Your little girl doesn't have her daddy because I couldn't get him out of that fucking truck." His broken words shattered against her heart.

"And you can't change that, either." She slid her arms around his waist and pressed herself against him. "I'm sorry, Sean. I'm sorry you made the choices you did. I'm sorry a man died." She leaned up and cupped his face. "But I am not going to be sorry that you came home."

He shifted and moved and crushed her to him. She held on, slinking her arms around his waist and clinging to the strength of the man that surrounded her. She buried her face in his neck and stood with him. Until they sank to the floor and still, she held him, unable to let him go. Unwilling to let him face the darkness alone.

She lay with him as he slept it off, letting her thoughts tumble over everything she'd learned that day. Sean had walked back from the edge of the abyss that long ago day in Fallujah. A decision that no one should ever have to make and a decision that no one who'd ever walked through a battlefield would ever forget. He'd lived with what he'd done and it had tortured him. Enough so that he would do anything to protect the man who had kept him from leaping into the abyss.

He'd risked his career and the Army he'd given his life to in order to protect one man. Loyalty: in the end, it was about loyalty. Something there was not nearly enough of these days.

He'd been alone and devastated. Just like she'd been once before. Haverson's loss was Sean's, but Sarah wasn't going to let him go through it alone. She paused, resting her hand over his heart. He moved suddenly, his big hand fisting over hers and holding her steady. She barely kept from squeaking in surprise as she met his gaze, stunned to find him at least mostly sober. She slid her free hand across his cheek. "You should sleep," she whispered.

"Will you be here when I wake up?" he asked, sounding more lost and alone than she'd ever heard him.

She smiled sadly. "Yes."

She lowered her forehead to his and simply sat with him. Moisture licked at her fingertips and she didn't know if the tears were hers or his.

"I failed him." Broken words, laced with regret. "I failed them all."

"No. You didn't." She shook her head and framed his cheeks with her fingers, tears tracing cool paths over her fingertips. She pressed her lips to his. "You're not God, Sean. You made the best decision you could have."

Sean swallowed and the words came easily. More easily than they ever had. "I was going to kill them all, Sar. When we lost Jack and the others, I wanted to hunt down every living thing in Fallujah and destroy it. I wanted to use the main guns on mosques. On houses. If it held a weapons cache or not, I wanted to destroy everything."

His confession was quiet, tainted with the darkness that had curled up and laid within him for so long.

She slid her palm over his curled fist until it rested on the scars covering his forearm. "But Kearney stopped you."

He nodded. "Yeah. Then he took an AK round in the guts. He was bleeding out until Haver"— he stopped and swallowed hard at the well of sadness that rose to block his throat. "Until Haverson got the bullet out and stopped the bleeding. It was touch and go for a while, though."

He couldn't keep the tension from his face. He half expected her to turn away from him and the darkness that resided inside him. Her fingers tightened on his arm.

"You didn't. You stopped." She paused. "You've remained loyal beyond what anyone would have called reasonable. Kearney's lucky to have you as a friend. What you might have done is not the same as what you did." She leaned up, cradling his face with one palm. "I know what kind of man you are." His eyes fluttered closed and she brushed her lips over each eye, feeling the moisture from his tears. "A good man. Kind. Decent. Loyal."

He didn't respond and Sarah again rested her forehead against his. He pulled her down gently until she lay curled against his body, her thighs twined with his. He buried his face in her neck and was quiet. After a long silence, she felt his body relax, his breath hot and even on her skin. She wrapped her arms around his shoulders and held him, wondering where they would be if they'd simply been able to do this years ago.

❧ 27 ❧

Sarah spent the night with Sean. Jamie had been able to stay with Anna but Sarah, like Sean, had to go to work the next day.

And Sarah had the added bonus of dealing with the fallout from her little explosion of temper, too. She was going to be in charge of burning shit, she just knew it. It was just a question of which shithole country she'd be doing it in.

Sarah saved her file and began printing off the investigation, tabbing the sheets by their respective exhibit number. She hadn't seen Major Wilson since she'd gone off on her the day before. She was reasonably certain she was about to have her career ended all because she couldn't keep her damn mouth shut.

She walked down the hall and felt like she was walking toward her own funeral. Her hands trembled. Her investigation was complete, at least as complete as it was going to get.

"Sarah, perfect timing." LTC Meister stepped into the command group. "Come into my office for a few minutes."

She sucked in a deep breath.

"Want to tell me what happened yesterday?" he said mildly.

She placed her hands at the small of her back and stood at the position of parade rest. "Sir, I was completely out of line and unprofessional. I lost my temper and my military bearing. I accept full responsibility for my actions."

God but it sucked being an adult. She felt like saying "she started it" but somehow didn't think that would fly in the current situation.

"Major Wilson tells me you're done with the investigation?"

She frowned at his completely ignoring what she'd just said. "I am, sir."

"And?"

Another deep, steadying breath. "Sir, I'm not convinced a crime wasn't committed but that's for CID to figure out. I have reason to believe they were laundering money and that their local national contact who was helping them was killed in an escalation of force incident."

Meister's voice was calm, unflappable. It was unnerving really. Did the man ever get upset? "What do you think?"

"Sir, I think people will do some terrible things in war," she admitted softly.

Meister nodded slowly. "It's been a hell of an arrival to the unit for you, hasn't it?"

"It has, sir."

"I have a job for you, if you're interested."

Sarah went deathly still, waiting to hear if she was going to be supervising the shit-burning pits in Afghanistan. "Sir?"

"Lieutenant Colonel Gilliad would like you to be the rear detachment commander for his battalion."

Her skin tightened over her bones. Her mouth moved but no sound came out. Her leg started throbbing, reminding her of the command she'd lost because she'd stood up to her last commander.

"After watching you dig into this investigation—and put up with Major Wilson's shit—you've made a reputation for yourself in a very short time." He held up his hand when she opened her mouth. "I know what happened downrange last time and I'm very much aware of what's going on here. You were given an impossible mission and expected to perform a super human task. I won't tell you that the impossible won't be asked of you again here. But I will tell you that you have a chance to take an organization that's struggling and help rebuild it." He took in a deep breath. "Being a rear detachment commander is a thankless job. You have two bosses, your forces are deployed across the battlespace and you're responsible for a hell of a lot more than most commanders." He tipped his chin. "Unless you'd rather not command?"

She opened her mouth again and no sound came out. She cleared her throat and tried again. "Sir, Major Wilson...did she tell you I failed a PT test?"

"A PT test that you should not have been required to take until you were fully healed." He paused. "That has been addressed. We're strict in this unit, Sarah, not unreasonable."

Her throat was thick, her chest tight. "Sir, it's my turn to deploy. I haven't..." A deep, trembling breath. "I haven't pulled my weight. Someone else should not have to go because I'm staying behind."

He rounded the desk then and gripped her shoulder. "Sarah, you have more than pulled your weight in this war. You've sacrificed more than most. Even if I needed you downrange—and make no mistake, I do—I can't take you away from your daughter. Your family...your family has sacrificed enough."

The tears she was fighting spilled down her cheeks and she couldn't take a deep enough breath to fill her lungs. She merely nodded, unable to find words that would get past the block in her throat.

He squeezed her shoulder again. "I hope you can figure out how to work with difficult people without cussing them all out," he said dryly.

"I'll work on that, sir." Her hands trembled and her breath wouldn't fill her lungs. "Thank you, sir. I won't let you down."

"I know you won't."

She stepped out of his office, needing air. Space. Something. Escaped down the hall to her office. Sat silently at her desk, staring at the picture of her and Jack the day they'd graduated from Officer Candidate School.

She wasn't going to have to leave Anna.

She was going to stay behind when Sean deployed. A thousand emotions twisted in her heart. She covered her mouth with her hand. Her eyes burned.

Her breath lodged in her throat. A lump blocked her air. She swallowed hard and blinked rapidly. Her mind started racing, revving up slowly to the hundred miles an hour that she remembered so well from her previous time in command.

She looked down at her phone. At the photo of her and Anna. Hot relief prickled over her skin.

There was a quiet knock on her door. She turned to see Claire looking down at her. "You know, for someone who has a job across post, you're here an awful lot," Sarah said, trying in vain to lighten the mood in her heart. She'd gotten her wish.

"I make excuses." Claire tipped her chin at her. "You okay?"

"I'm going to be the rear detachment commander."

Claire said nothing for a long moment. "You really did fuck up, didn't you?"

Sarah laughed because it was so sad that it was true. Rear D was a difficult job at best. "Scared," she admitted. "A little nervous."

"You won't be downrange with Sean," Claire said finally.

"That's part of it." Her heart ached in her chest, burning with fear, with sadness. With relief and guilt that she would not be on the team going forward. "This isn't going to be easy," she whispered.

Claire stepped into the office and pulled her into a quick hug. "I'm here for you. Just like always."

Sarah sank into her friend's embrace. Claire had been there for her in so many ways over the years. "Thank you."

Sean looked up as Sarah stepped into his office and closed the door. He felt rough and ragged, the strain from the last couple of days etched into his skin. His eyes were dark and weary, filled with sadness and grim determination. Her heart broke for him a little more.

"I hear you're in need of an XO," she said lightly.

"Yep. Apparently, I'm getting a kid from the battalion headquarters. Miller, I think is his name."

"I hear good things about him. Not sure if he'll be able to hang with you and Morgan, though."

"He used to work with Ben Teague. Apparently, he's got quite a sarcastic little mouth on him."

"That will keep things interesting," Sarah said, sinking down into his couch. "How's Kearney?" she asked.

"He's okay. He's been talking to the chaplain. Kitty felt bad for him and is talking to him again." Sean cleared his throat roughly. "I think it's going to be a long time before Kearney's steady on his own again."

Sarah looked at him, her eyes filled with something unreadable. It had been a long time since he'd seen that look in her eyes and the memory of the last time he had was not a good one.

"How are you?" she asked softly.

He pressed his lips into a flat line. "Coping." It had been less than a day since she'd spent the night with him. Less than a day since he'd woken up with her tangled in his arms, her cheek pressed to his shoulder. She'd stayed. She'd checked on him. By text. With e-mails.

And now, by stopping in to see him. But looking at her now, he wasn't sure what was on her mind. She was quiet, and far too still.

"Sarah?" He shifted then, moving to sit next to her on the dingy couch.

She fisted her hands together in her lap. "I'm going to be the rear detachment commander."

Something close to joy surged in his heart but judging by her expression, she was not feeling the same emotion. He brushed his hand over her cheek, urging her toward him. "This is not a bad thing." He rested his head against the top of hers, holding her close, terrified of ever letting her go.

"It's not about me." Her eyes filled. "I...don't want to lose you, Sean. And last night...I felt like you were gone somewhere that I couldn't follow." She did not look away. "I haven't done what you've done during this war."

"And I don't want you to. I don't want you to have the memories I've got. The nightmares. I know you don't want to do the Rear D but..." He cupped her face. "But I won't apologize for being glad you won't face this deployment."

Her smile was flat. "This is why we broke up in the first place," she whispered.

"No. We broke up before because I was an ass who didn't want his wife to be a soldier." He stroked his thumb over her skin. "I respect and admire the woman you've become, Sarah. But I can't be sorry that you won't have the nightmares that follow me home after the war." He brushed his lips against hers. "Please don't ask me to be sorry for that."

"I...I can't lose you, too." Her voice broke. Her arms slipped around his waist as the vicious sob racked her body. He held her while she cried. There was nothing else he could do. His throat closed as she released the emotions she'd been struggling to contain.

Her fear was real.

Her fear was his.

Because in the short time she'd been back in his life, he'd grown to care about her more than he'd thought possible—with anyone, let alone Sarah. He held on to the woman in his arms, wishing there was some way he could guarantee that he would be safe, that he would come home to her and not leave her alone.

He couldn't even protect his boys when they were home. Grief threatened to rise up again. He closed his eyes, letting it come, not fighting it.

It helped, releasing it.

It hurt when she leaned back to look at him and knew she saw the red around his own eyes. "I'm sorry," she whispered.

"I wish I could tell you that it will be okay," he said, cupping her cheeks. "I'd give anything to promise you that I would come home. To give you that security." He brushed his lips over hers. "But I can't make that promise. And I can't ask you to wait for me." He lowered his forehead to hers. "I won't do that to you again."

She closed her eyes, covering his hands with hers. "You're an idiot," she said.

He laughed then and pulled her close. "This is not news."

She leaned up, brushing her fingertips over his cheek then threaded her fingers with his. "I don't know how much time we have in this lifetime." She lifted her gaze to his. His heart pounded in his ears. "But however long it is, I want to spend it with you, Sean."

His eyes burned again and he jammed his thumb and index finger into them, pushing away the moisture. It was a long time before he spoke. "I want that," he said. "I want to be there for you. For Anna. I know...I'll never be her dad but..."

"Her dad was a good man," Sarah said. "And so are you." She rubbed her thumb over his. "You won't be perfect. None of us are. But we can try. And we can do it together. And we can do the best we can."

He reached for her then, pulling her against him, needing the feel of her body against his. Needing the assurance that she was real.

"I'd very much like it if you'd spend the night," she whispered.

"Like a sleepover? Should I bring a toothbrush?"

She slapped his chest. "I'm serious."

He crushed her to him then, kissing her fiercely, pouring a thousand unsaid things into that kiss, things he was still searching for the words to say. "I am, too."

S ean wanted nothing more than to take a shower and sit on the couch with Sarah and Anna. He was back from a forty-five day rotation at the National Training Center and he was hot and tired and had never been more nervous in his entire life.

Okay, that wasn't entirely true. He'd been this nervous once before. But that was a long time ago and there was a hell of a lot more riding on tonight than ever before.

He walked into Sarah's house, a space that she had welcomed him into. It felt like home.

Because it was.

He opened the front door and stepped into a wall of chaos. Six little girls screamed by him in a cloud of frilly ribbons. Sarah stuck her head around the doorway to the kitchen. Her eyes lit up when she saw him and she crossed the space to him. "Hey, you didn't tell me you were coming home tonight."

"Snuck back early. Didn't want to miss munchkin's birthday," he said, dropping his duffle bag by the door. He pulled her tight and close, savoring the feel of her against him. "God you smell great."

"That would be cake," she said against his neck. "Anna has decided she wants princess cupcakes for her birthday and since it's already after five and there's nowhere for me to pull these out of my fourth point of contact at the moment, I'm making cupcakes."

"Rear D commander and maker of cupcakes." He nuzzled her neck. "You are a woman of many talents. Marry me." He stiffened as soon as the words were out of his mouth.

She leaned back. "You okay? You're acting funny."

"I'm...Shit." He took a step back.

"Sean?"

"Hell, I didn't mean to do this right now." He pulled the small black box out of his pocket. "I wanted to take you to dinner and do this right but..."

Her eyes filled and she bit her lips, saying nothing.

"I'm going back downrange in a few more weeks." He closed his eyes. "And I know that's not time for a real wedding or anything but...I want to go knowing that...if something happens to me, you'll be taken care of. I want the official stuff lined up."

"Jesus, what happened at NTC?" she said.

"Nothing. I...I've been trying to figure out how to do this and well, basically I just screwed it all up, didn't I?"

She wrapped her arms around his waist. "It'll go down in history as far as terrible proposals go," she murmured against his mouth. "Is it wrong that I don't want to do this part?"

He stilled, bracing for her to say no to him again. Everything they'd built was still so fragile, so unsettled. "What part?"

"The prepare-in-case-something-bad-happens part." She rested her head against his chest. "Part of me wants to be stupid and say no so that if we're not married, the war won't take you away from me."

He tipped her chin up to look at him. "You're smarter than that," he whispered.

"Not really thinking rationally at the moment." Her eyes shimmered with tears.

"I know." He crushed her to him then. "I know." He pressed his lips to the top of her head. "I won't push you. If you want to wait, we can wait."

She tightened her arms around his waist, then leaned back. "I'm terrified." She brushed her lips against his. "But I would very much like to be your wife."

Sean's fingers shook as he slipped the ring on Sarah's finger. The last of the knots binding his heart fell away and he held her close. Something simmered between them, desire and something more.

"What time are the kids going to bed?" he asked against her lips.

She smiled and it was brilliant. "Not soon enough."

Later, after giggling girls were in bed, he lay in the bed she shared with him. The scent of vanilla twined around his body, beckoning to him in the dark corridor of his dreams. Warmth wrapped around him and tugged at him, dragging him fully into the moment with her body pressed against his. Petting, sipping kisses as he slid her clothes off. A keening need rose inside him as she sighed and shifted closer. Her breath was cool against his neck and one palm rested above his heart. He curled his fingers over hers, enjoying the softness of her skin. Her name was a whisper on his lips. A prayer.

Her hand slid lower and crept beneath the edge of his T-shirt to rest on his stomach. He rolled until they lay facing each other. He cradled her neck in one hand while her head rested on his arm. She kissed him then, slow and deep, and Sean lost himself in the feel of her response. When she eased away, he mourned the loss of her touch. His fingers twisted in her hair as his heart pounded in his ears. Her response overwhelmed him. He drowned in her taste and the sensations of her body and her soul reaching out to claim him.

He lost himself in her and realized that he'd found everything he'd been looking for. She shivered at his touch, at the stroke of his fingers across her belly. He rolled with her, until she lifted her hips beneath him, telling her with his body what he lacked in words.

He held her face cradled in his palms and felt the wetness. He tasted the salt of her tears against his lips and waited until she opened her eyes. He saw doubt and fear and a thousand points of love looking back at him.

His heart tightened in his chest. He threaded his fingers with hers, savoring the feel of her ring pressing into him. She wrapped her arms around his neck and he felt her deeply indrawn breath. Her fingers slipped beneath his shirt and she traced her nails over his skin, even as she arched beneath him, her sex rubbing against his erection, creating the most forbidden sensation.

Her smile was sad as she stroked his cheek. He pushed up on his elbows and watched her, savoring the sensation of her beneath him.

"What?" she whispered when he didn't move.

"I think I'm still in shock," he said, cradling her cheek.

"About what?"

"That you said yes." He kissed her then, deeply as he slipped inside her. Slowly, he moved deeper, deeper until she encircled him.

He cupped her breasts and his body tightened at the softness in his palms. He stroked her softly and felt her breathing quicken as he freed her from the restraints. She tasted like vanilla and sweetness and the quiet gasps aroused him more than any other sound he'd ever heard.

His chest hair crinkled against her nipples even as his erection stroked her. The feel of his body above hers stroked a heat to life inside her that was light and dark, love and desire all twined together. She rocked beneath him and he gave himself over to the heat threading through his blood and dragging him under to a warm place.

Her soft gasps as he dragged his teeth over the soft skin beneath her ear sent him closer to the edge. He barely smothered a gasp of his own as she urged him to move. He barely stroked her but felt her drenched sex swollen and soft. He wanted her. He ached for her.

And when she guided him inside her, he forgot about the worry, about the next deployment and focused only on her. She met his slow thrusts with her own, rising up to take him deep inside her. Her thighs wrapped tight around his waist and he stayed there, lost inside her and completely found.

She kissed him then and when she lifted her hips to his, he ceased to think at all, drowning in the pleasure of her touch. And when she shattered beneath him, his own climax ripped from his body with such a force he nearly lost consciousness. She shivered and quaked beneath him even as the last pulsing bursts destroyed him.

He rolled until she was on top of him, their bodies still joined, and felt sleep pulling him down like a drug. The only sounds in the silence were the two wounded heartbeats, beating in sync. Whole. Healed.

Together.

Thank you for reading AFTER THE WAR. I hope you enjoyed Sean and Tracy's second chance love story. Find out what happens when an unstoppable force who follows the rules meets an immovable object who breaks every rule she's ever crashed into in **LAST ONE HOME!**

Sal has dedicated his life to being a soldier. There's nothing funny about being in charge. So of course the universe sends him Holly, a wise cracking, rule breaker who pushes his every button. Sparks fly when these two get thrown together - the question isn't whether they get burned but whether the fire consumes them both.

One click LAST ONE HOME, a fiery enemies to lovers romance NOW!

If you enjoyed After the War, please consider leaving a review.

Keep reading for an exclusive first look at LAST ONE HOME, the final installment of the Coming Home series.

EXCERPT FROM LAST ONE HOME

Fort Hood,

Captain Sal Bello sat in command and staff, his fingers seeking out the lighter in his pocket, and wondered when the meeting from hell was going to be over. The sergeant major's voice was distant and far off. Sal struggled to pay attention. Something about missed appointments and too many soldiers on sick call.

Sal would have given anything for his first sergeant to be in this meeting instead of Sal, but Delgado was picking one of their superstars up from jail. Again.

And damn it if it wasn't one of the platoon sergeants this time. For some stupid incident at a bar last night. Pizzaro was pretty much on his last leg with Sal, but Delgado was determined to convince him Pizzaro was just going through a bad spot since his divorce had been approved last week.

Delgado always had Sal's back. If he said Pizzaro was going through a rough spot, then that's what it was.

He just wished this meeting would end so he could be done dealing with this stupidity and get back to what was really important.

Training his men for war.

The lighter was smooth and warm beneath his fingers. It calmed him. Gave him patience for the bullshit that garrison life involved. Crap like these meetings, where they went over every single missed appointment instead of training men to put rounds on target.

Half the time, Sal felt like he wasn't even in command. He just sat in meetings all day.

Because that was what God had intended for him, right? He was a warrior, not a personal assistant. If someone couldn't make it to an appointment, why was that Sal's problem?

"Captain Bello."

Sal paused where he was turning the lighter over in his hand. "Sir."

Lieutenant Colonel Gilliad's voice penetrated Sal's focus on the lighter. "What was my guidance regarding missed appointments?"

Sal ground his teeth and refused to look up at his battalion commander. It was borderline disrespectful but Sal just about out of fucks to give. And that was saying something considering he'd been in command for less than ninety days. "That if we have any more missed appointments, we're going to have to personally explain each and every one to the brigade commander."

It burned on a fundamental level that as a company commander, a man who was supposed to be a leader of men, he was reduced to little more than glorified babysitting in garrison life.

They should be on the range, blowing shit up. Learning how to control hallways and buildings with two- to four-man teams.

But they couldn't even get to the goddamned doctor's office on their own.

Sal ached for the war. The simplicity of it. The madness and the dirt and the evil chaos.

It was at least a devil he knew. This garrison life...he didn't know how to do this.

"You disagree with my guidance, captain?" Gilliad asked.

For a brief instant, Sal imagined there was a good angel on one shoulder that slapped her hand over his mouth and kept him from speaking.

But the devil on the other shoulder shot her before she ever lifted her hand.

"Yes, sir, I do." Sal finally looked at his battalion commander. "Sir, we're wasting our time with this stupidity. Appointments? Really? Next thing, you're going to tell me that someone won't deploy if they don't have their government travel card."

Gilliad's eye twitched. Beside him, Sarn't Major Cox looked like he wanted to throttle someone. Probably Sal.

Silence ticked by. Another moment and an uncomfortable cough from one of the lieutenants who worked in operations.

The lighter in his hand was smooth and warm. The letters reminded him of what he was. And what he wasn't.

Finally, LTC Gilliad spoke and the calm in his voice was razor thin. "While I appreciate your candor, Captain Bello, it behooves you to remember rule number one in this battalion."

Sal knew rule number one all too well. Do what the boss tells you. Sal ran his thumb over the well-worn words engraved into the stainless steel in his palm. "Roger that, sir," was all he said.

The meeting continued dragging on as LTC Gilliad went up one side of Headquarters Company for having the worst stats in the battalion. Sal almost felt sorry for Captain Martini but then he remembered all the reasons why he hated officers like Martini.

And no, hate wasn't too strong a word.

Officers like Martini lived inside the lines. They didn't wipe their ass without first checking it with the boss. Even when his first sergeant was arrested, Martini refused to color outside the lines.

The meeting was almost over. He just had to keep his mouth shut for a few more minutes. Sal turned the lighter in his hand, focusing on the strength in the words etched beneath his fingertips.

They all stood when the boss left the room and Sal was halfway down the hall before he could no longer pretend he didn't hear Sarn't Major Cox calling his name.

He closed his eyes and stopped.

Because of all the senior leaders in the battalion, Cox was the one person Sal actually respected.

And that was a rare, rare thing these days.

"Walk with me, sir," Cox said, falling into step with him.

So Sal walked.

Because good NCOs were next to god and even wiseass captains with bad tempers listened to them if they were smart.

They stepped outside into the brilliant Fort Hood morning sunlight. It was blinding, reflecting off Cooper Field across the street at the Division Headquarters.

They walked in silence for a few minutes. Sal had been around long enough that he knew Cox would speak when he was ready.

Cox sighed heavily. But he shocked the hell out of Sal when he reached out and gripped his shoulder. "I'm not sure what your malfunction is, sir, but I strongly recommend you figure it out. Go to therapy, start drinking. Get a puppy. Something. The boss is losing his patience with you."

"Roger, sarn't major." He really wasn't in the mood for a pep talk about getting his attitude in check. He knew this already. Hell, everyone knew this.

He just didn't care. He was tired of dealing with all the drama of garrison life. He was not a counselor. He was not a divorce attorney and he damn sure wasn't a personal finance manager. And yet, garrison life seemed to assume that he was all of those things.

"Where's Delgado?"

Sal frowned. "Picking up Pizzaro from jail."

"Again?"

Sal bit back a smart-ass reply. "Roger that, sarn't major."

"And how long before I see that packet on my desk?"

Sal stiffened. He'd been waiting for this conversation. Hoping to avoid it, honestly. He had misgivings about Pizzaro but Delgado wasn't wrong. "I need platoon sergeants, Sarn't Major. I can't have lieutenants running around Fort Hood unsupervised. God only knows what trouble they'll get into."

"Partying isn't the problem, commander, and I think you know that. It's the getting arrested part that's causing problems." Cox let the silence hang.

Sal finally couldn't stand the silence any longer. "Sarn't Major, you know this is bullshit, right? We're wasting time in meetings over missed appointments and you're busting my balls over one of my platoon sergeants in a bar fight?"

"Captain Bello, I like you. But if you don't figure out really quick that there is more to commanding soldiers than teaching them to shoot a motherfucker in the face, you're not going to be commanding soldiers very long."

"What else is there?" Sal asked. Yeah, he was feeling belligerent. He *hated* the idea of having to break in a new first sergeant and he damn sure didn't like feeling like this was going to be a permanent change instead of a temporary one.

"Leadership is about preparing your men for war."

"That's what I'm trying to do, Sarn't Major. That's why I need men like Pizzaro on this next deployment."

"I'm not going to tell you how to run your company, sir, but I think you need to take another look at what's happening inside your formation. Pizzaro is a symptom of a larger problem." Cox jammed his finger in Sal's general direction. "If you want to take these boys downrange, get on board with what the boss wants. You might command your men but don't forget that your job is to execute his commands. That's the way the army works, son."

Sal slipped his hand into his pocket and felt the cold comfort of the worn out steel lighter.

It reminded him of what he was.

And what he wasn't.

And reminded him that men like Cox, men who understood what the war would demand of them, were rare. They were not the enemy.

First Sergeant Holly Washington knocked on the battalion sergeant major's door. Her stomach was in knots but not because she was afraid of him.

No, it was something much more personal.

She'd served with Sarn't Major Cox many moons ago. And today, standing outside his office, the memories were piling up, beating against the wall she'd carefully constructed to keep them at bay.

One day they were going to break free and she was going to have to have a come-to-Jesus with her past.

But today was not that day.

"Get your sorry ass in here, First Sergeant," came Cox's reply.

She sucked in a deep, bracing breath and stepped into his office.

He'd aged. It had been almost ten years since she'd seen him last. His hair, what was left of it, was whiter now, graying at the temples. His face more lined and darker from the sun.

But his eyes. His eyes were still the same. Glittering and dark and filled with an intensity that most people found downright terrifying.

She had been one of those people, once upon a time.

Until the night her world had gone to hell and the only person standing by her side when the debris had been cleared was then First Sergeant Cox.

He ignored her. Kept typing whatever he'd been working on before she stepped into the office.

She didn't move. Not one inch.

Finally he removed his hand from the keyboard and clicked the mouse. "Close the damn door."

She kicked it shut with her boot.

And found herself buried in an enthusiastic hug that lifted her off the ground and crushed the air from her lungs.

But it did nothing to tear away the smile that spread across her mouth.

"Holy shit it's good to see you, kid," he said when he finally put her down. "You haven't changed a bit."

"Good to see you, Sarn't Major," she said. And it was. Too damn good.

"Really glad you told me you were coming here," he said after a while. "Sit down, tell me about things. You in-processed?"

"Finishing up."

"House?"

"Out at Stillhouse."

"Good."

She braced for the inevitable family question and was grateful, so damned grateful when he skipped it.

He remembered. He knew.

And he was as good a man as she remembered for not bringing it up.

"Well, I've got a hell of a job for you."

"So I gathered from your e-mail," she said, sitting on the small, dingy couch in his office. "You know I like a challenge."

"Oh you're about to get the challenge of a lifetime," he said, and his grin was pure evil in the way that only a sergeant major's could be. "You're taking my support company. The support battalion still can't seem to find me some leadership so I'm finding my own."

"I thought we were friends," she said dryly. Support companies had a dangerous mission no matter where they were in country. They were always on the roads, making sure the front line fighters had the beans, bullets, and bandages they needed to keep fighting.

They also came with their fair share of problem soldiers.

He shook his head. "I wanted you in my ops cell but I need your ass in one of the line companies." He leaned forward, his expression shifting. "I had a first sergeant arrested a couple of weeks ago for threatening to kill his kid. Another one just had a heart attack."

"Sounds like you've been having a blast," she mumbled.

"Never a dull moment around here, that's for sure."

Holly nodded and said nothing, the situation hitting far too close to home.

"Anyway, you're going to have your hands full. You're my senior first sergeant now that Sorren went and had a heart attack."

She narrowed her eyes. "I'm sure the boys are just going to love that." She didn't try to restrain her sarcasm. Not around Cox.

"You're probably going to get into a dick-measuring contest on day one but it's nothing you're not used to."

Holly raised both eyebrows and smirked. "I think I'm offended."

"No you're not," Cox said. And he wasn't wrong. She'd known him too long. And more importantly, he'd known her too long. He knew exactly what she was likely to do when someone tried to break bad with her.

It was always fun to watch the shock when the guys realized she wasn't going to take their shit.

"Anyway, I need your help. The other first sergeants can't seem to get their legal packets done. I need you to help me there. We've got some real pieces of work that I need out of my Army."

Holly shook her head. "I think I'm supposed to have some obligatory remark about how you're being sexist by assigning me to work on paperwork."

He flipped her off and she almost choked on the laugh. "God, it's good to see you," she said when she stopped laughing.

"And you know why I need your help. We've got to clear out the formation. And I think Delgado in Diablo Company is deliberately shielding his men."

Holly lifted one eyebrow and fought the wave of anger that rose quickly from the dark recesses of her memory. She was used to the feeling. It was her constant companion these days, as the officers around her seemed to care more about numbers than the men and women they led.

And that caring meant putting bad soldiers out of the force.

Soldiers who could not or would not soldier needed to find another job.

"Do you need proof?"

"I need the packets done, Holly. We've already fired the entire chain of command in every company. We're going to war with the Army we have. We've got to make the best of it."

Holly nodded and folded her hands together, leaning forward. "So are any of the commanders worth a damn?"

"You're going to have fun with Diablo Company. Bello is a loose cannon depending on what day of the week it is. He's chafing under garrison life and the way the commander wants to run things. And his first sergeant…I'm not sure I trust Delgado."

"And you can't fire him, huh?"

Holly couldn't help the wry look that she knew called bullshit on Cox's statement. He didn't miss it because a slow flush crept up his neck as he laughed.

"Nice," she said.

"I need your help with Delgado and Diablo Company. Captain Bello thinks his first sergeant is right about everything; he doesn't listen to but a very few people. And he's got some baggage."

"Don't we all?"

"His is a little unique. Ask him about it sometime."

Holly sighed. She loved Sarn't Major Cox like a father but the man really liked putting her in tough situations. "Couldn't you just tell me and be a pal?"

Cox shook his head. "Nah. What would the fun be in that? I'm going to love watching you put him in his place."

"I shall endeavor to make a scene, if only for your enjoyment, Sarn't Major. But understanding his psychological trauma and hang ups doesn't affect whether or not I get to do my job."

Cox didn't smile. Instead his mouth got that twisted half grin that told Holly she was already in over her head. The only question was how deep.

"You're not going to tell me about this guy, are you?"

"I think Sal Bello is someone you have to experience for yourself," he said.

She shook her head and rolled her eyes. "Whatever you say, Sarn't Major. You need me to run two companies with one potentially crazy-eyed captain, I'll do it. But only because it's you asking me to," she added after a moment.

"I knew you'd be a sport."

"How much am I going to regret what you just signed me up for?"

"Not sure. But it's going to be fun to watch. I've wanted to see you in action since I first found out you got promoted to master sergeant."

"I live to keep you entertained." She stood, recognizing the gauntlet for what it was and started toward the door.

Cox may have been there when her life had gone to hell but he'd never babied her. He'd never held her to a lesser standard. He'd pushed her harder after that night. Never let her quit even when she wanted to.

"Holly."

She turned back to face him, bracing for his next words.

"I'm glad you didn't let the son of a bitch win," he said quietly. "We need leaders like you. Now more than ever."

Her throat tightened and she nodded briefly. "That's why I'm here," was all she could manage.

ONE CLICK LAST ONE HOME NOW!

AUTHOR'S NOTE

Thank you for reading After the War.

Sean and Sarah are the first characters I ever wrote and though this version has been edited and revised a lot, it's still a version of the first story I ever put on paper. I started them way back in 2007, when my husband was deployed for the second time and I was in Officer Candidate School. I remember the first day I wrote the first line. I was sitting in Building 4 at Fort Benning, Georgia, waiting for class to start. One of my classmates who'd deployed was ripping one of the members of his platoon a new one for something that seemed so trivial at the time. But it wasn't. It was something he'd seen matter downrange. And that was the spark that started everything: what does war do to men and women who lead soldiers? And how does it affect their decisions when they're home, knowing they are going back to war?

I've made some of those decisions now. I hadn't when I started writing this book. But those decisions influence my writing now in a way they couldn't before I'd gone to war myself.

Second, this is probably the darkest book I've ever written. I don't expect everyone to love it. I wrote about some of the dark realities of war that I haven't tackled directly before, because I felt like it was the right time and the right characters to engage with these issues. I expect there will be mixed reviews of this one, if not outright hatred of this book because the choices that Sean and Kearney and Smith had to make are not easy ones. They are not easy to understand if you haven't been there and even if you have, we all come at these situations from different points of view and different moral world views.

Third, Sarah is probably the most difficult character I've tried to write. She's made choices that many people probably won't agree with and may even despise her for. But they are choices that women in the military - especially mothers in the military, have to make all the time. I have made and wrestled with many of the decisions Sarah faced and I used my writing about them as a way to turn them over and examine them in the safe space of a novel.

Fourth, I wrote this book out of fear. My husband was on his second deployment. After his first deployment, we both knew what that meant. His first tour in 04 was bad. When we decided to stay in after he came home, we knew it meant he was going to war and that I too, would get my turn. We stayed knowing we had two little girls counting on us. There were a lot of reasons why we stayed and many more reasons why we probably should have gotten out. This book is an exploration of those choices and the fear that comes with them along with the pride and fulfillment that comes with being a soldier for both men *and* women.

It's taken me almost 8 years to get this book right. I hope it resonates with you and I hope that even if you hate it, you'll think about it long after you finish it.

Warmest Regards,

A MESSAGE FROM JESSICA SCOTT

Dear Reader,

Thank you so much for reading. If you'd like to make sure you never miss a new release, sign up for my newsletter at http://jessicascott.net/subscribe and please like my Facebook page at https://www.facebook.com/JessicaScottAuthor/. You can also join my reader room, affectionately known as The Pint for sneak peeks, giveaways and general all around shenanigans.

If you enjoyed the story, please consider leaving a review. Word of mouth is incredibly important for helping other readers discover new authors. I appreciate any and all reviews (whether positive or negative or somewhere in between).

Until next time!
Jess

THE COMING HOME SERIES

Because of You

I'll Be Home for Christmas: A Coming Home Novella

Anything For You: A Coming Home Short Story

Back to You

Come Home to Me: A Coming Home Novella*

Carry Me Home*

A Place Called Home*

Take Me Home*

Homefront

After The War

Last One Home*

THE FALLING SERIES

Before I Fall

Break My Fall

After I Fall

Catch My Fall

Until We Fall

NONFICTION

To Iraq & Back: On War and Writing

The Long Way Home: One Mom's Journey Home From War

BOOKSHOTS

Dawn's Early Light

Author's Note

The Coming Home series and Homefront series were originally published as separate series. I have rebranded them to get things organized as they were originally intended.

Come Home to Me: A Coming Home Novella* was originally published as part of the Homefront series

Carry Me Home* was originally published as Until There Was You as part of the Coming Home series

A Place Called Home* was originally published as All for You as part of the Coming Home series

Take Me Home* was originally published as It's Always Been You as part of the Coming Home series

Last One Home* was originally published as Find My Way Home as part of the Homefront series

ARTIFACT OF BETRAYAL